PRAISE FOR AWARD-WINNING AUTHOR JEAN R. EWING

"Writes with true Regency wit and charm."
—Jo Beverley on *Scandal's Reward*

"One of the finest treasures of the genre."
—Mary Balogh on *Rogue's Reward*

"Talent and wit shine from every word."
—Margot Early, 1995 RITA Finalist
on *Valor's Reward*

"A brilliant star."
—*Affaire de Coeur* on *Virtue's Reward*

"Bright star Jean Ewing shines with excellence
. . . another irresistible hero!"
—*Romantic Times* on *Folly's Reward*

PRAISE FOR *LOVE'S REWARD*

"Plot and romance hold hands to a captivating conclusion.
Intriguing and witty . . . a cloak and dagger of the
highest quality. Be sure to read *Love's Reward*.
One for the keeper shelf."
—Pamela James, *The Literary Times*

WATCH FOR THESE REGENCY ROMANCES

LOVE'S REWARD

Jean R. Ewing

Zebra Books
Kensington Publishing Corp.

http://www.zebrabooks.com

ZEBRA BOOKS are published by

Kensington Publishing Corp.
850 Third Avenue
New York, NY 10022

First Printing: December, 1997
10 9 8 7 6 5 4 3 2 1

Printed in the United States of America

"What, have you come by night, and stolen my love's heart from him?"

A Midsummer Night's Dream

Chapter 1

"It is a question of power," said Lady Elizabeth archly. "I have it. You do not."

"Really?"

Fitzroy Monteith Mountfitchet raised a brow and settled more deeply against the upholstered back of the chaise longue. He seemed a little foxed, his sprawl too relaxed to be seemly, his elegant coattails crushed haphazardly beneath him.

Lady Elizabeth laughed. She stood gracefully at the fireplace, her slender figure enhanced by a gown of exquisite apricot silk. Diamonds flashed fire at her neck as she moved. "Men have power everywhere else in this wicked world. Why should not ladies wield it somewhere? So we have chosen our battleground and this is it. A gentleman gives way to a lady's wishes here, does he not?"

Fitzroy swung his feet up onto the chaise longue and leaned back. The red gleam from the banked fire was swallowed into black shadows in his carelessly tousled hair and cast a frantic, carmine glow over his strong cheekbones and firm mouth. He was dressed for the evening: white linen cravat, tightly fitted ivory breeches, white stockings, black dancing shoes, all tinged to pink by the firelight. Music drifted into the chamber and delicately decorated the air, a lace-edge of sound. Somewhere in the house an orchestra played waltzes and country dances. He glanced up at her from narrowed eyes and smiled.

"In the bedroom? Undoubtedly. Guinevere glances from her window at Lancelot, and Camelot falls into ruin. Let Helen but smile, and Trojans and Greeks war to the death. Men are helpless when it comes to a beautiful woman."

Lady Elizabeth billowed about, allowing the soft fall of her skirts to outline her legs. The flattering firelight brought a warm flush to her smooth cheeks and cast shadows across her delicate jaw. Her voice was soft, teasing. "You speak of the heroes of romance? Bachelors all, of course! There is such a charming inevitability to it, isn't there? The unattached warrior and the married lady set fire to history and fable, while the poor husband boasts cuckold's horns and finally consoles himself with a noble death. Why are you not married, Lord Tarrant? The rest have wives, do they not? All of Wellington's *jeunesse dorée:* Lenwood, Hawksley, de Dagonet, Deyncourt? Lord Lenwood even has a daughter, I hear. They say he has become distressingly domestic with some provincial little wife, and never comes to town except to badger the peers about factories and working hours. It's too boring."

A slight wariness crept into his features, but his voice remained casual. "So I hear. What do you suppose is their connection to myself, madam?"

"Oh, stuff! It's common knowledge: all that derring-do against Napoleon. You were one of them—one of the secret scouts who organized the partisans—worth a brigade to our Iron Duke!"

Fitzroy held his right hand up to the firelight and studied it. The smooth palm was square and strong; his carefully manicured nails gleamed faintly. He had a sudden vision of that same hand scarred by calluses, its elegant lines blurred with dirt. For four years he had used it to wield sword or pistol, and for the more tedious daily toil of the campaign.

"We are at peace with France now, if not with each other,"

he said. "I have not seen any of them privately since. It's a long time ago."

"It is not even two years! The Iron Duke boasts that you conquered more Spanish hearts on the dance floor than Frenchmen on the battlefield. I can see why." She moved closer, with a sultry little laugh. "Then the Peninsular heroes came home to conquer hearts in England. Now they are all married—except you."

He glanced up at her and dropped his hand. "How lovely for them!"

Idly opening and closing her fan, she watched him, fascinated. "So did those black Spanish ladies spoil you for golden hair and fair skin? I refuse to believe it. Don't you find me attractive, Lord Tarrant?"

Fitzroy let his head drop back against the arm of the chaise longue. He wasn't sure if he felt relief or frustration, but he moved easily into the pretty flattery that the situation obviously demanded now. "I find you delectable, madam. Why do you ask? Why else do you suppose I am here, in your boudoir, while Lord Carhill entertains your guests in his ballroom without you?"

She made a small moue. "I told him I had the headache and would slip away for awhile. I shall have to reappear in an hour or so, of course, or face husbandly tantrums, but until then no one will miss me."

"Nor suspect?" Fitzroy laughed. It was rich, throaty. "And do you think an hour enough, madam?"

In a whisper of silk, Lady Elizabeth stepped up to the chaise longue and dropped down beside it. "Tarrant! Don't be silly! How much time do we need?"

He turned on his elbow, caught her head in an outstretched hand, and held her there for a moment, examining her features. She looked up at him under her lashes, a gesture of pure coquetry, and ran her tongue along her upper lip. He pulled her toward him. Lady Elizabeth bent like a willow as he lifted her face up to his and began to kiss her. The fire glow on her cheeks darkened to a hectic crimson flush which ran up into

the edge of her flaxen hair. Fitzroy slipped both hands behind
her head, and let his fingers caress her ears and jaw and the
nape of her neck as his mouth searched hers. She moaned
against his lips, a little sob of desire.

A log fell in the fireplace with a distinct crack. He released
her. Lady Elizabeth collapsed back onto her knees, panting a
little, her breasts rising and falling rapidly beneath her deep
décolletage. The diamonds leapt, sparkling in the light.

"Ah, Fitzroy, I knew how it would be with you." It was
almost a sigh. "Come, my darling hero! How can I let you
remain unconquered? Let me enslave you." She smiled at him
and slid one white hand onto his chest as if to tug at his cravat.
He caught and held it.

"Your maid will not come looking for you with salts?"
The question was lazy, unconcerned, but he kept her hand
imprisoned in his.

"I have locked the door. The key is here." Lady Elizabeth
laughed as she touched her cleavage. "She cannot enter. As
you cannot leave. Unless you wish to retrieve the key for
yourself? Perhaps I will let you beg me for it."

He ran his tongue lightly over her fingertips. "I am imprisoned, then?"

She leant forward and touched his jaw with one forefinger.
"Admit that I have mastery over you, Fitzroy! You want me,
don't you? Then take me, darling, as Lancelot seized Guinevere."

"Here on the chaise longue?" A faint trace of derision
colored his voice.

"Why not?"

Fitzroy kissed her palm. "I'm not sure I shall."

"What do you mean?"

He stood up, pulling her with him. In a hiss of apricot silk,
still clinging to his hand, Lady Elizabeth found her feet. He
was a full head taller. Releasing her fingers he forced her to
step back, away from him, and folded his arms across his chest.
He swept his gaze over the delicate gold evening slippers and

up to the fine border of gold embroidery at the neck of her gown and let it linger there for a moment.

"Take off your dress, madam."

Lord Carhill's lovely wife laughed, a little nervously. "What?"

Leaving her standing alone on the Aubusson carpet, he dropped back to the chaise longue and looked up at her. "Since you have so cavalierly locked out your maid, I assume you can manage without her? So, pray, take off your dress."

She looked confused. "But I thought we would . . ." Her voice trailed away.

"No," he said softly, "you thought that I would. But I am not prepared to do all the work when this little rendezvous was your idea. So let us take all the usual first steps as read. I have been plied with excellent wine and titillated with coteries of lovely women. We have flirted and danced and you have looked at me just so over your fan. One of your lackeys has discreetly extracted me from the ballroom and placed me here in your sumptuous boudoir. You have told your husband a small falsehood and have managed to join me. We have exchanged compliments. We have kissed. There is less than an hour left. So take off your dress, madam, and let us get to it."

Lady Elizabeth stared down at him, her eyes dilated. With a small, shaky laugh, she reached up to the clasp on her diamond necklace.

"Oh, no," said Fitzroy softly. "Leave the jewels, sweetheart. Just the dress, if you please."

There were two sets of small buttons at the shoulders of the apricot silk gown. Lady Elizabeth began to unfasten them, one at a time. Fitzroy lay relaxed on the couch and watched her. Her dress fell in a soft crumple at her feet and she stepped out of it. A tightly laced corset lay beneath it, rich with white ribbons and lace, over a fine white chemise, almost transparent, stitched with a delicate border of silver embroidery. She was breathing a little fast.

"Now the lacing," he said. He was faintly amused. "You won't need all that whalebone, madam."

Lady Elizabeth pouted. "But I shall need help with the back laces."

"Alas, I don't feel inclined to give it. Never mind, I suppose we can manage with the corset on, like swimming in the willows."

Her flush became fiery. "How dare you! This is outrageous!"

"Is it? How about the stockings? Can you manage them by yourself?"

"How can you expect me to undress like this, while you watch me?"

He grinned and stretched with deliberate unconcern, genuine humor coloring his voice. "Why not? You don't imagine that if you undress like this I shall avert my gaze, do you?"

Lady Elizabeth lost her temper, just enough to be provocative. "It's indecent! Not even Carhill would demand such a thing! You must look away."

Fitzroy closed his eyes. "Do you mean to tell me that you deny your husband his God-given rights to your person while offering yourself to any passing guest, and then have the effrontery to suggest that shedding your clothes in front of him is improper? Original, madam, but hardly logical."

She stamped her foot. "I must have been mad to invite you here. I thought you were . . ."

"What?" Fitzroy opened one eye and looked at her. "What did you think?"

"I thought you were Don Juan, if you must know! That's what they say, isn't it? Yet you have no more gallantry than a . . . than a barnyard rooster! Dear God! What is the matter with you? Are you incapable?"

Fitzroy stooped to the carpet and retrieved the key, where it had fallen unnoticed. "Not incapable, madam," he replied calmly. "I just prefer to choose my own mistresses."

Lady Elizabeth turned her back and caught up her apricot silk. "Dear heavens, you are a bastard, aren't you?"

"Indeed not. I am the most impeccably legal heir to my father, and my mother is a lady of irreproachable propriety and always has been. I am certain that she would never have strayed from her marriage vows. Unlike you, madam.''

She struggled into her dress. "What the devil can you know about it?'' she asked furiously. "You obviously have little interest in females. Do you think you have succeeded in humiliating me? There are hundreds more like you, footloose young dandies, wasting themselves on dissipation and fashion!''— *Though there are only a handful as wickedly attractive as Lord Tarrant, of course, and with such a very dashing and mysterious reputation!*—she banished the thought. "I can see why you aren't married like the others!''

He sounded merely tired. "I have no interest in marriage, madam.''

She spun about, triumphant, and pointed her finger at him. "Then you prefer boys! A common enough vice, of course. But you are an earl's son. How can you not want an heir? Are you so unable that you fear you can't get one?''

"Your sleeve is twisted.'' He turned the key in his hand. "At the back.''

She tugged at the sleeve and rapidly fastened all the buttons. "I feel sorry for you!'' Turning to the mirror, she patted her hair and adjusted her neckline. "What lady would willingly have you, in spite of that air of the conquering hero? Don't tell me you are a virgin, Lord Tarrant?''

The question was obviously absurd, and she knew it. But Lady Elizabeth, Countess of Carhill, was not prepared in any way for what he said next, nor for the deadly self-derision with which he said it.

"I have been married. She is dead.'' And suddenly he looked up at her with something close to anger in his face. "It was not my intention to humiliate you. I thought you were enjoying yourself, and that it was rather at my expense. Now, if you'll excuse me, I shall rejoin your guests and your husband before it is noticed that I am gone. I trust your headache will be better shortly?''

"You were *married?*'' She caught at his coat sleeve as he stood up. "Fitzroy! I had no idea. I am sorry. It was in Spain?''

"Don't be distressed." *So did those black Spanish ladies spoil you for golden hair and fair skin?* He ran one hand gently down her cheek, then leant forward and gave her a light kiss. "How could you have known?"

She gazed up at him and put one forefinger on his chest. "I am not distressed anymore. You are quite foxed and you are hiding a broken heart. You made me take off my dress just to get the key, didn't you? That was very wicked of you!"

He took her fingers and touched them with his lips in a practiced gesture of gallant submission. Then he kissed her once more, lightly, on the mouth. "But you are very beautiful, Lady Elizabeth. I would have enjoyed your shedding your gown even without an ulterior motive." He strode to the door and unlocked it, then tossed her the key and winked, a wink filled with seductive humor. "Since, as it happens, I do not prefer boys."

He stepped into the hallway and closed the door behind him.

Elizabeth, Countess of Carhill, stared at her reflection in the mirror for a moment. So she had been misled and she had failed. She supposed she ought to be angry, for although she had acted as she had promised, she was deeply disappointed. Dear God, the man was glorious—like a dark, exotic hero from some lost myth from the Arabian Nights! But she did not feel humbled, she only felt puzzled. If Lord Tarrant had not intended to become her lover, why had he agreed to come privately to her room?

The footman intercepted Fitzroy as he made his way down the stairs. The man looked faintly surprised to find him there. "My lord? There is a message for you. If you would follow me?"

Fitzroy was not expecting it. He usually made the contact himself. Did Lord Grantley think that Lady Carhill was the one? If so, he was very plainly wrong. She was looking for nothing more than a new lover. Fitzroy walked rapidly after the footman and was let into a small room off the hallway, paneled in oak. Dressed in a long cloak, a woman was waiting at the fireplace. A small bag lay on the floor beside her. As Fitzroy closed the door she spun about and stared at him. Her fair skin was slightly flushed and beads of dampness lay along her dark hairline. Her face reflected his own strong bones. She had something of the family cavalier grace. Yet she was obviously close to tears.

"Fitzroy! Oh, thank heavens! The most dreadful thing has happened! You must come away at once. There may just be time if you act quickly enough."

He walked up to her and laid his hand lightly on her forehead. "I thought you were unwell, Mary. You still have some fever, you silly child. Why the devil have you come out alone like this? Is someone with you?"

She caught at his coat sleeve. "Oh, I'm fine, really! It's just a cold! I brought Smithers. I had him send to your house to get your phaeton for me. Listen. It's urgent—indeed, it's a disaster!"

Fitzroy helped her to a chair. "Then it is Quentin. What has he done now? Ravished Cook in her rocking chair? Gamed away my best team to some card sharp from White's? Whatever it is, I shall take care of it. So don't cry like a goose, I beg of you."

"I am *not* crying! It is just this silly cold." Lady Mary wiped her eyes and looked ruefully up at him. "If only it were just that! No, Quentin has run away with a girl—stolen her out of school! And he was foolish enough to take one of Papa's carriages. The ostler told my maid, and she finally found enough courage to tell me what was afoot. Oh, Fitzroy! What on earth are we going to do about our mad brother?"

Fitzroy wrung his hand through his hair. He was torn between genuine distress and laughter. "Damn his eyes! To wish him posthaste to perdition would be a good start. But first, you will sit there, my dear sister, and compose yourself. I will get you a glass of wine, then you may tell me the whole. Quentin was probably foxed. He will wake up beside the poor wench in the morning and regret the whole thing. Then he will no doubt beg me to pay off her father and provide for the babe, so the Black Earl doesn't find out. And for the sake of family honor, and as an alternative to blowing out his brains, I shall do it.''

Lady Mary blew her nose. She was shaking a little, but she allowed him to ring the bell and ask the footman to bring wine. ''It is *serious*, Fitzroy.''

His voice was very gentle. ''I don't question it.'' He stroked the hair back from her damp forehead and gave her his own clean handkerchief. ''Most of the scapegrace things Quentin does are serious. Why else have I been trying to extricate him from them since he was born? Does Father know?''

''I don't know. Oh, dear Lord, I hope not!''

''Then perhaps I can catch them before any harm is done, and return the foolish child to her convent.''

Mary wiped her eyes again and smiled suddenly. ''She was at Miss Able's Academy where I went myself. It's very select. Miss Able will die of chagrin.''

The door opened and the wine was delivered. As soon as the servant had gone, Fitzroy turned back to his sister.

''Tell me what you know, from the beginning.''

''This isn't just a mad start, Fitzroy. And I don't think money will suffice this time. Apparently he's had it planned for weeks. He met the girl at a weekend house party given by some mutual friends. In spite of his reputation, it's rare that he's actually not received, of course. After all, Quentin is your brother!''

Fitzroy grinned at her. ''I should think it counts a great deal more that he's a son of the Earl of Evenham. After all, am I so very respectable?''

Sipping at her wine, she grinned back. ''Barely, I suppose! But being our father's heir is bound to give you an entrée everywhere, isn't it? And Quentin benefits from that. He certainly uses it. Otherwise, there's no comparison between you.''

''For I have the courtesy of being Viscount Tarrant, and Quentin must make do with being just a plain mister. I wonder sometimes why he has not shot me over it. So he met this schoolgirl and arranged an elopement? Who is the intended bride?''

Lady Mary set down her wine and looked up at him. "That's the worst of it, Fitzroy. It's not just any schoolgirl. It's Lady Joanna Acton, and she's not even out!"

"Dear God!" Fitzroy collapsed into a chair. Then he dropped his head to his knees to bury his face in his hands.

Her voice was shaking. "It is very bad, isn't it? If she's ruined, Lord Acton will demand a match—"

Fitzroy looked up. He was fighting back a desperate, wild laughter. At the look of open despair on her face, he let it loose. "A wedding? Then Quentin's cat *will* be out of the bag!"

Lady Mary was filled with indignation. "How can you laugh? She's the Earl of Acton's daughter, Fitzroy!"

He sprawled back in his chair and met her gaze. "But that's not really the worst of it unfortunately, dear sister."

"What can be worse? Oh, Fitzroy, will you please go after them?"

"Of course." He stood up and rang the bell. A footman appeared at the door. "Lord Evenham's carriage for Lady Mary, if you please. And have my phaeton brought to the door. We are leaving. Tell Lady Carhill that I am regrettably indisposed. Her excellent wine and the heady intoxication of the company force me to retire early from her enchanting entertainment."

The servant bowed deeply and stepped out.

"I have brought you a change of clothes, Fitzroy." Lady Mary indicated the bag. "And Smithers is already waiting with your phaeton. I just hope that unholy team of yours won't overset you. I was terrified coming here, perched up there above those huge wheels like a crow in a tree!"

Fitzroy leaned down and kissed his sister with a tenderness that would have seriously surprised Lady Carhill. "Bless you, my child, for your bravery, sense, and foresight. With my bays in harness, it's the fastest thing on the turnpike."

He opened the bag and pulled out a driving coat, buckskin breeches, and tall boots. While Lady Mary modestly averted her eyes, Fitzroy changed rapidly from his evening clothes and stuffed them into the bag.

"Oh, Fitzroy! What if her family finds out? Will one of her brothers call Quentin out?"

He thrust his legs into the breeches and pulled on the black boots. "Very likely, dear sister. And I have no doubt that it will be her oldest brother Richard, which adds some considerable irony to the whole situation."

"Why?"

"Like Montague and Capulet: 'Who set this ancient quarrel new abroach?' I am decent now. You may look up."

She glanced into his face, alarmed. "What ancient quarrel?"

"Lady Joanna's brother is Captain Richard Acton—more correctly known as Lord Lenwood—my erstwhile comrade in the Peninsula, who now resides, so I hear, in domestic bliss at Acton Mead. He has a wife I have never met and a baby daughter. And he has hated me ever since those last days in Spain."

"Hated you? Good Lord! Why?"

His expression closed a little, but it still held an undertone of raillery. "Lord Lenwood has a regrettably old-fashioned idea of the gallantry due to the female sex. I had the misfortune to trample on his tender sensibilities." The pause was momentary, but it was enough to cause Lady Mary a moment's wild speculation. *What had happened in Spain, and why would Fitzroy never tell her?* But Fitzroy went on with nothing in his voice but humor. "And now, it seems, my rakehell brother has run away with Lenwood's little sister, and probably ravished her under a hedge. Add this family mishap to my other transgressions, and Richard Acton will doubtless shoot me on sight."

Ten minutes later, the phaeton thundered north out of London. Fitzroy had given his team their unsteady heads. The horses lunged into the harness, excited at being allowed to gallop into the night. He was leaving behind all his business in town. He hadn't even made his report to Lord Grantley, a serious breach of duty and manners.

Ruthlessly, Fitzroy thrust aside every other concern but the tyranny of this immediate crisis. Richard Acton's little sister Joanna, for God's sake, and his own prodigal brother, Quentin. He supposed she must be a beauty. Quentin would never bother with a plain miss. Yet his usual entanglements were with opulent opera singers or bad but beautiful actresses. Why the devil had Quentin decided to elope with an English schoolgirl, for God's sake, and an earl's daughter to boot? And why the hell this particular earl's daughter?

The last time Fitzroy had seen the chit's brother, he had been known simply as Captain Richard Acton. Although the title, Lord Lenwood, was his then, he rarely used it. But Lenwood was a splendid soldier and a man of infinite integrity. He and Fitzroy had served together on more than one dangerous, dirty mission against Napoleon and forged the kind of friendship that only shared combat could bring. Yet on that last day in the camp outside Orthez, Captain Richard Acton had threatened to shoot down Captain Lord Tarrant if their paths ever crossed again—and for very good reason. If their roles had been reversed, Fitzroy doubted that he would have been as forbearing.

Fitzroy concentrated on the flying manes of his horses and the singing cadence of their hooves. Acton and Mountfitchet. Montague and Capulet. It seemed that the devil was determined to pile difficulties onto his head. He didn't have time for one of Quentin's foolhardy escapades just now. Yet Fitzroy hoped to God that word of this latest misadventure wouldn't reach the ears of his father, the Black Earl. Lord Evenham had a short temper and very little patience with his sons reenacting the classics.

Let Helen but smile, and Trojans and Greeks war to the death.

With a slightly grim smile, Fitzroy thought about the lovely Lady Carhill and how delectable she had looked in her shift. He hoped he had not made her into a permanent enemy.

Chapter 2

Joanna sat in the parlor of the Swan Inn gazing distractedly into the fireplace. She was beginning to wish she had chosen someone other than Quentin Mountfitchet for this particular adventure. For now he was getting visibly drunk. He sat opposite her in a large wing-backed chair, his booted feet tossed up onto a stool, and he was working his way quite steadily though several bottles of claret.

"We are stuck here for the day," he said. "Do you mind very much?"

His voice was not slurred, and he did not look in the least disheveled. Brown hair curled gaily over his handsome forehead. His cravat was still neatly tied in the *mathematical*. His green eyes were only faintly bloodshot, and there was just the slightest increase in his air of abandonment. Obviously Mr. Mountfitchet could hold his liquor, even after a night without sleep. Nevertheless, it did not bode well for their early arrival at Harefell.

"Are you quite sure that the curricle cannot be repaired until tonight?" Joanna could not hide the exasperation in her voice. "Then, pray, why do we not take the public stage?"

It took him just a moment too long to reply. "Lost all the blunt, Jo. I am sorry. Rotten run of luck, don't you know?"

Joanna stood up and flung down the gloves she had been holding. She was wearing her pelisse, although the parlor was warm. "Only my brothers call me 'Jo', sir! And I am perfectly well aware that while I sat in here and ate my breakfast alone, you indulged in a few rounds of whist with some other gentlemen in the common parlor. I am also aware that you lost very deeply. You told me so at least thirty minutes ago when you first rejoined me in here. Yet you seem to be making no efforts to mend the situation, and I refuse to believe you do not have credit. It is clear dawn. We have been here for three hours. The sun is shining on a frosty world, bright with promise. The rooster cried out his possession of the midden some time ago. So why on earth are we still sitting in this parlor, Mr. Mountfitchet? Good heavens! If you do not care to accompany me any further, I shall go on by myself."

She picked up her gloves and began to walk toward the door. In a few long strides, Quentin was there before her.

"Oh, no! That would be beyond the bounds of anything. You are very pretty, my lady, and charmingly young. It would be dangerous for you to attempt to travel alone. I rather fancy sharing your company for a little longer. After all, I brought you this far. Don't you think you owe me something for that?"

She had no idea that he could move so fast! He stood with his back pressed against the door and his arms folded very deliberately across his chest. He grinned at her and tossed back an errant lock of hair. The grin sent dimples into both cheeks.

Joanna looked at him quite calmly. "Yes, I know you admire my raven locks. You told me so at Fenton Stacey when we first met. And although I feel quite ragged for lack of sleep, you remain a perfect replica of a Greek coin. Your profile is flawless and your cravat the very model of attractiveness. An entire night of debauchery has barely disarranged it. All that is quite beside the point."

He laughed with genuine delight. "A night of debauchery? My dear child, I would like to show you one! Then you would not be so careless with language. It seems to me that we spent five hours in fast driving before we arrived here, and less than three hours in debauchery—which sadly was mine alone.''

Joanna shrugged with considerable eloquence, a dismissal of this perfectly correct statement. She felt quite exhausted from her night without sleep, and she was rapidly losing patience with her escort. ''You are the one careless with words, sir. If I remember rightly, in the garden at Fenton Stacey you compared my eyes to a summer sky, when they are quite black. As black as my hair, in fact.''

''A winter sky—at midnight,'' he corrected, still blocking the doorway so that she could not leave. ''Like the darkness we drove through all night. I was creating poetic images, my dear.''

''And now you are truly foxed,'' continued Joanna as if he had not spoken. ''And think to enact a small drama for your amusement. Very well. I wonder why you did not make the attempt before now. If it will be enough for you to let me pass, you may kiss me, if you like.''

He narrowed his eyes a little. ''May I? And have you ever been kissed, Lady Joanna?''

She turned away and walked to the window. Pushing hard at the catch, she opened it and looked down into the courtyard below. ''By someone like you? No, I haven't. But I think it might be quite an interesting experience. You're a rake, aren't you? I imagine you've had lots of practice.'' Her voice changed suddenly as she put both hands on the sill. ''Good Lord! How outrageous! That team is ready to drop!''

Quentin was looking just a little disconcerted. ''What?''

''A man just arrived in a high-perch phaeton, of all things! Beneath a liberal spattering of mire one can see that the wheels are picked out in yellow and black in the very latest mode. There is an exactly correct amount of seriously shiny brass. It is a most expensive rig to risk among the flyers and wagons, yet it would seem that he has driven that showy town carriage at breakneck speed along the turnpike. His cattle are quite soaked with foam.'' Joanna leaned further from the window.

"You might have more care for those poor horses, sir!" she yelled. "Do you think to call yourself a gentleman?"

Fitzroy leapt down from the phaeton, handed the reins to an ostler, and looked up. Some termagant was shouting at him from an upstairs window. He had driven hard and fast in pursuit of his father's curricle. It had been absurdly easy to trace. After leaving Miss Able's Academy, Quentin had obviously made no effort to cover his tracks, and had attracted notice at each toll gate and posting house by the speed with which he was traveling and his liberal dispensing of vails. By the time the sun was coming up over Bedfordshire, Fitzroy knew he would catch up with the fugitives long before they reached Scotland. But he was also painfully aware that Lady Joanna Acton had just spent an entire night in his profligate brother's company. He was not at all sure what he was going to do about it when he caught up with them.

Nevertheless, his last change of horses had put him not more than a few hours behind them. He would make inquiries here at the Swan, get a quick bite to eat and fresh horses, before pressing on once again. The sound of a young female voice dropping invective on his tired head was the cap to an already exhausting journey.

"Do you think to call yourself a gentleman?"

She was leaning from a window, the thin morning sun shining on impossibly rich black hair piled on top of her head in a mass of curls. Above perfectly molded cheekbones, her eyes were impenetrable. Deeply black, they seemed to be all pupil under glossy black brows which arched provocatively up at the center. Her color was high, bringing a deep flush to her cheeks. For one absurd moment, he thought of the fairy tale: hair black as ebony, skin white as snow, lips red as blood—Snow White, who lay in a glass coffin and waited for a prince to awaken her with a kiss. Their eyes met for one burning instant before she blushed and looked down. A moment later a brown-haired gentleman appeared at her shoulder. The man looked at Fitzroy, then he laughed aloud. With a wink he pulled the girl away from the window, only to take her exquisitely delicate chin in his hand. He searched her lovely face for a moment while she stared back up at him. Then he began to kiss her far too thoroughly on those blood-red lips.

Fitzroy's driving whip bent almost double in his hands. *Quentin, for God's sake!*

Lady Mary had retired to her bedchamber with every expectation of going straight back to sleep. She felt feverish and ached most uncomfortably in every limb, but she was filled with relief that this dreadful family emergency was in Fitzroy's competent hands. For as long as she could remember, Fitzroy had been rescuing Quentin and shielding him from the wrath of their father. It didn't occur to her that he could ever fail. A sleepy lady's maid had just helped her to undress and put on her night rail, when the entire house reverberated to the sound of a slammed door, agitated voices, and heavy footsteps ascending the stairs. To the astonishment of the maid, the door to Mary's chamber burst open and the agitation swept into the room.

"Evenham! Pray, Mary is ill!"

Lady Evenham, Mary's mother, was clutching at the sleeve of a handsome dark-haired gentleman who bore a striking resemblance to his oldest son, Fitzroy. He had the same height and dark, deep-set eyes. His black hair, graying only a little at the temples, framed a face with the same strong cheekbones. But there was no mistaking the air of absolute authority with which he moved and spoke. One imperious gesture waved the maid away. With a quick curtsey, she fled.

Now, heaven help me, breathed Mary to herself. *The Black Earl, himself. Father.*

Lord Evenham strode across the room to stand over her. He looked splendid, in a dark blue evening jacket with a discreet scattering of gold: his watch chain, his rings, his cravat pin. "Your mother believes you too ill to speak, Mary, but I am given to understand that, in spite of your indisposition, less than an hour ago you made Smithers fetch Fitzroy's phaeton. You then had him drive you to Lord and Lady Carhill's ball—which earlier you declined to attend with your mother and myself—at two o'clock in the morning. There you had a private interview with your brother Fitzroy, who has now disappeared with said phaeton. Will you please tell me what possible emergency could justify this extraordinary behavior?''

Mary looked down at her hands clasped together in her lap, and felt a hot flush creep up her cheeks. She felt completely miserable.

''The child has a fever, Evenham. She should be abed.''

The earl turned to his wife. ''Exactly, madam. She also has a kind heart and a foolish brain. What she intends to withhold from us is that Fitzroy has gone in pursuit of Quentin, who has taken my curricle in order to effect an elopement. An *elopement*, madam! He has stolen a schoolgirl from Miss Able's Academy for Young Ladies and is taking her to Scotland as we speak. If Fitzroy does not catch them in time to avoid scandal, an inflammation of the lungs will seem like a blessing in comparison.''

''Get into bed, Mary,'' said the countess quite calmly.

Mary looked at her father.

''Go ahead!'' He waved one hand. ''It is none of it your fault. However, I would ask that you inform *me* before you go scurrying to Fitzroy, if such a situation ever arises again in the future. You may worship the very sole of his boots, Mary, but Fitzroy is as determined to bring disaster to this family as his brother is. And worse! He is the heir!'' He struck his fist once into the palm of the opposite hand. ''So before you go into a decline, I pray you will tell me the name of the girl Quentin has seen fit to ruin. Otherwise I shall have to get the information out of the servants, an indignity I prefer to avoid. Out with it, madam.''

Mary climbed into bed, pulling the covers up to her chin. She kept her eyes firmly fixed on the painting which hung on the opposite wall. It was a portrait of eight pigeons which she, Fitzroy, and Quentin had kept as children. Tails spread, rust, gray, salmon, and ivory, a rich bloom on their feathers, the birds were arranged in an elegant group in the foreground. Evenham Abbey lay spread out behind them, its medieval arches and crumbling towers a picturesque ruin. In the days of Henry VIII, it had been a rich prize for the king to hand to his most loyal supporter, a man who had married one of Catherine of Aragon's Spanish ladies-in-waiting, but had been prudent enough to change his religion when his sovereign required it. An ignoble enough beginning to Evenham power and prestige, the wealth which had come from all that abbey land, stolen from the monks. She took a deep breath. "It is Lady Joanna Acton, Papa. I'm very sorry."

There was silence for a moment. The earl crossed to the fireplace and courteously helped his wife to her feet. Lady Evenham walked to the door and allowed him to open it for her. He did so with practiced grace, and she stepped into the corridor as if entering a measure in the ballroom. The earl said nothing until he was about to close the door behind him. It was just one sentence, but the implacable words were quite distinct.

"Then it is Fitzroy who will pay for this," he said.

The pupils at Miss Able's Academy were expected to rise at six and wash in cold water in preparation for their devotions in the school chapel. Thus it was still dark when Miss Able was informed that Lady Joanna was not in her room, and that several of her things had gone missing. Miss Able called immediately for Joanna's little sister, Lady Matilda Acton.

Milly stepped into the headmistress's study still sleepy, but she kept her back straight and met Miss Able's pale eye with more defiance than was seemly. She was dressed in a simple muslin gown and cotton apron over ankle-length pantaloons. Her blond hair was worn in two bright golden plaits. The plain dress only enhanced Milly's quite exceptional beauty.

Miss Able was seated behind her desk, but Milly had to stand, head up and shoulders straight, for as long as was deemed necessary to teach little girls correct deportment and respect for their elders. Since in the past this had stretched to over an hour, she exaggerated the stance, just enough to annoy without giving Miss Able any room to correct her, even though her left stocking was uncomfortably twisted in her shoe and she hadn't had any breakfast. Milly thought about Joan of Arc before her inquisitors and bore it stoically.

"Your sister appears to have left us, Lady Matilda. Did she speak to you about it?" Milly curtsied. It helped the stress on the back to move whenever the opportunity presented itself. "Report to me exactly what she said, if you please. Exactly."

Milly's blue eyes were perfectly serious, her small chin quite steady. She curtsied again and hoped the rustle of her skirts would cover the rumble of her empty stomach. Miss Able's pupils were expected to control such unseemly expressions of bodily function.

"Yes, ma'am. She said that she intended to go where there was hot water to wash with in the morning, where no one would ask her to memorize enormous stretches of meaningless text instead of introducing her to the modern poets, and where there wouldn't be any more interminable sermons from dried-up old ladies in abominable wigs. I remember her words exactly, Miss Able. My sister Joanna is very fond of the modern poets. That is what we all read together when we visit our brother Richard at Acton Mead: the modern poets, and Shakespeare, of course. Richard's wife, Helena, has a wonderful voice for reading aloud."

"I'm sure Lady Lenwood allows you to hear only what is proper," said Miss Able, her voice tight. "What else did Lady Joanna tell you?"

"When I asked her if she planned to run away alone, she told me not to be silly, that a gentleman was going to meet her with a curricle at the end of the lane at midnight and that she would be quite safe. I am not in the least concerned for her, Miss Able."

There was a dreadful silence, then Miss Able let out a groan. To Milly's amazement, she put both hands over her face and groaned again. All her horror at the news that the little girls knew that she wore a wig melted instantly away. She concentrated on the one piece of information appalling enough to destroy her.

"A gentleman?" she said at last, with an odd little choke.

"Yes, Miss Able. He is the Honorable Quentin Mountfitchet, a son of the Earl of Evenham, you know, so it is quite all right."

The pale eyes squeezed shut. "Pray, Lady Matilda, will you please ring the bell for Miss Sandhurst."

Milly rang the bell and a small, thin lady entered the room.

Miss Able looked up. Her skin had the look of mud in December. "Miss Sandhurst, we are faced with a calamity. Lady Joanna Acton has run away with a gentleman in a curricle, a gentleman with a most unfortunate reputation. She has been gone since midnight. There is no alternative but to send a message to her family immediately."

Miss Sandhurst turned white, then green. "Oh, my! The Actons? Lord and Lady Acton? Oh, my!"

"Will they come here, Miss Able?" asked Milly. "And Richard?"

The headmistress looked sharply at her noble pupil. It was as if frost crept over the mud, sending a craze of ice shards across the ground. "Lady Matilda, you will be pleased to write me an essay on the benefits of the regimen at this school. Two thousand words. By nine o'clock sharp. You will place particular emphasis on those requirements which are designed to secure the physical, moral, and spiritual health of the pupils, and thus convert heathen children into English ladies whose future calling is to serve as the wives and mothers of this great nation. You may go."

Milly curtsied and left, filled with enough admiration for her sister's escape to almost offset the burden of writing two thousand words of hypocrisy. She had been kept in Miss Able's study just long enough to miss breakfast.

"Oh, Miss Able!" exclaimed Miss Sandhurst, her eyes filled with tears. "Alas! By the time you send word to the earl and countess at King's Acton, it will be too late, surely?"

Miss Able stood up. "Nonsense. Lady Matilda is a spoiled, disrespectful child, but she shall have her wish. Lord and Lady Acton are probably in London. A message will reach them without delay. But we shall also send immediately to Acton Mead, which is hardly a stone's throw from here. Lord Lenwood may take on the responsibility for the redemption of his sister. And I would like to see his face when he gets this message. He came here last spring with his wife, as you may recall, and was most impertinent to me, most impertinent indeed. These young gentlemen who think of themselves as reformers must shoulder some of the blame when their sisters kick over the traces as a result."

Fitzroy went up the stairs two at a time. The stunned inn-keeper had not hesitated for a moment to tell this imperious gentleman where he had served breakfast to the dark-haired beauty. Of course, it was his best upstairs parlor. And her escort, a most dashing young fellow, had spent liberally enough on wine. Yet this new gentleman not only wore a silk shirt and waistcoat worth enough to buy an ostler's services for a year, but drove a high-perch phaeton that might have belonged to a duke. Perhaps it did belong to a duke. In which case, the ducal family would be prepared to pay handsomely for the innkeeper's assistance. For there was something distinctly havey-cavey about these goings-on, now, wasn't there? It wasn't every day that a young couple arrived in a curricle, with no servants and not much luggage, to be followed by a second gentleman, distraught and angry, setting a bruising pace in a phaeton. And the two gentlemen had the look of brothers.

At the door to the private parlor, Fitzroy stopped and took a deep breath. A deeper rage than he had expected had seized him by the heart the minute he had seen Snow White welcome Quentin's embrace. He had the horrific, repellent fear that he wouldn't be able to trust himself if he carried a weapon. There-fore he had left his pistols and sword cane with the innkeeper. Fitzroy told himself that it was only because this time Quentin had involved the family honor. She was the Earl of Acton's daughter, for God's sake. Even without the complications posed by the feud between himself and Lord Lenwood, the ramifications of this were unthinkable. Yet he knew his rage was due to more than that, and he had no idea why.

Steadying his breathing, he rapped on the panel. There was silence. He knocked one more time and tried the knob. It turned easily in his hand. With that dark rage still eating at his heart, Fitzroy stepped into the room. Quentin's tall figure blocked the light from the window, the sun casting an unlikely halo around his brown head. He was entirely absorbed. Lady Joanna Acton was encircled in his arms, and he was still kissing her. Fitzroy had the distinct impression that Snow White was kissing him back. The perception turned in his gut and filled his mouth with ash.

Damnation! Damnation! He was too late.

Joanna was not surprised when Quentin began to kiss her. She had been expecting it ever since she had climbed into his carriage outside Miss Able's Academy. She discovered that she had made the right choice to run away with a rake, after all, for what Quentin was doing to her lips was quite agreeable. She softened against him and tentatively opened her mouth just a little. He tasted of the claret he had been drinking, a warm woody fragrance. He deepened the kiss, entirely stealing her breath as he slipped one hand down to her waist, pulling her more closely into his body. His mouth covered hers, a little too greedy, almost oppressive. Joanna was determined to learn from the experience, though she wasn't sure how much she liked this new development, when the door opened behind her. Quentin pulled away, wiping moisture from his lips, and laughed.

Joanna turned to see the gentleman of the high-perch phaeton standing in the doorway. He was tall and lean, with wide shoulders and strong, graceful limbs enhanced by a very expensive, fashionable caped greatcoat. For some reason he was wearing an evening shirt and cravat with buckskin breeches and boots. His hair was as dark as her own, wildly curling over a brow contracted into a black scowl, his clear, smooth tan flushed a little with color across the high cheekbones. More than handsome, he had the look of a vampire, of demons flying out of the night: magnetic, enchanting—and out for blood. He leaned back against the door jamb and crossed his arms over his chest as if to contain that surging power. Oh, dear God, those dark eyes would pierce her to the heart!

"How very charming," he said with a derisive curl to his lip. "True love in a tavern. How do you do, Lady Joanna? Do you think that this gentleman will offer you the protection of his name as well as his heart and his passionate embraces? Or are you content to become his harlot and tend to your flock of bastards with a glad heart and a forgiving nature? For that is all you will get. And while you are waiting for him so faithfully in your nice little parlor, the innocent children clamoring at your knee, he will be fathering other little by-blows on other mistresses, with just as much enthusiasm as he brought to your bed. I hope you enjoyed it."

Joanna felt the hot, dreadful wave of anger and embarrassment start somewhere near her knees and flood uncomfortably up through her body until it set fire to her face. She wanted to cry, but only from anger. *How dare he!*

"Ah, Fitzroy," said Quentin, still holding her against him. "The officious older brother, always on my track. Good morning, my lord. Allow me to present Lady Joanna Acton. Lady Joanna, my brother, Lord Tarrant, an honorary viscount. Of course, you know that, don't you? Your brother Richard holds the same courtesy rank, the mark of an earl's heir, and just enough in Fitzroy's case to make him think that he can be bloody imperious and insulting whenever he likes."

"It would be easier, Quentin," said Fitzroy with the same deadly mockery, "if you were to release Lady Joanna from your lecherous grip. Then I could knock you down and murder you without compunction. I left my weapons with mine host, but I'd be happy to strangle you with your own neckcloth:

neater and less sanguine than lead or steel. After all, we are in the presence of a lady, whether or not she is inclined to act like one. She might not mind bearing you a brood of bastards, but she would probably faint at the sight of your blood.''

''You are unarmed, brother? How damned noble and impertinent of you!'' Quentin smiled at Joanna. There was no humor at all in his expression. ''Shall I kill him for you?'' he said, and laughed.

Chapter 3

The message was waiting for the Earl and Countess of Acton as they returned to Acton House in Park Lane at four in the morning: a short note from Lord Evenham, sealed with his crest.

Lord Acton tore open the paper as a manservant helped him off with his coat and hat. Moments later he turned deep red, his skin mottling above his tight cravat, a heavy, aging Henry VIII oddly out of place in the clothing of a gentleman of the nineteenth century. Lady Acton looked at her husband and wondered why in almost thirty years of marriage she had never quite grown used to it.

"For heaven's sake, Acton," she said sharply as she drew off her gloves. "What has happened?" She was very clearly Joanna's mother. Of her six children, only her second daughter had exactly her coloring—the black eyes and rich dark hair—and exactly her exquisite bone structure.

The earl was choked. With a violent gesture he waved away the butler and the footmen who stood ready to attend to their master and mistress. As soon as the hallway was empty of servants, he thrust the note into her hands.

"Read this, madam, if you please."

Lady Acton read it rapidly. "Oh, dear Lord!" She looked away across the grand entry hall, and her lovely dark eyes blurred suddenly with tears. "Joanna!"

"Is that all you have to say, madam, when your daughter runs away with an infamous rake?"

The countess seemed to regain her composure as easily as if she slipped on her cloak, yet it was as if an abyss had opened somewhere deep inside her, an abyss of dread and cold fear. Yet a lifetime of being a duke's daughter and an earl's wife had taught her how to cover up any weakness and shield her emotions behind a shell of serenity. She turned now to her husband with cool derision in her voice.

"But at least he is the son of an earl. I suggest we invite Lord Evenham here at his earliest convenience—for breakfast, perhaps. In the meantime, you should send for your man of business. Settlements will have to be drawn up."

The earl tore off his cravat and opened his collar. "Settlements! Damn his eyes! It is a crime to abduct an heiress, even if she is willing. Good God, that a daughter of mine could be so foolish! Will none of my children make a suitable match? Look at the brood you have given me, madam!"

He grasped her arm and dragged her toward the painting which dominated the entryway. It was a faintly sentimental portrait of the countess surrounded by her children, painted at least ten years before: three boys and three girls, one of them a baby in a lace cap staring solemnly from the countess's lap.

"Look at them!" He indicated the oldest boy. The youth stared back at his father, proud, defiant, his silver-blond hair a striking contrast to his deep black eyes. "Richard! What was he—sixteen, seventeen? It wasn't long after this was daubed before he was wasting his youth in vice and dissipation in God knows what depraved corners of the globe."

"He became a soldier, a perfectly honorable occupation."

"He is my *heir,* madam! The next Earl of Acton, for God's sake, joining the Peninsular Campaign as an ordinary cavalry captain, then coming home to marry a penniless chit from

Cornwall that he had known for only two days! And you call that honorable behavior? Madness, madness! He could have had any heiress in the kingdom!''

Lady Acton gazed at the painted face, greeting her with eyes that were so like her own. Her first-born. She had been just eighteen, far too young, frightened, and in love with someone else. But Richard had come into her life, a helpless infant with such tiny, perfect features and great trusting black eyes, and sunk an unbreakable hook into her heart. Lord Acton had handed him to a wet nurse and ordered his young wife to dry her eyes and act the countess. Of course she had done so.

''As it turns out, Helena's family was perfectly respectable and she was heiress to a small property. Richard loves her.''

The earl was gripping her arm hard enough to bruise it. ''Love! Yes, he's as devoted to her as any cowherd to his milkmaid! Yet it was not the blood suitable for my son and heir, madam, however charming the girl. And now she has produced a daughter!''

''She and Richard will have more children. You may thank the love that you so despise for that!''

''Yes, a splendid match for Lord Lenwood! A chit with a pretty face who loves him!'' The earl pointed next to a grave girl who seemed to be the odd one out in a family of stunning good looks. Gawky and awkward, frozen in paint on the last brink of childhood, she had straight chestnut hair and plain brown eyes in a face that was all bones. ''And there stands her older sister, Eleanor, who made a botch of her Season and turned down an offer from the future Duke of May.''

''My brown hen!'' Lady Acton smiled. ''And now she is Countess of Hawksley, and her husband a hero of Waterloo. Eleanor can hardly be faulted for her marriage, Acton.''

''Hah! It was a damned close-run thing! But Joanna is determined to outshine all of them! Quentin Mountfitchet, for God's sake!''

''It is no secret what Quentin is. But there is nothing inherently unsuitable in a match between the families. And they must marry, of course. Even if Lord Tarrant has discovered them by now, they have spent the night together unchaperoned. Though I am very sorry for it, for I have no doubt that the marriage will be an unhappy one.''

With an oath, the earl turned away, but the countess caught his arm so that he spun back to the painting. She pointed her finger, the rings on her elegant hand sparkling in the candlelight.

''Can none of our children content you? Look at Harry— the only one of all of us who is laughing! Your favorite son, with my hair and your eyes. Beautiful, faultless Harry! You don't mention *his* marriage?''

The earl's face seemed to have become spongy, as if his features had lost the bone beneath them. ''I won't—'' The earl choked on the words. ''Harry is as good as dead to me, madam. And after such a foul *mésalliance,* do you think I shall let Joanna ruin herself? Oh, no. They *shall* marry, madam. If Joanna is determined on a rake, she shall have one. But she has brought dishonor to this house. To elope is a scandal, even if he were a royal duke! I'm damned if I intend to act happy over it.'' He wrenched from her, and thumped away to disappear up the stairs.

Lady Acton stood alone in the echoing hall, gazing at the two youngest children in the portrait: John, a little lad in petticoats, grown up now and at Eton, and Milly, the baby. Then she looked at Joanna and felt the familiar tug of the child who was most like her. Joanna was scowling, clutching a doll in one hand which she dangled by its legs, and hanging onto Harry's coattail with the other. Stormy, difficult Joanna, who had just doomed herself to a loveless marriage with a man who would break her wild heart. There was no way out of it. Within two days, all of London would know that Lady Joanna Acton had brought shame and scandal to two of the greatest families in the land. An immediate wedding was the only solution. Joanna must marry Quentin Mountfitchet without delay.

Lady Acton turned away from the portrait and went up the stairs after her husband. There was a great deal to discuss.

* * *

"Shall I kill him for you?"

Joanna's mind seemed to blur into a horrified blankness as Quentin said the words. The tall, black-visaged stranger, Quentin's brother, Lord Tarrant, did not move. He leaned, still nonchalant, still smiling, with his back to the door, yet his presence seemed to dominate the room. He said nothing.

Her attention snapped back into focus, and she stumbled away from Quentin to drop into the chair beside the inn fireplace because her legs would no longer hold her. She felt faint, for heaven's sake. She had never been weak, or had the megrims. What on earth was the matter with her?

Quentin went to the window and closed it. "How noble! And how typical of you to disarm yourself before facing me. When you are such a good shot it would be the action of a cad, would it not, to draw a pistol on your own brother? If you allowed your finger to tremble for an instant on that hair trigger I should be dead. Now, since my aim is less sure, I have no such scruples. When I point my weapon it might well go off, but the ball might not pierce your heart. I might shoot your arm, or your knee, or take off an ear quite by accident." He grinned and ran his left hand through his hair as he turned back to face Lord Tarrant. "I wonder what portion of your anatomy you would miss the most?"

"Go ahead," said the demon visitor. He had still not moved from his post at the door. "I am an easy enough target."

Joanna saw the reflection first: the sunlight glinting on the engraved metal of a small pocket pistol. Quentin held it steadily in his right hand with the barrel pointing directly at his brother's heart. He began to lower it slowly, one inch at a time.

"A bullet in the heart? In the ribs? In the belly? Or lower yet?"

"Stop it!" she shouted. "For God's sake! Quentin!"

"He is foxed, Lady Joanna." The dark eyes seemed unconcerned, relaxed. "Hadn't you noticed? Your darling swain is barely in possession of his senses. What is a little more murder and mayhem to a rake in his cups?''

Quentin smiled, still slowly lowering the barrel of the pistol. ''You should know, my lord, all about murder and mayhem. Yet without your right arm, you would be hard pressed to practice that stunning swordsmanship. Without your knee, alas, no more dashing exploits on horseback. Without your ear? No more music and thus no more dancing, the gentle art that allows ladies to soften in your arms. For, of course, you know even more than I about being a rake, don't you?'' He moved the pistol down another inch. ''Although if my hand should tremble in the next minute or so, that career also might be over for good.''

''Would that be enough atonement for Juanita?'' said Lord Tarrant very softly.

Joanna saw Quentin tighten his fingers slightly, and a lethal concentration came over his face. Her momentary paralysis disappeared. She leapt from her chair and threw herself at Quentin, wrenching at his sleeve, and in the same instant Lord Tarrant threw himself violently to one side. The pistol jerked. A bright flash, black smoke, and a deafening explosion roared in the small room. She clung to Quentin's arm. In a blur of powerful movement, Tarrant had rolled, landed back on his feet, and closed the space between them. She felt Quentin stagger as Lord Tarrant slapped him hard across the face. The viscount was taller than his brother, more powerful, and Quentin crumbled, the pistol falling to the floor. There was the clatter of steel on wood, then a sickening thud as the brown curls hit the hard boards. She fell with him, bruising her shin and her elbow.

''You're a bloody fool, brother,'' said the demon's voice almost in her ear. ''To drink so much damned cheap liquor.''

Ignoring Joanna, Lord Tarrant took his brother by his lapels and shook him. She stared up at him. How fine and smooth his skin was, so darkly shadowed at the clean jaw! Joanna felt the most unholy impulse to reach up and mark it with her nails. The intensity of the feeling left her shaking. She sat up and looked at her escort. Quentin seemed to have passed out. He lay supine on the oak floor boards, breathing steadily, a small smile at the corner of his mouth. Suppressing her confusion of emotions, Joanna struggled to her feet and limped back to her chair. Lord Tarrant stood up and dusted off his hands, still gazing down at his brother. After a moment he picked up the pistol and thrust it into his own pocket.

"Was it your intention, Lady Joanna," he asked quietly, "to get me killed?"

"For heaven's sake," she snapped. "It would seem to be *you* offering violence."

He turned his head to look at her, his dark, piercing gaze emphasized by his strong brows and the lush black lashes. She met it with clear defiance, expecting to see a murderous rage in those handsome features, but her challenge dissolved into bewilderment. Lord Tarrant's face was lit with a kind of desperate laughter, his dark eyes brilliant with awareness, his mouth curved by an amusement that seemed merely cruel to her. Once again she had the odd sense that she was out of her depth, threatened, endangered more by this man than she had ever been by his brother, the infamous Quentin Mountfitchet.

"I trust you are not seriously hurt?" he asked, still with that dark raillery in his eyes.

"Oh, good heavens, no! I'm fine. Or at least, as well as might be expected for someone who has just been cursed at, deafened by a pistol, thrown to the floor, and accused of abetting murder. May I assume Quentin will recover?"

"All too soon, I fear. How long has he been drinking?"

"Only three hours or so, since we've been here—and from the flask he had in his pocket as we drove, of course. Though I believe I would trust him more foxed than I would you sober. What a shame that he's not much of a shot!"

"Oh, no, my lady," said Lord Tarrant softly. "He was lying. Quentin is a dead shot, even three sheets to the wind."

Joanna gazed at him in a kind of mesmerized horror. "And you goaded and challenged him unarmed? Did you know he had a pistol?"

"I thought it very likely."

"Then you are mad!"

"Am I?" he asked. "But you are the one who ran away with him."

"And would have been thankful if you had refrained from interfering." There was a pounding on the stair leading up to the room. Joanna turned away from him, and drew herself up like a duchess as Miss Able had taught her. "Perhaps while you are explaining all this to mine host, you would ask for tea to be sent up? Made with *freshly* boiling water, if he would be so kind."

The innkeeper flung open the door. "My lords! I pray of you! This is a respectable house!"

Lord Tarrant laughed. He walked up to him and laid a hand on the man's shoulder in a convincing imitation of casual camaraderie. "And so I trust, sir. My brother imbibed a little too much of your excellent claret and has passed out. In falling his pistol discharged accidentally. No one is hurt, but sadly there is a shocking hole in your plaster. I shall cover all your expenses for repair and any inconvenience, of course. In the meantime . . ." There was a flash of coin in his hand, which the innkeeper accepted with alacrity. "It has caused a sad start to this lady, and she would like some tea, made with *freshly* boiling water."

"In a warmed pot," added Joanna. She was far too hot, so she pulled off her pelisse and settled herself with what she hoped was dignity in the chair beside the fire.

Their host, his eyes round as he caught sight of the gentleman sprawled unconscious on his floor, bowed and stepped out.

Joanna watched silently as the demon lord caught Quentin around the shoulders and dragged him to the chaise longue at the side of the room. The heels of Quentin's top boots squeaked a little on the polished floor. Then Tarrant picked his brother up bodily and dropped him onto the plush surface of the couch. He did it easily, as if Quentin were no weight at all. He stood looking down at him, his dark brow still contracted.

"No doubt you see me as the malevolent spirit," he said

suddenly, "come to interrupt your escape into blissful matrimony. What on earth attracted you to the idea? Your bridegroom
is totally sodden. Whether I had interfered or not, he would
not have made it much further today."

Joanna stared up at him, her expression icy. "We shall never
know, shall we?" she said with emphasis. "Since you took it
upon yourself to beat him into unconsciousness. And he is not
my bridegroom!"

Lord Tarrant turned and strode across the room to stand
over her. He was very tall. Joanna was determined not to be
intimidated, so she stood up. She still had to look up into his
face, and she was mystified by what she saw there: a derisive
anger, and the dark shadow of something almost like despair.

"Oh, really?" he said quietly. "So you intended to live with
my brother in sin? An earl's daughter, a schoolgirl, not yet out,
hopes to set up unlawful housekeeping with a drunken rake.
How very bold and original of you!"

Joanna gazed stubbornly into his face. "What can you know
about me? Nothing! You understand nothing! Nothing at all!"

He stepped closer. Since the backs of her knees were against
her chair, she could not move away without ducking or sitting
down. Either movement seemed a concession of defeat, so
Joanna stood her ground.

"I understand this much, Lady Joanna: that you spent the
night unchaperoned in his company; and that you welcomed
Quentin's lecherous attentions in the full view of everyone in
the coach yard without care for discretion or reputation."

"Reputation!" said Joanna. "It won't matter to me in the
least."

"Obviously not, since you arrived here like this at a common
posting house, alone with him. How do you suppose the two
earls will react, your father and mine?"

How very powerful he seemed, breathing strength and an
easy athleticism! Joanna felt the force of it like a weight, pushing for her surrender. "I have no idea how Lord Evenham will
react since I've never met him. And as for my father? I don't
care. Neither my brothers nor my sister Eleanor married to

please him. My father's reaction was to swear to arrange every detail of my future, as if I alone can make up for all their transgressions. He is determined to force me into a suitable marriage as soon as possible—the limp son of the Duke of May has been suggested—and I shall defy him over it just as they did. But I do not intend to become Quentin's mistress!''

Lord Tarrant laughed. A rich sound that transformed him from a merely dangerous demon into a fiendish one. ''Indeed? Then why did you kiss him?''

''I wanted to see what it would be like.''

''Dear God!'' He was standing very close. He laid one hand softly along her cheek. ''And did you like it? Hardly a wise experiment!''

''Why? Because Quentin is a rake? Why are females denied all experience and kept at home like decorative ornaments, when gentlemen can plunge into the world and discover it for themselves? Don't you think that the female sex has as much intelligence and as much talent? But how can any of it be developed, how can any of it grow into something real, if we aren't allowed to make mistakes?''

He didn't answer for a moment. Joanna could feel the warm, caressing touch at her jaw, insistently summoning agitation. She bit it back. His other hand stroked her hair away from her ear, delicate, subtle, his fingers meeting at the sensitive nape, and staying there, moving softly. She stood like a rock, staring up at him, while the ripples of sensation began to flow out into her blood. His fingers stroked over the lobes of her ears and rubbed gently down the line of her throat to her pulse, beating wildly in its own rhythm of madness.

Joanna was trapped against the chair. She tried to move back, but her knees buckled and she was forced to catch his coat in her hands to prevent herself falling. He was strong, and steady, and dangerous. Her senses were filled with her awareness of him: his dark eyes with their fringe of long lashes; his masculine scent, of the wild woods and leather and horses. Both hands moved back up her throat, over her chin, to brush gently at her cheek, one thumb caressing the corner of her mouth. Joanna felt the warm, sweet trail of it, like a melody on her skin, promising strange and perilous delights.

"And what was it like?" he asked softly.

Her voice was biting. It took everything she had not to let it tremble instead. "An interesting experience."

He smiled. "Interesting? How very clinical! But pray, don't tell Quentin your assessment of his skills, will you? He would be mortally wounded that you were not more impressed. But then, how many dull kisses have you suffered as a basis for comparison, Lady Joanna?"

Fitzroy expected her to show some fear, or defiance, perhaps, or even blushing maidenly vapors. After all, how much experience could she possibly have? He ran one finger slowly along the deep curves of her upper lip. Her eyes dilated into pools of black, as dark and deep and full of mystery as the mere at Evenham Abbey on a midsummer night. He felt his very bones respond, an answering flare of desire, deep and urgent, imperious in its demand. Without compunction, his blood burning in him like lava, he bent his head and kissed her. Then Fitzroy forgot everything as he felt the angry, passionate tremble of her lips beneath his.

Had she invited this? Was this was she wanted? Joanna had no idea, but her body bent against his and his mouth compelled her response. She felt as if an ocean roared in her ears, as if gale-force winds tore at her, tossed her like a barque helplessly on the white-topped waves. Oh, this was not simple or merely agreeable! It was searing, frightening, tyrannical in its dominance of her senses, a glorious blaze of sensation melting her to the very core. She wanted to rail at him or tear him apart, yet she was melting, melting, like butter in the sun. It wasn't fair!

There was a rattle at the door and a sharp knock. Fitzroy spun about, rage in every line of his taut body, his hands still gripping Joanna by the arms. A maid stepped into the room carrying a tray with cups and a silver tea service. Precariously balancing the tray, she dropped a curtsey.

Joanna stared up at Lord Tarrant, her lips bruised and her

blood on fire. The wild, high song of the sirens echoed in her veins, waking her to something new and infinitely desirable, so that she would never be content again. Why? Why had he done that to her?

"You ordered tea, my lord?" the maid asked a little nervously, glancing up at Tarrant and Joanna. "For your brother's wife?"

"This lady is not his wife," he replied in chilling tones. "She is our sister."

"No, she is not," said a man's voice from the open doorway. "She is mine."

Chapter 4

The tones were flat, hard, and filled with a virulence that Joanna could hardly believe came from her brother. She watched him, tall and blond, step into the room and close the door behind the fleeing maid. A deep line was etched between his brows. He was tired, obviously. It was a long ride from Acton Mead, and no doubt Richard had come fast on horseback as he had traveled so often in the Peninsula.

"What the devil fool start is this, Joanna?" he asked coldly, ignoring Lord Tarrant entirely. "Get your things together. I'm taking you home."

She hated to wound him. Joanna loved Richard dearly. But she had no intention of being returned in disgrace to her family, or worse, to Miss Able's Academy. "I can't come, Richard! I'm sorry."

Fitzroy had already released her. He leaned casually against the mantel, one hand at his hip. He was essentially unarmed. Quentin's pistol in his pocket had been discharged and he was carrying nothing else to defend himself. He had no doubt that Richard Acton, Lord Lenwood, would be carrying a loaded weapon and would like any excuse to dispatch him. But Richard would never shoot at an unarmed man. Quite simply, he had too much honor. And in spite of what had passed between them two years before, Fitzroy had no desire at all to see Richard Acton die. So even if Richard demanded a duel, Fitzroy would have to cravenly refuse; Acton was only a moderate shot, after all. It was odd to feel so safe in the presence of a deadly enemy. Fitzroy buried any other emotions behind a cool sarcasm.

"Your sister, my dear Lord Lenwood, intends to marry my brother Quentin. That's him over there on the couch—sadly insentient."

"I do not!" said Joanna with emphasis. She sat down.

Fitzroy's dark eyes narrowed. "Alas, my lord, she will not allow me to soften the blow. In fact, she intends to live with him in sin. It must be delightful for you to find me here to witness it."

Richard dragged his gaze from Joanna and focused on Fitzroy as if he had to force himself to look at Medusa. His voice was quiet, even courteous, though every line of his body betrayed his loathing. "It is not, Lord Tarrant. It is far from delightful. I had hoped never to have to speak with you again."

"No," said Fitzroy. He turned his back and strode to the window. Richard might see him as the head of the Gorgons, but he had no desire to witness his glance turn anyone to stone. "I can see that. Indeed, I am sorry enough about the whole bloody business myself. Nevertheless, I am here. And Lady Joanna is right. She cannot simply go home as if nothing has happened. If you would like to take off your coat and gloves and sit there by the fire, we may have tea. It would be a shame to allow it to get cold. Mine host has had it made with freshly boiling water."

"I would rather leave now. Joanna?"

She couldn't bear to see Richard look at her like that. Although Joanna would always be closer to Harry, Richard was the oldest and she had looked up to him with something close to awe throughout her childhood. His wife, Helena, had been more than kind to her when she had been an unhappy and awkward fledgling one strange and magical Christmas at

Acton Mead. "I can't, Richard, truly! Go home to Helena and baby Elaine. It's too late. Lord Tarrant is right."

Richard tore his dark eyes away from her and faced Fitzroy again. His rigid control only thinly masked the deep sorrow in his expression. "Very well. Pray, tell me the worst, Tarrant."

Fitzroy stood in silence for a moment. Then he spun about and crossed the room to sit down by the fireplace. He poured tea and handed a cup to Richard. It was taken in stiff fingers, but Richard also dropped into a chair.

"Lady Joanna and my brother have just spent the entire night together. Nothing can change that. And alas, Quentin gave no thought to concealment when they arrived. He announced his own and your sister's names without compunction in the public rooms. He was very foxed, I understand. Innumerable respectable travelers are thus privy to the sad facts. Among that busy number, so mine host informed me, are Lady Pander and Mrs. Charlotte Clay, two ladies of execrably slow wit and fast tongue, who were enjoying breakfast together. Such a delicious piece of scandal would have been welcome spice to add to their curried eggs and Bedfordshire muffins. By tonight all of London will know about this imprudent elopement. A marriage is the only possible outcome, whether you mind so very much or not."

Richard set down his tea without tasting it, and crossed his booted legs at the knee. The vertical line cut deep between his winged brows. His eyes were now locked on Fitzroy's face. "I am very aware that she will be forced to marry Quentin. Do you think that I care because he is a drunken rake? Who knows? If he loves her, he may reform. It has been known to happen." Richard smiled, entirely without mirth. "Oh, no, Lord Tarrant, the reason I mind so very much is that you will become her brother."

Joanna's tea also sat untasted. It had developed an unpleasant oily scum on the top. "Stop it," she said. "I do not intend to marry Quentin Mountfitchet. I cannot be forced into it!"

Richard slammed his fist onto the arm of the chair. "For God's sake, Joanna! In law you are Father's chattel. He may dispose of you as he wills. How the devil do you think you can stand up against him?''

Joanna, her color high, was furious that her voice trembled at all. ''Not easily, but I shall. How you men love to order the lives of females! What do you think this is about? You sit there, both of you, like avenging angels, disputing my fate as if it were yours to dispose of. You make the assumption that I am with Quentin because I am dazzled by his address, and charmed into silliness by the winks and kisses of a libertine. For God's sake! Am I not allowed a mind of my own, and plans, and ideas for the future that I want?''

Richard stood and took her by the shoulders. ''Dear God, Joanna. And you thought that this was the way to get it? You have given Father no option, dear girl.''

Fitzroy leaned back in his chair and gazed up at his enemy through narrowed lashes. ''You have not asked her, Lenwood, what future she wants so very badly.'' He glanced over at Joanna. ''Why don't you tell us, Lady Joanna? If you are not eloping and not in love with my sodden brother, then why have you run away with him?''

Joanna still looked up at Richard. ''I needed an escort, that's all. I knew there was no chance to escape by myself. When I met Quentin at the house party at Fenton Stacey, he offered to help me. So I took him up on it. He's a fast driver and in possession of a carriage, which I am not.''

''So he took my father's curricle,'' said Fitzroy dryly. ''And thus alerted the household.''

''If it was so urgent, you might have asked me.'' Richard dropped his hands and turned away. He seemed austere, the control back in place, his features set in lines of stone.

''And you would have taken me?''

''That might have depended on where you were going,'' replied Richard.

Joanna stood up and laid her fingers on his sleeve. ''Richard, you and Helena have your own lives. You aren't responsible for me. I've made up my own mind. I shan't marry Quentin Mountfitchet, and I don't care if all this has put me beyond the pale.'' She waved one hand around the room, casually including the still unconscious figure of Quentin, breathing softly on the chaise longue. "I could not stay at Miss Able's Academy another minute. I'm going to Harefell Hall, if you must know!''

"For God's sake!" said Richard on a sudden exhalation.

"Would you mind very much," interrupted Fitzroy calmly, "telling us what the devil you expect to find at Harefell, Lady Joanna?"

Joanna turned to him. "A group of artists, of course! There was a lady, Mrs. Barton-Smith, at Fenton Stacey who told me about it. I intend to paint—not silly watercolors suitable for ladies, but real paintings—and the owner of Harefell Hall allows any artist to live and work there, ladies as well as gentlemen, with complete artistic freedom!"

"Dear God!" Richard sat down and dropped his head into his hands.

"You didn't know, Lord Lenwood?" asked Fitzroy wickedly. "You have so much concern for your sister, yet you had no idea that she harbors a longing to be a painter?" He turned to Joanna. She gazed at him with pure fury, her color high. "Rather a bold ambition for a lady—not the painting, but the desire to join the infamous community at Harefell. I have had occasion to visit there myself. I enjoyed it." Fitzroy stood up and stretched, then strode again to the window. He continued over his shoulder with a deadly edge of humor to his subtle voice. "I don't believe much painting or sculpture gets accomplished—in fact I am sure that it doesn't—but they do hold splendid, wanton, and very dissolute orgies." He paused for a moment to let all the implications of this sink in, before turning to face her with that infuriating, supercilious smile curving the corner of his mouth. "Did you know?"

Joanna only knew she was scarlet. Chagrin burned in her like smoldering pitch. She hated her own impotence in the world and this impossible, arrogant certainty only highlighted it, forcing her to face her ignorance and naiveté, and the fact that she had just made a complete fool of herself. "But Mrs. Barton-Smith said . . ."

Richard interrupted. "Of course she didn't know! What the devil do you think my sister is?"

"She is nothing to me, Lord Lenwood."

Fitzroy saw the flush wash up her cheeks as she dropped back to her chair. The humiliating color stained those perfect, high cheekbones, making her black eyes brilliant in contrast. They shone with unshed tears, restrained with a determination and bravery that took his breath away. She blinked them back, leaving her long lashes damp. The gesture was painfully vulnerable, and feminine, and defenseless. Dear God! She had ruined her future for a chimera, a dream that did not exist.

He looked away and took a deep breath. His own brother, Quentin Mountfitchet, had not flinched from leading this innocent to her damnation, and he himself had reacted by kissing her as if she were a doxy. Let Richard Acton shoot them both down. Joanna could not be saved, and Lord Tarrant had just spent the last hour proving that he was no better than Quentin, that they were both equally beyond the reach of grace, beyond any hope of salvation. The bitter knowledge rose in his throat like bile. Fitzroy watched almost blindly as a coach pulled into the yard below, a chaise and four with two outriders and an all too familiar crest emblazoned on the panel.

She is nothing to me, Lord Lenwood. Fitzroy's mouth twisted into a caricature of a smile. He had just seen his doom. All the many possibilities that the situation might have contained now began to collapse together into one inevitable and appalling certainty. The veins stood out starkly on his hands as he spread his fingers over the window frame. What the hell! What the *hell* did it matter?

He thrust his fist hard against the wood, making the latch rattle, before he turned back to face them. Richard sat next to Joanna, holding her hand in his own with a natural tenderness. She buried her face against his coat.

"I'm sorry about all of this, Lord Lenwood," Fitzroy said quietly. "It has no doubt been damnable for you to be forced into my company in such a way. But the situation is about to be taken out of our hands. The Black Earl has arrived, Lord

Evenham, my father. He is descending from his carriage as we speak, and he bears the rattle of wedding bells at his coattails and the sour taste of the nuptial toast in his mouth.''

"He will make Quentin marry me?" asked Joanna faintly, rubbing away the trace of tears.

"Oh, no, my dear," Fitzroy said softly. "You are safe from that. He cannot do so. You see, Quentin is already married."

There was a flat silence as Richard gazed blankly at Fitzroy for a moment, then Joanna began to laugh. "Married!" she exclaimed. "Quentin has a wife? Then I am free, after all!"

"You will never be free again, after this!" Fitzroy said fiercely. "That is what Richard has been trying to tell you, for God's sake. An elopement can always be covered up and turned into a respectable marriage, but for a young lady of your station to run away with a married man destroys her forever in the eyes of society. And whatever you may think or desire, your father has absolute legal control of your person. He may take what revenge he will. I'm sorry, but there's not a damned thing that your brother can do about it."

"Would you be kind enough to tell us about Quentin's mysterious spouse, Tarrant?" asked Richard, his voice cold and deadly.

Fitzroy smiled at him, a smile that could only be interpreted as an insult in the circumstances.

"She is a singer, some years older than Quentin. They met when he was nineteen. In an excess of youthful passion he carried her off to Scotland, married her, and fathered two children. Two years later she abandoned the children and left him, but unfortunately not for another swain. She turned to religion and leaves a life of blameless chastity, seeking converts in the marketplaces and wynds of Edinburgh. The bawdy songs of the stage have been supplanted by ardent hymns of praise and invocation. Yet unless she is caught in adultery, he cannot divorce her. My father has paid for spies and set up traps, but the fervor of her faith sustains her in her holy purity. Quentin could legally force her to live with him, but he cannot stand her prating company. So he sends her money, pays for care for his offspring, and drowns himself in drink. Only the family knows of it. Ironic, isn't it? We Mountfitchets don't seem to have much luck when it comes to matrimony, do we?"

Richard flushed, an angry burn of color that washed over the fine bones of his face, then left him unnaturally white. "Damn you!" he said quietly. "It is not by my choice that we mention your marriage, sir."

"No," replied Fitzroy coolly. "Least said, soonest mended, indeed."

Joanna stared at two men, the brother she loved, and the dark, forbidding man who had tracked her down and kissed her so ruthlessly. Quentin's wife made no difference to her. She had never intended to marry him. But what on earth was she going to do now? And how was her father going to react when he heard about this?

Two hours later, her face blotched with tears, Joanna had her answer. The Black Earl, Lord Evenham, had swept into the room carrying a package of papers from Lord Acton. He handed them to Richard in silence. Joanna watched her brother turn white with shock as he read the covering letter. He barely glanced at the other documents.

"For God's sake! But my father doesn't know what this man is!" he exclaimed. "It is impossible!"

"It is done, sir!" snapped Lord Evenham. "You will please apprise my son Fitzroy of the contents."

"What man?" asked Joanna. The tension pressed around her like a thick bank of ice.

Richard thrust the papers at Fitzroy and dropped back to the chair beside her. "Joanna, listen. There are things in life that cannot be undone. But if he harms one hair on your head, or causes you a moment's disquiet, I shall happily kill him."

"Who?" said Joanna, feeling the blind panic undermining her determination as a storm surge attacks dunes. "Kill whom?"

Fitzroy rapidly perused the letter. He looked up with a hard, clenched line at the corner of his mouth, and an unholy light of deviltry in his eyes. "This man, my dear," he said, indicating himself. "There is only one rogue around whose very existence stirs up murder in every peaceful breast. Richard means me, of course."

"What is it?" Joanna stood up. She wanted to break the air and see it shatter in shards. "What does Father say?"

Fitzroy refused to reply. He turned to the Black Earl, his movements fluid and deadly, like a swordsman facing an enemy. Lord Evenham stood at the window, tall, imposing, elegantly inhaling a pinch of snuff. As calm as when he had first entered, he was in complete, quiet command, an absolute, certain authority, without bluster or excess. He met his eldest son's cold anger with equal implacability.

Fitzroy held up the letter and faced that merciless will with an identical determination and dark, icy depths in his voice. "You have arranged this, sir, for your own ends. You know that I will not stand aside and see Quentin hanged, but do not think that by forcing my hand in such a way you will avoid seeing the singer's little waifs finally inherit Evenham Abbey. I will do it, but you may have my oath upon it that there will be no joy in it for you and Mother."

"I will see you wed, sir." Lord Evenham closed the lid of his snuff box with a small snap. "And if force is what it takes, so be it. You have a duty to your house and to your blood. Your little Spanish bride has been dead for two years. As the next Earl of Evenham, it is incumbent upon you to take another wife. Lord Acton and I have agreed to the settlements. But do not think for a moment that Lord Acton is bluffing about Quentin, or that I will intervene. If you refuse, you will see your brother hang, sir."

"And which do you think is more trying to my tender sensibilities, my lord?" The subtle voice betrayed depths of sarcastic awareness. "A hanging or a wedding?"

Joanna stood up. She was shaking. "Whose wedding?" she demanded.

Fitzroy turned to her and grinned. He looked wild, dangerous.

"Why, yours and mine, my dear," he said gaily. "Our fathers have agreed without consulting either of us. Lord Acton will overlook my family's stain to your honor if I redeem your reputation by marrying you. Otherwise he will have his revenge on that poor clay." He indicated the still flaccid figure of his brother, breathing more noisily now on the couch. Quentin groaned and turned over. Fitzroy held up the two sheets of paper that Richard had handed him with the letter. "This is a legal complaint drawn out against Quentin Mountfitchet for the kidnapping and rape of Lord Acton's daughter; and this is a special license for the marriage of Lady Joanna Acton to Fitzroy Monteith Mountfitchet, Lord Tarrant. It is up to us which one is acted upon."

"What?" exclaimed Joanna. "This is absurd! I won't marry you!"

"Oh, no, my dear, on reflection I think you will, though it is as far from my inclination as it is from yours. Sadly, I am quite a catch, however black my character." And suddenly hating the hostility he saw in her face, Fitzroy turned to Richard. "Unless you think that when you tell Lord Acton what kind of man he is forcing is daughter to wed, he will change his mind?"

Joanna caught at her brother's sleeve. "You can stop Father from doing this, surely?"

"He won't care," said Richard, gently touching her cheek. His eyes were bleak with devastation. "Unfortunately Lord Tarrant doesn't make a false claim about his value on the marriage mart, Joanna. As heir to Evenham, he's a fine catch. If he had murdered and ravished his way across Europe and back again, Father wouldn't mind. But you will always have the backing of your brothers, sister mine. Either Harry or I will happily cripple or dispatch him for you, if you ever say the word."

"And if I still refuse to marry him?"

Richard closed his eyes for a moment, distress clear in every feature. "Then Father will press charges against Quentin and see him hanged, and you will live out your days confined to King's Acton, publicly disgraced. There will be no reprieve and certainly no painting. He means it, Joanna. Quentin may deserve death, but only you can decide what to do. I hope that it will be to tell all the Mountfitchets to go hang!''

"Lord Lenwood!" exclaimed Fitzroy, mocking. "When did you ever suggest that an innocent man should meet such a fate? I am as much a victim of my brother's indiscretion as your sister, am I not?''

Richard's eyes flew open and met Fitzroy's derisive gaze. "For God's sake, Tarrant, show her the letter!''

With an elegant bow, Fitzroy gave Joanna her father's letter. Rage sputtered from the page, echoed in the ink splattered across the paper by a pen breaking under too forceful a fist. Lord Acton had learned from Lord Evenham that Quentin was already married. The two earls had agreed to the only solution: Joanna must marry his brother, Fitzroy, or they would both suffer the consequences. She closed her eyes for a moment. Surely her mother could soften him? But, no, at the bottom of the letter was a terse note in Lady Acton's flowing hand.

"He is not to be moved this time, Joanna. After what happened with Harry and the others, like the lamb you are to be led to the slaughter. Your father has no compunction in destroying the tree along with the fruit thereof. I'm very sorry, my dear girl, but not every forced marriage is a bad one. You must make the best of it that you can.''

Let us destroy the tree with the fruit thereof, and let us cut him off from the land of the living, that his name may no more be remembered. It was one of Miss Able's favorite passages from Jeremiah. Lady Joanna Acton had done something even more unforgivable than her brother Harry, who had married a Scottish governess, and her father was not going to excuse her. He was prepared to see Quentin Mountfitchet hanged at Newgate if she did not give in—a slightly uneven return for the loan of a curricle and an escort to Harefell, however ineffective he had been in delivering her there. And even if she called

Lord Acton's bluff over Quentin, her own future was doomed: to live out her days in that great marble mausoleum, King's Acton, cut off forever from the world. She could stand it, perhaps, and surely they would not really hang the son of an earl?

Joanna glanced up at the ring of faces. "I cannot," she said. "I cannot marry this man." She turned to Lord Evenham. "My lord, you will not allow my father to harm one of your sons, surely?"

"I must have a suitable heir in the direct line in the next generation!" replied the Black Earl without blinking. "If it is necessary to sacrifice one useless son to compel the other to do his duty by his house, then so be it!"

Fitzroy watched Joanna with an oddly conflicting range of emotion. She was headstrong, willful, spoiled. She was at least ten years his junior, little more than a schoolgirl. She was beautiful. And at a glance she looked—if one did not concentrate too long on the pure English skin and the full curve of upper lip—decidedly like Juanita, his Spanish bride, who had died in circumstances that had made honorable Richard Acton want to execute her husband without compunction.

Fitzroy turned to his father. "My lord, if you would kindly allow me a few moments alone with my future bride, I would be most grateful."

"I shall be waiting in my carriage, sir, to escort the young lady back to town. You may have five minutes. Then I would be pleased if you would do something to sober Quentin and bring him back with you in your phaeton. Smithers may retrieve my curricle, and this unfortunate incident will be behind us. Lord Lenwood, perhaps you would like to accompany us?"

Richard bowed his head and with one quick, agonized glance at Joanna, followed Lord Evenham from the room.

Joanna could not bear to meet his gaze. She let her eyes wander across the dull plaster—there were faded prints on the walls, of birds and flowers—then up at the low, timbered ceiling where traces of paint hung in small green peels, so

that the beams had the look of lichened tree trunks in an
ancient forest. The Swan was Tudor, no doubt, with its lead-
paned windows and crooked doorways. How odd that in this
busy, modern world, so many post-houses should still echo a
long-lost past.

"Evenham Abbey is Tudor, also," said Fitzroy quietly. Yet
there was still that echo of anger and derision there. "Stolen
from the monks for the benefit of my ancestors. Strange that
such a hallowed place should spawn such an unholy family,
isn't it?"

"They will not hang Quentin," replied Joanna.

Fitzroy dropped into the chair opposite hers. He stretched
out his long legs and let his head fall back against the high
wing. "Are you prepared to take that risk? I am not."

"I thought you hated him. Aren't you glad to have an excuse
to see him hanged?"

"I do not hate him." It was said flatly, without emotion.

There was silence for a moment.

Joanna studied the carved leaves trailing up the edge of the
stone fireplace. They were a little battered and blunted by time,
the veining blurred, the stems chipped away. "It is absurd. I
was not abducted; I went with him of my own accord."

"The law is often absurd, and Quentin has broken it. To
carry off an heiress is a hanging offense whether you claim
you were willing or not, and we have two earls determined to
press charges—your father to save your reputation, mine to
force me into marriage at any cost. Once the charges have been
made, the law will grind out its own inexorable course. No one
will be interested in your opinion."

"So what are we to do?" Joanna knew she had been defeated.
She could not stand alone against the force of all of them: her
father, the Black Earl, and most of all this man with his spoiled,
sarcastic humor.

He laughed suddenly, with a wild, reckless lack of restraint.
"Why, we shall marry, of course, like the dutiful children we
are—it will be the first honorable act toward a lady that I have
been seen to commit in a long time—and thus I shall save

your reputation. Then we shall set up a splendid pretense at housekeeping in my house near town. We shall receive the wellwishers with smiles and a sham of wedded bliss. But privately you won't ever need to see me. I have my own pursuits.''

Why should it wound, when she had no desire to marry him? Yet it did. ''Involving women, I suppose,'' she said tartly.

Fitzroy grinned at her. ''Of course. I shan't make any demands on you. You may live as you please. As I shall continue with my own life. I have urgent business in town at this moment which interests me far more than taking an unwilling bride.''

The painting above the mantel was a watercolor, not badly done, of a riverbank and a rustic cottage. ''I should want a studio.''

''Very well. You may have an entire floor, if you wish. In fact, you may do any damned thing you please with the house. I don't imagine I shall be there much. So, you see, marriage to me will bring you what you have been longing for: freedom to paint. Ironic, isn't it?''

She felt the force of his dismissal of her pierce like an arrowhead. It settled somewhere inside her rib cage, threatening to fester. *But I have never wanted to marry! And he is offering me my heart's desire, more clearly than my own plans for Harefell. It doesn't even matter if he means it. Because if he breaks trust, Richard and Harry will retaliate, and—like Quentin's wife—once I am married, I can always run away. A married woman is free of her father, at least.*

''You don't want children?'' she asked.

He took up the poker and rearranged the coals. Joanna's attention snapped back to him. He had lovely hands, square and strong. There was a cold bite to his voice. ''I most particularly don't want children. There is no other revenge that I can have on my father for this except to deprive him of that grandson from my loins that he so desperately craves. So Quentin's little singer will be the mother of the next earl.'' The dark eyes glanced up, implacable, but with just that hint of derision. ''You will not again be subject to my unwanted attentions. I have enough females to satisfy my natural male needs. And once we are married you may take whatever lovers you please, as long as you are discreet about it and produce no bastards. So let that one kiss be the first and last expression of lust between us. Even if you invite me, madam, it will never happen again.''

Chapter 5

Fitzroy accepted the brandy from Lord Grantley with a polite bow of the head. A rattle of carriages and a splashing of horses' hooves could be faintly heard in the London street outside, broken by the steady tolling of church bells. It was raining. The light coming in through the tall windows into Lord Grantley's study in Whitehall was dull and flat, leaving the room washed in tones of gray.

"We were wrong, my lord," Fitzroy said. "It is not Lady Carhill. Greeks and Trojans mean nothing to her, and I was then forced to extricate myself from a very delicate situation."

Lord Grantley was a generation older than Fitzroy, his white hair curling away from a balding brow. The buttons on his ivory waistcoat stretched a little too tightly over a portly belly, but he embodied command. He stood looking down at his guest with a slight frown. "It's a damnable business, sir! So who is left?"

"After Lady Carhill? Lady Reed and Lady Kettering. Three ladies, two more campaigns of seduction." Fitzroy smiled up at the older man.

"You damned dog! Very lovely ladies, too, of course. It shouldn't be too difficult for someone of your famed talents."

Fitzroy took a sip of his brandy. "There is a small change in my situation, however, my lord." Lord Grantley raised a questioning brow. "I am to marry on Friday."

"Marry?" The word burst out, a tiny explosion of annoyance and shock.

"Indeed. Do not look so very surprised. It is a common enough human pastime—to tie oneself for life to a perfect stranger in a bond that can never be broken. Who does not marry? Aren't we all gluttons for punishment?"

"But marry! Now? To whom, by God?"

"The lady who honors me with her hand is Lady Joanna Acton—the famous countess's younger daughter. She favors her mother in looks, so you may believe that I have effected a coup, if you like." Lord Grantley still looked completely astonished. "Yes, I know that the chit's not even had a season. She comes to her nuptials straight from school, unsullied and refreshingly naive. Our fathers have arranged the match, a little gothic, but there you are. The wedding is to take place at King's Acton, a private affair, just immediate family. I shall thus be out of town for a few days."

"And you agreed to this? At this juncture? When Lady Kettering holds a ball this Friday? It might be critical that you attend. For God's sake, Tarrant, have you gone mad?"

"Very possibly." Fitzroy stood up. "But don't worry, my lord. A little delay will do no harm. It will keep our villain guessing, at least, and Lady Kettering offers another dance in a fortnight. Apart from missing this one upcoming ball, the marriage will not interfere in any way with my work."

Lord Grantley looked incredulous. "Hah! You would not say so if you had ever been—" He stopped and bit his lip. "But you were married, of course. I'm sorry. For a moment I had forgotten. I shouldn't have mentioned it."

"Yes," said Fitzroy darkly. His knuckles shone white as his fingers closed hard on the stem of his glass, but he was entirely unaware of it. "To Juanita, whom I willingly sacrificed for the cause in the Peninsula. But poor Juanita was an orphan, so my crime went unavenged. Sacrifice should not be necessary and would most certainly not be wise this time, unless it is mine, of course. Lady Joanna has several puissant brothers and her father is well known to you—not a man to cross lightly. I do not want any of the Actons breathing down my neck, so I shall try to be as discreet as you could possibly wish with the ladies.''

''But what will you do, sir, if the ladies do not wish for discretion?''

Lord Grantley could not see the expression on Fitzroy's face, and the subtle voice seemed entirely free of distress as he replied with a certain humor: ''I don't know, my lord. My duty, no doubt.''

Joanna returned to London in an oddly detached daze. It all seemed unreal. The journey with Lord Evenham and Richard, where the two men talked politely of commonplaces as if nothing momentous had occurred, passed in a blur. Her arrival at Acton House to face her father should have caused her at least some consternation. Instead, she walked into the house quite calmly to find that the earl had gone out, and her mother wished to see her. She went up to the withdrawing room which looked out over Park Lane to discover the countess busy at her writing case, compiling lists. It was too strange to comprehend. Everything seemed unchanged: the gilt chairs, the voluptuous goddess sailing across the ceiling in shades of blue and pink, her mother's calm, quizzical look as she tapped her perfect cheek with the feathered end of her quill.

''Ah, Joanna! But where is Richard?''

Joanna walked restlessly to the fireplace and back. ''He went straight home to Acton Mead. He said he didn't trust himself to meet Father until he had given Helena a chance to calm him down.''

''Very wise, no doubt. They will join us at King's Acton for the wedding. Pray, sit down, my silly child. Now, I have drawn up a list of clothes and other things that you will need.

And I have found you a wedding dress. Would you like to see it?''

"To be honest, Mama, I really don't care if I am married in sackcloth and ashes.''

"Ah, I was afraid it would be like that. Was Lord Tarrant quite impossible?''

Joanna's lips twisted just a little as she bit back a derisive grin. "Richard doesn't like or trust him. They almost came to blows.''

"A bad sign, I admit. Richard is usually an excellent judge of character. Does he think Tarrant merely offensive, or actually dangerous?''

"He is an arrogant, self-centered rogue!'' Joanna felt a faint stirring of dread as she said it. They weren't just words, were they? They meant something real, something quite appalling to face. She was to be tied to this man for life. Once it was done, it could never be undone. She must swear to love, honor, and obey him till death did them part. As the panic leapt into her throat, threatening to strangle her, she crossed the room to her mother. Having no idea that she was about to do it, Joanna dropped to her knees and laid her head against Lady Acton's lap. "But then so am I. We shall be well matched. Mama, I'm so sorry!''

Lady Acton touched her daughter tenderly on the cheek, then brushed a wisp of dark hair back from her forehead. "You are not selfish, Joanna. You are just filled with too much passion and too much burning longing for life. You will find love, my dear, either within this marriage of convenience, or out of it. And at least there will be children.''

Joanna rocked back on her heels and gazed up at her mother. "I don't want children! What if I want something of my own, that isn't dependent on a man or lived through him? I want to *paint,* Mama! Can't you understand that? And a woman can't do anything of her own, nothing real anyway, if she's gone soft in the head for a man and children! So if it has to be marriage, then very well, let it be to a self-centered, arrogant bastard like Fitzroy Mountfitchet. At least he will leave me alone!''

And to Lady Acton's considerable distress, Joanna fled the room.

Fitzroy came to call the next afternoon. He was charmingly polite to Lady Acton and the earl, and calmly civil to Joanna. She returned his greeting with an even cooler one of her own. But she dressed in a stylish pelisse and bonnet and went with him in his phaeton to inspect his house, where they were to reside together in wedded bliss when they returned from King's Acton.

It lay a few miles from town in several acres of grounds. He led her through the rooms, from the kitchens in the cellar to the servants' rooms in the attics. It was an elegant, formal house, decorated in the latest style, reflecting nothing of its occupant's personality or taste. Finally he took her into a sitting room with large windows facing a quiet lawn to the north.

"You may have this room for your studio." He went to the window and looked down into the garden. "I have given orders for the furniture to be removed and the carpets put in storage. Will it do?"

"I should like the wallpaper peeled and the walls white-washed, please," replied Joanna.

He turned to her and raised a brow. "For God's sake! Are you serious? The house is leased. The wallpaper?"

"You said I might do anything to the house that I liked." Joanna forced herself to face the insult of his incredulity calmly, while she hated herself for caring at all. "And I have a list here of supplies I shall need."

She reached into her reticule and pulled out her wish list: easels and canvas stretchers, pigments and brushes, oils and charcoal sticks.

Fitzroy took it and gave it a perfunctory glance. "Order anything you like," he said. "You may have it all charged to

my account. I shall see to the whitewash, if it is so important
to you.''

It shook her that he could be so very calm and casual about
it—to take on a wife he didn't want and tear down the wallpaper
to satisfy her whim.

"I didn't really think that you meant what you said at the
Swan Inn.'' Joanna heard the uncertainty in her own voice.
This man, Fitzroy Monteith Mountfitchet, was going to be her
husband. It was to be for a lifetime. A lifetime of frosty
exchanges and this rigid, barely controlled civility. She didn't
know him; she even felt a little afraid of him, perhaps, but
there was no reason for them to be enemies, was there?

"I meant every word that I said. I promised you a studio.
Here it is. If you wish it painted purple, it's of no interest to
me.''

What had Helena said to her once? *We all of us need all the
allies we can get, I think.* Joanna took back the list, folded it,
and thrust it into her reticule. "Thank you for this, at least.''
She fought for the strength to swallow her burning pride and
find something of the grace that Helena had tried to teach her.
"I don't suppose this marriage is any easier for you, is it?''

He dropped to the window seat, crossing his arms and staring
up at her, still with that hint of derision at the corner of his
mouth. The dull daylight behind him struck bronzed lights in
his dark hair where it fell forward across his forehead, a shine
of burnt sienna and cadmium red against that deep, rich black.
"Good God! Nothing is easier than marriage! A few words
spoken in public, a signature, and it is done. After all, I have
done it before.''

It was as if he had slapped her. An overture of peace was
to be met by more mockery! A quick rush of anger brought
the same sarcasm to Joanna's voice. "No wonder Richard
would like to shoot you! Was she a singer, like Quentin's
wife?''

She did not expect him to reply, but he didn't hesitate. "No,
she was Doña Juanita Maria Gorrión Navarro—a nice Spanish
lady.''

Your little Spanish bride has been dead for two years. As the next Earl of Evenham, it is incumbent upon you to take another wife. Had he loved her, this Spanish lady?

"You fought in the Peninsula under Wellington. I know. Richard told me while we were traveling back from the Swan. I suppose it's where he learned that you couldn't be trusted."

His face was unreadable. "And what else did he tell you?"

"Nothing. How could he? Your father was there." Joanna tossed her reticule to a table and dropped onto a Sheraton chair. She knew that her back was rigid and her chin perfectly level. Miss Able would have been proud.

"Very well. Let me fill you in, Lady Joanna, before some busy gossip does it for me. In 1812 we fought the French for Badajoz. It was a long and bloody siege, followed by a long and bloody rape of the town. The soldiers looted and drank for three days, and the officers were powerless to stop them. Perhaps you have heard that Wellington referred to our men as the scum of the earth? This is one reason why. Juanita's entire family died in a fire set by Englishmen. I found her hiding in the stable. She was sixteen. I married her. Two years later, before the battle at Orthez, she was killed."

Joanna could not keep the horror and sympathy from her voice. "I'm very sorry. How did she die?"

He smiled, a hollow, dead gesture, filled with disdain. "If you want the details you must ask Richard. He was there when it happened. And the other thing that Richard can tell you is how beautiful she was. Indeed, she not only shared your name, Joanna, but she looked very much like you. It is not relevant. There is nothing else that you need to know. Now, do you have any other questions or desires concerning this house?"

The vampire might as well ask if you cared to dine.

"No," said Joanna faintly. "None."

It was a long three-day journey to King's Acton. Joanna left with the earl and her mother the next day. It was considered more discreet in the circumstances for her to be married in the church at the Acton country seat than in town, whatever the inconvenience to all concerned. King's Acton was in the west of England. It meant that it was impossible for her sister Eleanor and her husband to travel there from Norfolk and arrive in time, and it was out of the question for Harry and Prudence to be summoned from Scotland. Milly and John would remain at school. Richard and Helena would attend, of course, since Acton Mead also lay west of London, and various elderly relatives from both sides of the family were prepared to lend their consequence to the match in order to avoid the least hint of scandal.

The Earl and Countess of Evenham with their two sons would travel separately. Their daughter, Mary, was unwell; she had developed a cough and it was considered unwise for her to travel. Joanna remembered her from earlier days at Miss Able's Academy. Lady Mary was some years older and had left school when Joanna was still quite young. But she had noticed her, a tall, grave girl with strong bones, who was kind to the little pupils. Joanna felt an odd disappointment that she wasn't to meet her again very soon. Then she had to gulp back a wave of most inappropriate laughter when she heard that Quentin would serve as groom's man. Would he stay sober long enough to hand his brother the ring?

They were all tired and worn to irritation when the carriage finally turned in at the great iron gates and swept up the immaculately kept driveway to King's Acton. Joanna gazed without interest at the woods and park, scattered now with early spring flowers—snowdrops, aconites, celandines—beneath the faintly greening branches. The house massively dominated its setting. Ornamental stone spires pierced the sky along the entire length of the facade; a huge imposing portico presided over a sweep of steps. Joanna's grandfather had torn down the early seventeenth-century house and replaced it with this monument to his conceit. Joanna hated it, but she had been born here, in the great bedroom with the blue and gilt ceiling that dominated the west wing.

Richard and Helena were waiting in the echoing stone hallway with its rows of urns in their arched niches. As Richard welcomed his father and mother, Helena swept Joanna into her warm embrace.

"Joanna, you insane creature! Are you quite exhausted?"

Joanna returned the hug, then held Helena at arms' length and looked into those infinitely wise gray eyes. Her sister-in-law was as blond as her husband, with a deceptive frailty to her slim figure. "Where's Elaine? I shan't even take off my coat until I have seen her."

"Come, then. She's with her nursemaid. But I have set the household in an uproar by insisting that my baby be allowed to sleep in the room next to ours." She laughed. "That Richard and I share a room is already considered *outré* enough! All the protocol of King's Acton is shattered, and in the butler's eyes I can never be redeemed. But I'm not going to let Elaine be banished to that cold, hideous nursery wing where Richard spent his first years—and you, too, of course. Oh, dear. I hope I don't offend you?"

"Helena, you could offend no one. Come, let's go and see Elaine. Has she grown much?"

The ladies hurried away through great echoing corridors and up sweeping flights of stairs. At last they entered a massive bedroom and made their way across its rich expanse of carpet to a set of screens in front of the fire. There Helena had created a little cocoon of warmth, sheltered from the cold grandeur and resonant, hollow spaces. A fresh-faced young woman holding a baby on her lap looked up and smiled.

"She's asleep, my lady. Shall I put her down?"

Joanna gazed for a moment at the small round face, the immaculate, tiny curve of nostril and the sweet mouth, the upper lip curled like a rose petal. Elaine's eyelashes lay in a tan sweep on her flawless cheeks, and one small hand was clenched into a tiny fist against her chin.

"Oh, Helena. She's so beautiful!"

"Would you like to hold her?" Helena gently took her daughter from the nurse and set her into Joanna's arms. "You will probably need some practice with babies. They are the one consolation for having to live with a man." The nursemaid giggled, and Helena smiled at her. "Thank you, Betty. I'll put Elaine to bed. You go and find that handsome husband of yours and tell him what I said."

Still giggling, the girl left the room.

"How can you talk such fustian, Helena? You and Richard are besotted with each other!"

Joanna meant the words to be light and humorous, but her voice cracked. The baby was surprisingly heavy in her arms. She dropped to the chair vacated by Betty. Elaine fit so perfectly into the curve of her elbow. With one hand Joanna pulled the wool shawl away from the baby's chin. Her skin was so smooth! She had that poignant smell that clean babies always had, of milk and soap and lavender-water. With a strange sense of awe, Joanna studied the perfect fingernails and the little creases at the chubby wrists, and felt an unexpected start of tears pricking at her eyelids.

To her horror a splash of water fell onto the baby's cheek. Elaine's little face instantly puckered, but then she relaxed again without waking, only her mouth moving a little. Joanna fiercely brushed away her tears with one hand. Her eyes were beginning to burn and she could tell that her nose was turning red. How humiliating! Oh, dear God, how very humiliating! She could hear those implacable tones as clearly as if Fitzroy Monteith Mountfitchet stood next to her in the room: *I most particularly don't want children.*

Helena reached forward. Gently taking Elaine, she laid her in the cradle waiting beside the fire. Then she put her arms about Joanna and held her.

"This man of whom Richard refuses to speak—the dastardly Lord Tarrant. If you are to marry him, he will become my brother. I should like to know something about him. So if you want to talk about it, I'm here."

Joanna turned her face into Helena's shoulder, choking back

angry sobs. "I don't know anything about him! And it won't matter. We are to lead separate lives." She wrenched away from the comfort of Helena's grasp, and forced herself to laugh. "But there won't be any children, you see, and though I know it's what I want, I don't think I realized until now just quite how much I will be giving up!"

As a girl, once she had left the confines of the echoing nursery wing, Joanna had been given a suite of rooms of her own, as had her brothers and sisters. She hadn't spent much time there. Along with Eleanor and Milly, she had been sent away to school. Childhood summers had been spent with their grandmother at Acton Mead—the house that the dowager countess had left to Richard in her will—and Christmas had usually seen them as guests of some other household. Until Joanna had spent Christmas two years earlier with Richard and Helena at Acton Mead she had never taken part in any of the things that Helena considered normal Yuletide experiences, gathering holly and ivy, making a kissing bough. Then, these last two years while she had still been at school, she had spent other holidays with friends, often enough at Fenton Stacey with Lucinda Sail, where on her last visit she had also met Quentin and Mrs. Barton-Smith. Nevertheless, this formal suite of rooms had been her only fixed base, and she turned the brass knob and went in with a certain sense of homecoming.

Weak spring sunshine filtered through the windows and cast pale shadows over the gilt and white trim and the cerulean walls. The room was immaculate. The chairs, the writing desk, the brass fender, everything gleamed from the constant care and attention of the King's Acton staff. Joanna did not notice any of it. She took the key that she had hidden in the corner of the mantelpiece and crossed the room to a large chest that sat in one of the window bays.

It was filled to the brim with paper. She began to pull out the sheets, glancing briefly at them as she spread them across the floor: pencil sketches of trees and flowers; watercolors of the weed that had pooled up against the edge of the lake; a violent charcoal rendering of a storm-wracked sky that she had witnessed from the window of this very room when she was fourteen. And then there were the portraits: of Richard frowning over a book; of Harry in the orchard, bold and laughing, shooting down a row of clay jugs one after another; of little Milly with her sunshade, and Eleanor with an embroidery frame. The sheets showed a complete progression from the passionate, clumsy drawings of a child to the fast, accurate portrayals of an artist.

She picked up a drawing she had made when she was almost fifteen, of a pair of old boots that had been tossed aside in the stable. It marked the turning point. The first day she had known that she had really learned to *see,* and had felt the truth and essence of her subject—the very history and soul of the cracked leather—flow unhindered from her eye through her hand and onto the paper. Any woman could have a baby. Only she could do this.

Kneeling on the carpet she was completely absorbed, looking critically at her work. This one of the horses needed a more marked definition of shading, but she liked the overall composition of it, and the head of Richard's black gelding was excellent—that rolling eye, so full of pride and intelligence! The watercolor of the cabbages had a wild, intricate feeling that she loved—the leaves curling back on each other, layer upon layer—but she had spoiled it by working on it too long and muddying the colors. Now, this one, this drawing of Richard doubled over with laughter, was superb. She couldn't fault it.

There was a knock at the door. One of the maids, presumably, to make up the fire. Without lifting her head from an impassioned sketch of a dead bird, Joanna called out permission to enter.

The robin lay tossed and abandoned in a bank of snow, the feathers of one wing spread like the hand of a priest raised in benediction. But the head of the bird was twisted oddly on its body, the beak a little agape, the eyes mere slits of black. The snow was melting into bright, sparkling shards of crystal.

Joanna closed her eyes for a moment, remembering her rush of feeling when she had found it. Poor robin, never to sing again, never to see the sun or build a nest again, lying frozen and stiff in the cruel hand of winter!

She thrust aside the drawing of the bird and took up another.

"I had no idea," said a man's voice, completely without sarcasm or mockery.

Joanna looked up. There was a pair of boots standing next to her. Very black, very shiny boots, marked with small splashes of mud. Her eyes swept up over buckskin breeches and a dark blue jacket to a handsome face under a mass of curling dark hair. Fitzroy Mountfitchet stood over her in her sitting room with one of her drawings in his hands.

"So this is what Richard looked like before he became a soldier—he's always been a damned irritating fellow, hasn't he? Do you realize, my dear affianced wife, that these are quite extraordinary!"

Chapter 6

"What on earth are you doing in here?" Joanna inquired frostily. "Couldn't you wait until tomorrow to inflict your presence? That's our wedding day, isn't it?"

She began to get to her feet, struggling with her skirts. Fitzroy reached down a hand and helped her. Without treading on her drawings she could not move away, so she found herself standing far too close to him, with her hand still imprisoned in his.

Fitzroy gazed down at her, his eyes unreadable, a faint smile curving the corner of his lips. "I came to offer a truce. I have been unnecessarily harsh. Perhaps you would forgive me? I also came because your sister-in-law confronted me before I could even change my clothes. Lady Lenwood intends to dispatch me to hell and the devil, I believe, for my brutal treatment of you. She also quite correctly sees me to blame for the towering argument that her husband is about to have with Lord Acton. Richard would still stop our imprudent wedding if he could."

"Please, leave me alone!"

"This is what it's all been about, hasn't it?" He waved his free hand across her sketches and paintings. "There was no way

I could have known. For God's sake, Joanna! Every schoolgirl paints. Every parlor has its share of insipid, washed-out watercolors and cameo portraits done with blunt scissors. My sister Mary does the most frightful little scenes of shepherdesses in pastures of viridian and cadmium yellow, scattered about with daisies like sheep's eyes. I had no idea that you were anything else.'' He looked back down at her and something she had never seen before in his expression darkened his eyes. "You have been crying? I'm sorry. Is there anything I can do about it?''

Joanna was horrified to feel her eyelids turn hot and dry. Oh, dear God! She would *not* weep in front of him! "You? No, of course not!''

His expression hardened. "Devil take it, Joanna! I am not a monster of iniquity! I'm damned if I want this marriage, but I shan't torment you. I assure you I do not hold you to blame for the way events have turned out. Indeed, I hope you will be happy. For God's sake, don't weep about it!''

She hated him with a clear, passionate flare of loathing at that moment, without knowing why. Joanna only knew that she had been caught out somehow, defenseless and exposed, as if she were discovered in the center of a ballroom without clothes, and that he had witnessed it. She twisted away from his grasp, but he caught her to him with both hands.

"Don't!'' he said. "You are gaining everything you want— not only a studio, but the full backing of my purse. I shall strip the wallpaper. You shall have supplies, models, complete freedom of action about this. Become the artist that you want to be, Joanna. I shall do nothing to prevent it, and marriage to me is what's providing the whole opportunity. It's not a cursed three-act tragedy!''

The tears spilled over, hot and humiliating, to burn down her cheeks, and her hatred flared, consuming any other emotion.

But before she could escape and unwittingly crush her artwork underfoot, he took her chin in his hand and kissed her. His lips moved over hers, seeking and tender. Joanna kissed him back with the full force of her fury, because she couldn't help it and because she didn't know what else to do—anything else would be a defeat, a desertion of pride. His solicitation disappeared. His mouth etched into hers, opening her lips, then he ruthlessly explored her warmth and moisture as he bent her body in his arms. At last he took her head in both hands and let his mouth rove over her face—to her sore eyelids and the sensitive place at the temple—with an exquisite gentleness that ravaged her and left her shaking and defenseless, before releasing her.

"You said," gasped Joanna, breathing hard. "You said you would never do that again!"

"I'm sorry." His eyes were wide and bleak. "It was meant to be something else. For a moment I thought I could . . . but it can never be undone." He stood looking down for a moment at her drawing of the dead bird. " *'Who killed Cock Robin? I, said the sparrow, with my bow and arrow—'* "

Turning abruptly, he left the room.

The waves of paintings and sketches lifted and settled again like leaves in November as he slammed the door behind him.

"Are you certain?" Lady Elizabeth, Countess of Carhill, put up a hand and nervously touched the blond curls tumbling against the back of her neck. "He is marrying the Acton girl? I admit I can hardly believe the news. What a devilish dark horse he is, to be sure."

Her companion leaned forward and poured more tea into a very dainty gold-rimmed dish. She spoke with a soft accent, hard to trace. "The rumor is that he has been forced into the match, a little gothic for this day and age, but she's quite a catch. She had a fortune settled on her by a great-uncle quite recently—all the girls did—so in addition to the dowry that Acton is bound to give her as his daughter, she's an heiress in her own right. Yet I hear that Tarrant is at daggers drawn with her brother Richard Acton, and Lady Pander has been saying that Quentin Mountfitchet tried to run away with her. Do you suppose that Lord Tarrant will first be cuckolded by his own brother or slaughtered by hers?''

Lady Elizabeth took a cup and stared into the swirling liquid. ''From what you told me, Lady Joanna Acton can hardly be much of a match for such a man! She is barely a schoolgirl, while he. . . . Do you suppose the wedding will make any difference to Lord Tarrant?''

''I shouldn't think so, except that he misses Lady Kettering's ball on Friday, and there will have to be some small punishment for that.'' The teapot remained suspended for a moment in one smooth, faintly olive-toned hand. The silver surface reflected an unusual ring on her third finger, diamonds around a large sapphire. ''Do you mind so very much, my dear? He is quite delectable, isn't he? The man certainly sends shivers down my spine; I have never made any pretense to you about that. So last Friday, why did it not go according to plan? They say he cannot resist a lovely woman. I thought you'd easily have made him your slave.''

''I did as I promised. I couldn't have done more.''

''Ah, no, of course, I'm sure you could not. Indeed, Lizzie dear, I hear you set up the most shameful public flirt with him—and it was not only because I planned it for you, was it?'' The teapot was set down on its matching silver tray without a sound. ''What did he say to you? Exactly now! There, see, you are quite put to the blush. He is so very witty, isn't he? Can't you share any of it with me?''

Lady Elizabeth glanced up at her companion. ''He was not witty. He was devastating. He defied me without any difficulty. If you thought that I would be able to humble or manipulate him, you were very wrong.''

The ladies' faces were reflected in the gleaming silver. The curved surface distorted them into two grotesque little caricatures, mocking both style and beauty, one dark, one fair.

''Never mind, my dear. Your failure demands only a small forfeit. May I have a little of your hair?''

''My hair? Why?''

''Why not? Then your debt to me is discharged.''

"Very well." Lady Elizabeth stood up and took a small pair of scissors from her reticule. "And now I must go."

The lady of the diamond and sapphire ring waited until the countess had left the room before she rose and stared at herself in the mirror above the fireplace.

"So Fitzroy Mountfitchet still makes fools of women! And thus he did not have to face his precious sister, and see her devastation that he was discovered in his hostess's bed while his brother eloped! *Dios!* I'll see him shattered yet, sobbing at my feet, and imploring my forgiveness."

Joanna shut herself into her room. She would not, could not go through with this marriage! The chorus of the old child's song echoed without meaning in her head: *All the birds of the air fell a-sighing and a-sobbing when they heard the bell toll for poor Cock Robin . . .*

She spent the best part of the evening pacing, trying to think through the alternatives. She was an heiress, but none of the money was accessible to her. If she ran away, her father would hunt her down and find her. If he decided to lock her in her room for the rest of her days, there was nothing that anyone could do about it, not even her mother. An appeal to Richard and Helena would only bring down the wrath of her father—even the power of the law —on their loving, peaceful household at Acton Mead, and very probably on the foolish Quentin. No, she had trapped herself, and worse, she had trapped Fitzroy Monteith Mountfitchet. No wonder he was angry, but how was she to cope if he didn't keep his word?

She asked for supper on a tray, pleading the headache, yet she felt maddened by the close confines of her room after spending the last few days cramped in a carriage. There was a small folly in the woods beyond the formal gardens, with a view across the lake. It was a place of peace, a place that had served as a retreat throughout her childhood, whenever she had raged against the confines and restrictions of being raised as a lady. Joanna waited until she knew that everyone else would be in the great dining room before slipping down the stairs and out into the garden.

The broken pillars of the folly shone a pale, ghostly white against the night sky. It was a replica in miniature of the Parthenon. As she walked rapidly down the path between the hornbeams, the marble columns seemed almost to float in a thin mist that curled up off the water. Joanna wondered with a strange sense of precognition why she should not be surprised that Fitzroy Mountfitchet was standing there in the mist, gazing out across the lake. She stopped, her heart thudding uncomfortably against her ribs, and watched him.

Power and elegance lay in every line of his figure. It was the quality she had tried to capture in her drawing of the horses—a pure, animal beauty—the beauty of a man, relaxed and easy in the strength of his youth. Joanna closed her eyes and forced herself to face it with a painful honesty. She did not want the man, but she wanted that beauty. It had entranced her from the first moment she had seen him, turning with feral, athletic grace to look up at her from the yard at the Swan Inn. She was fascinated by it, and her very fascination made her afraid, for it gave him power over her.

" 'The world is too much with us,' " he quoted softly, although he did not turn and face her. " 'Late and soon, / Getting and spending, we lay waste our powers: / Little we see in Nature that is ours . . . ' Your mother said you might come here."

"My mother?"

"It did not seem politic to impose my disruptive presence on either you or your brother Richard for the evening meal. I made my excuses to the countess, only to find that you had made your excuses, also."

"I did not want to face them all over the dining table. Do you think it would be pleasant for me to make small talk with Quentin, or your father?"

The darkness flowed around her like a protective shield. Why was it easier to talk to a stranger in the dark—when it was hard to read expressions or see those revealing changes in the eyes?

He turned, leaning his back against one of the pillars and looking up at the frieze overhead. "Why do you suppose in our age of enlightenment and reason that we build replicas of pagan temples and visit them in moonlight? As we conquer Nature with our roads and canals and new factories, at the same time we worship her. It doesn't make much sense."

"Do you worship Nature?" Joanna felt lost, out of her depth. There was a cool remoteness to his voice, entirely without hostility.

"No, but you do. You are a pagan, Joanna, whether you know it or not. That is why, when it is so abhorrent to you, I won't take part in forcing you into this marriage any longer. Why should you care for convention?"

"What about Quentin?"

"I shall get him out of the country."

"Where would he go?"

Fitzroy laughed. The ironic, bitter edge had returned, revealing no merriment at all. "To the devil, no doubt. It is what I've been afraid of for years, but this marriage is a sorry answer, isn't it?"

Joanna looked down. She felt embarrassed to face him, because she had realized that she wanted the marriage, if only she could trust him to give her the freedom he had promised.

"Not really," she said. "I don't mind so very much. I shan't impinge in any way on your life, and I've thought about what you said. You are giving me what I've always wanted: the chance at a life of my own, with the time and means to paint. It is you who's getting nothing in return."

He folded his arms across his chest. "No, I prefer it to the alternatives, if you are indeed willing. I shall have my father off my back and Quentin close enough that I can still reach him. The rest doesn't matter. But I have nothing to offer you of what young ladies usually want in a husband. You won't get my attention or my interest. I shan't be available to you, or supportive of you. I shall try to keep up appearances in public, but in private I shall always be preoccupied with other concerns that I will not share with you. Is that what you want?"

"I shall be in my studio. I don't care what you do. I might as well ask if you care that I won't give you anything that a wife usually gives a husband. You men are so very one-sided in your assumptions, aren't you?"

The thin, weak moonlight caressed his profile, casting the bones into strong relief in shades of indigo and ivory black. Joanna wished she had her sketchbook and her charcoal. She would like to draw him like this, in bold, strong strokes that would express as much of her own anger and distrust as reveal any truth about him.

"No doubt. Very well, then, we do understand each other."

"And you will not kiss me again?" asked Joanna. "How can I trust anything you say? What you have demonstrated so far is that your word means nothing!"

He dropped his head and looked at her. The dim light shadowed his strong features and hid the intensity of his dark eyes, but she could see the wild humor that made him so very attractive curling the corner of his lips.

"Have I? I said I would not act in lust. I will not and did not. I kissed you in your room because you were unhappy and I thought I could comfort you. I did not mean it to become anything else. It was arrogant and foolish of me, and I'm sorry."

"So it ends there?"

The humor colored his voice again, a little mocking. "You will be my wife; I shall have every legal right to force myself on you if I wish. Yet on my honor I swear without reservation that I will never do so. Apart from any other consideration, I am in pursuit right now of some very lovely ladies who are only too eager to slake my baser male needs. Be reassured, Joanna. My word means a great deal."

"Then I take the bargain," said Joanna. "Because it's all I shall ever have. And if this is your assurance that you will not take out your resentment and your rancor on me, then it's good enough. It is not my fault if I look like your first wife and bring back painful memories."

"No," he replied calmly. "It is not that. Indeed, you are nothing like her."

"Though I would like to know why Richard hates you."

Only the tiniest hesitation betrayed him. "You must ask him."

"I have. He said it made no difference now, so he wouldn't tell me. Nevertheless, I will marry you tomorrow. Good night, Lord Tarrant."

Joanna returned to the house and flung herself onto her bed fully clothed, pulling the pillow over her head. Yet she could not bury or deny this appalling, unlooked-for, meaningless sense of desolation. *I thought I could comfort you.* Oh, how dare he!

Fitzroy dressed for his wedding with a quiet and unhurried deliberation. He had soaked in a copper tub of hot water and allowed his valet to shave him, the blade of the razor moving with a gentle, firm touch over his jaw and upper lip and the exposed, upturned curve of his throat. What a great deal of trust to put into the hands of another human being! And what greater trust the valet placed in his master, that he would not move suddenly, and deliberately thrust his own noble jugular into the wicked blade—

Who'll be chief mourner? I, said the Dove, I mourn for my love, I'll be chief mourner.

He dried himself and stood for a moment before the mirror. It was still the honed, athletic body of a soldier, vibrant with power and masculine strength, like a pagan warrior in the insolence of nakedness. But there was a ragged discoloration down one thigh, the trace of a saber cut. He had been lucky not to lose the leg. Another scar marked his back, only inches above the heart, as close as he ever wanted to come to death. But now the warrior had to be transformed once again into a gentleman—an English gentleman in the second decade of the nineteenth century, going to his wedding. Fitzroy's mouth twisted into a small grimace. His valet stood at his elbow with his smallclothes draped over one arm.

Step one: pull on the short linen drawers and shrug the shirt over one's head: a shirt of cambric, delicately stitched with small ruffles and insets of needle-point lace. Two: slide into the stockings and silk knee breeches, buttoned up each side to fit snugly at the waist, then the flat-heeled black shoes. Three: don the white waistcoat and have one's valet help one into a coat cut so tight that it would be impossible to get it across the shoulders without tearing out the seams unless that help was provided. And lastly: lift one's chin like a child, while the faithful valet tied collar and cravat and arranged one's hair, since the jacket prevented a man from lifting his arms above his waist. Fitzroy had a sudden fierce longing for the simpler days of the Peninsula. But of course, the last two years there had not been simple. Juanita had seen to that.

There was a scraping at the door and a footman came in with a tray.

"A message for you, my lord, delivered by hand. The man waits for a reply."

Fitzroy recognized the seal and the signature. It was from Lord Grantley. He tore open the note. It was curt and to the point. *"Drop everything. Return to London immediately. Another man has been killed."*

"Is there a reply, my lord?"

It took a moment to swallow his shock and anger. *Which man?* His valet had already opened Fitzroy's writing case and stood waiting, pen in hand. Fitzroy strode over to him and took it. He wrote a few words on a sheet, sanded them, folded the sheet, and sealed it, using his signet ring to make a deep mark in the warm wax. Fury burned in him like a chimney fire. *Which man this time, for God's sake?*

The footman took the paper, bowed, and walked out.

"My lord," Fitzroy had written. "I shall be pleased to obey your summons. However, I regret that I am obliged to get married first."

* * *

In the grounds of King's Acton, the church of Acton All
Saints had stood as an unchanging symbol of eternity since it
had first been rebuilt in the twelfth century. Parts of the nave
were Saxon and there were a few later improvements, like the
rood screen and the Jacobean pulpit, but the square tower and
soaring arches of the Normans dominated the building. Joanna
had been driven from the house in the landau so she would not
soil her white satin dress and wedding shoes, even though the
door of the church lay only a few hundred yards from the east
wing of King's Acton, sheltered by a small grove of trees.
Church and house, oddly juxtaposed together, spiritual and
worldly power in each other's pockets for centuries, and both
estates agreeing that men should have power over women, to
limit and define their lives.

Helena was with her, helping her with her skirts and veil
and the bouquet of orange blossom—the branches stolen from
the orangery, the flowers made of silk. It was a clear, crisp
day, and the woods were filled with birdsong. Joanna vaguely
noticed a groom standing near the church gate holding a fretting
thoroughbred by the reins, but she could not think about it or
what it might mean. She felt sick with nerves. Helena walked
with her to the church door, gave her hand a quick squeeze,
then she slipped inside. Lord Acton, tightly corseted in his best
clothes, held out his arm for his daughter. No one paid any
attention to the bridegroom's valet, standing quietly to one side
with a small bag and a pair of riding boots.

She didn't know if there was music or not, or whether the
small groups of guests, Acton and Evenham, turned to watch
her slow progress down the aisle. She knew they were all there:
Richard and Helena and Lady Acton; the Black Earl and his
wife, Lady Evenham; a scattering of aunts and cousins. The
angry power of her father at her side dominated her senses, as
if she kept time with a barely restrained mad bull. She vaguely
noticed the stone flagstones beneath her feet and the worn brass
plate in the floor that marked the fifteenth-century grave of Sir

Lionel Acton. He lay forever in full armor, next to his elongated wife and their sixteen tiny children: the ones who had died in infancy even smaller than the three who had reached adulthood. Had that tall, thin medieval lady in her flowing robes felt this afraid on her wedding day? Her husband had been a warrior, very probably a brute, yet she had borne him all those children only to see most of them die as babies. *It won't do!* Joanna told herself. *Everyone in your family has courage, and they always had, as far back in time as anyone can remember! How can you let yours fail you now?*

Joanna raised her chin and looked up. Fitzroy Monteith Mountfitchet and his brother Quentin stood waiting for her at the altar. Quentin gave her a wavering, boyish smile. He was obviously foxed, his brown curls dropping carelessly across his forehead. She barely noticed him. Her eyes were locked with the dark gaze of her bridegroom. Fitzroy had seemed to be frowning slightly, as if preoccupied with something far more important. He looked remote and formal, and impossibly handsome in his impeccable clothes, accentuating his height and his breadth of shoulder. A shaft of sunlight burst through the high windows and fell suddenly across his face, across the rich black hair and the strong nose, the molded cheekbones and firm mouth. Yet as their eyes met, Joanna could see concentration pool in them, and to her immense surprise, he smiled.

She hadn't expected it, but it gave her a warm rush of courage. She could feel the physical impact of it, making her blood sing and her step firm. His smile sent deep creases into his cheeks, and lit up his mysterious dark eyes with humor: not that mocking, sarcastic humor, but a deeply intelligent, offered invitation to share with him in the absurdity of this moment—two strangers in all their stiff finery putting on a show for the world—and Joanna found the courage to go through with it.

She placed her hand in his and spoke her vows with a clear, strong voice. "I take thee, Fitzroy Marmaduke Jeremy Monteith Mountfitchet to be my lawful wedded husband, to have and to hold—"

Marmaduke! No wonder he didn't want to get married, when

it meant a public recitation of his whole name! She felt a sudden spurt of most inappropriate laughter and looked up into his face. Joanna didn't know how to read that odd mixture of expressions, but one thing was clear: there was no hostility to her in his eyes. There was humor there, and something wildly uncaring and distant, along with something else that looked like sorrow and a fierce burning anger. But none of it was directed at her, except the intelligence and wit. Lord Tarrant was offering her his support and something close to an apology, and Joanna made it through her wedding service without disgracing herself.

"... man and wife. You may kiss the bride."

Fitzroy touched her chin and kissed her briefly, with an impersonal courtesy, before escorting her from the altar and into the vestry where they were to sign their names. The cool, light touch of his lips on hers made her knees as weak as the spring sunshine and turned her blood unexpectedly into something heady and sweet, like mulled wine. What a strange thing, that his kisses could be so different, yet each still move her to the very soul! Above their heads the church bells began to ring out in a joyous peal, the clamor of notes jangling into one strange harmony, and the guests came forward to offer congratulations. It seemed odd, since she had been forced into marrying a stranger, that their parents and relatives should press greetings on them as if it were a real marriage.

"Come, then," boomed Lord Acton. "Let us return to the wedding breakfast! Take my girl, Tarrant, and give her sons, by God!"

"You will forgive me, my lord," said Fitzroy with a correct bow. "The son-making will have to wait. Urgent business recalls me to town, and I must go without my breakfast and my bride."

He was stripping off the tight jacket as he spoke, and signaling to his valet. The man stepped forward with the bag.

"To London?" asked Lord Acton in tones intended to freeze everyone where they stood.

"Regrettable, but necessary. You will excuse me?"

"By God, you shall not do this, sir!" It was the Black Earl, Lord Evenham.

For a moment it seemed that the two earls were ready to attack him, that Lord Acton would even use physical, brute power to restrain his daughter's bridegroom on his wedding day. Joanna felt the most unseemly, wild surge of giggles, which she instantly suppressed. They were prepared to manhandle a viscount into bed with his bride? Did they think they could force him?

Fitzroy remained entirely calm. "Alas, Father, I shall."

The surge toward him stopped. Fitzroy had pulled a small pistol from his pocket. Lord Acton had raised his cane; it hung like a barber's pole above his head. As Joanna fought her indecorous urge to laughter, Fitzroy caught the bag and his boots from his valet, stepped into the private space where the vicar donned his vestments, and locked the door behind him.

The scandalized guests poured out of the church, only to see Fitzroy run from the side door and swing onto the thoroughbred which had been standing at the gate. He had stripped off his wedding clothes and thrust himself into breeches, boots, and riding coat. The horse spun and reared, before galloping off toward London. Fitzroy briefly doffed his hat and waved it, while that feral, secret mix of determination, desperation, and hilarity lit his face.

Joanna watched him go with mixed emotions. She was abandoned in full view of her family and his, and the handful of servants and tenants who stood ready to applaud and throw rice at the happy couple. She supposed she ought to be angry—what could be more humiliating to a bride, after all?—but it had been so very splendid! To face down her father and his in the church with a pistol!

"For heaven's sake, my lords," said a cool voice. "Everyone is hungry. Let us go back and eat." It was her mother, Lady Acton. She smiled at Joanna and winked. "Let Quentin escort his new sister-in-law. We shall all feel a great deal better for our breakfast.''

Quentin grinned and offered Joanna his arm. She took it and allowed him to help her into her carriage. What the devil did it matter if her bridegroom absconded? He would never touch her, and although he might kiss her, she was sure that he meant it to go no further. It would never be a real marriage—and she didn't want one. She wanted the freedom he had offered her: the freedom to paint. And then she saw Richard's face.

Chapter 7

As soon as they arrived back at King's Acton, Joanna waited for the opportunity to get her brother alone. First she had to sit through the interminable wedding breakfast. It took place with an odd, constrained civility, the polite conversation led by her mother. Lady Acton seemed to have no untoward emotions at all about what had happened, but there could be no toasts, nor speeches, nor congratulations, since the bridegroom was missing. The other guests rose to the occasion, even Richard and Lord Acton who were obviously scarcely speaking.

Joanna knew that Richard must have privately confronted her father about Fitzroy. Yet there would be no public scenes or outbursts, just a quiet demonstration of good breeding in the face of calamity. Even Quentin behaved properly, though barely, since it was too early in the day for him to be truly three sheets to the wind. Yet there was a real concern on Helena's face, and that implacable, blind fury on Richard's.

At last it was over, and Joanna was able to get her brother alone in a quiet corner. "It doesn't matter, Richard," she said. "Pray, let it go."

He took her arms in a grip that hurt. "For God's sake,

Joanna! How the devil can I let it go? By God, I knew he was base, but I had no idea that he'd dare to show this much effrontery—to you, to Mother, to his own family! How the hell do you expect me to overlook such an insult?''

''You will *not* call him out!'' insisted Joanna. ''I want your word of honor on it, Richard. It's the only wedding present from you that I care about.''

Richard looked down at her with the eyes that were so like her own. ''I'm not sure you have the right to demand that!''

''Then who else has the right? I am the one most insulted, aren't I? And who are you to demand that a bridegroom be publicly solicitous and caring? You left Helena alone for weeks after you married her!''

''Because I was forced to. Yet I did not leave her at the church door after our wedding. By God, I should have found a way to stop this! The world would be a better place without him.''

Joanna wrenched herself away from her brother, yet the depth of his anger and despair bothered her more than she wanted to admit. *Richard is usually an excellent judge of character. Does he think Tarrant merely offensive, or actually dangerous?* She thrust aside the memory of her mother's words. More to the point, Richard was only a mediocre shot, whereas she had no doubt that Fitzroy was a superb marksman, as Quentin had boasted. A duel might be fatal for Richard.

''But I have every intention of living with him, and I don't want my husband and my brother meeting at dawn like two cocks in the ring!''

Richard looked incredulous. ''Why the devil would you want to live with him?''

''Where else do you suggest that I live?''

''You can come to us at Acton Mead. You'll always be welcome there, Joanna, you know that.''

''Oh, you silly man. Of course I know it, but I don't want to be constantly underfoot and in the way, intruding on you and Helena and the perfection of your marriage. Lord Tarrant has promised me a studio and complete freedom to use it. Do you think I intend to turn that down?''

The deep vertical line had appeared between Richard's brows. ''And what will he demand in exchange? Joanna, you cannot comprehend what a man like that can do, what he may require—''

''Not his marital rights,'' said Joanna flatly. ''So put your mind to rest on that score. He swears to defy his father over it; we shall live in celibate harmony, marked by his never being there. I'm sure that Lord Tarrant has no lack of mistresses.''

''No, I know for a fact that he doesn't,'' replied Richard faintly.

Joanna wanted to ask him again about Juanita, about why he distrusted her new husband so deeply, but she couldn't bear the anguish she saw on his face. So instead she hugged him quickly, and tried to bury her insistent, dreadful unease.

Fitzroy rode hard and fast, picking up a fresh horse every five or ten miles. It was at least two days to London. When he finally rode into Whitehall it was early dawn, and he had not slept at all the previous night. He had stopped briefly at his house on the edge of town, calling for hot water and a change of clothes. However urgent the summons, whether the very kingdom was at stake or not, no gentleman would call upon another unshaved.

Thirty minutes later Lord Grantley ushered Viscount Tarrant into his quiet study. He gave his guest one shrewd glance, then asked the servant to bring coffee.

''Very well, my lord,'' said Fitzroy curtly as soon as the footman was out of the room. ''Which man?''

''Sit down, sir. You cannot help him now. I'm afraid it was Flanders. He was stabbed in a tavern in Whitechapel. There was nothing to say that it was not just a random brawl, except—''

Fitzroy dropped into a chair and steepled his fingers together against his brow. ''Except that he was my groom in the Penin-

sula, and two other men who served closely with me there
have been similarly killed—not the officers who might still be
carrying weapons to defend themselves, but the men. Dear
God! I have been back from Spain for two years. What the
hell is going on?''

Lord Grantley gazed at him steadily. ''That is what you are
supposed to be finding out!''

''With how much to go on? The dying words of Herring,
my poor batman, for God's sake, with a ball through the lung
and trying to make jokes about it, after I had been sent a
message that he was down on his luck and in need of a visit.
Instead I arrive like Azrael, and see him shot down in front of
his wife.''

''But he did have a message for you. And it may be vital,
sir!''

Fitzroy dropped his head into his hands, his strong fingers
buried in the dark hair. ''A message! Some mumbled words
about a threat to Lord Wellington, and the conviction that one
of the ladies I danced with on a particular evening will be given
secret information, and is expecting me to pursue her favors
at a ball she will hold on a Friday. She will identify herself
with a response to some inane statement about Helen of Troy,
and the reward for my cooperation will be the details of the
plot. It's like a damned melodrama. In the meanwhile, men are
dying for no other apparent reason than that they were once
contaminated with my presence during the Peninsular Campaign. It makes no sense at all. It would make no damned sense
even on the stage.''

''But Green and Herring and now Flanders have been
attacked, Tarrant. And Wellington's safety is crucial to achiev-
ing a lasting peace in Europe. It is barely a year since Waterloo,
after all. Since the duke has been in France there has been
more than one assassination attempt. Though Cambrai is proving safer than Paris, we have to take this seriously.''

Fitzroy closed his eyes and pressed his hands over them,
leaving his hair curling in wild disarray over his forehead. Lord
Grantley watched him for a moment. The young man's body

was limned in lines of exhaustion. Grantley was not surprised
to see the trace of moisture on the square palms when Fitzroy
dropped his hands and looked up, nor the too bright shine of
his eyes, though the bite of sarcasm in his subtle voice remained
unchanged.

"You think for one moment that I do not? Lady Reed holds
a ball this coming Friday. I am invited. Let us hope to God
she is a devotee of the Iliad."

The day after her wedding Joanna packed everything she
owned and retraced the slow journey back to town with Lord
and Lady Acton. She spent one night at Acton House on Park
Lane, then the next morning several footmen and grooms
accompanied her to her new home, the house where Fitzroy
had shown her the room she could use as a studio. As the
menservants carried boxes and trunks up to the suite set aside
for her private use, she went straight to that elegant drawing
room on the north side of the house. She opened the door with
a certain sense of trepidation, then stared in amazement. It had
been completely stripped: no furniture, no carpet, the walls
gleaming with a fresh coat of white paint, and there were a set
of packages at the side of the room. Joanna immediately opened
them. Everything she had wanted: easels, pigments, canvas. He
had remembered. The fearsome Fitzroy Monteith Mountfitchet
had kept his word.

He was not at home. He had left no messages. The servants
quietly accommodated her; she was expected, but that first
evening she dined alone. It was possible that he did not return
that night at all, for Joanna retired to her lonely bed at midnight
without having seen him or heard him come in. She thumped
at her pillow with her fist and told herself that she was far
happier that way.

The next morning she set up her studio, and then she was
truly absorbed, mixing pigments and preparing a palette. She
had no idea that it was already afternoon when the door opened
and a footman came in.

"There is a lady to see you, madam."

"A lady? Did she leave a card?"

A pale face beneath a sleek cap of dark hair peered in past the footman. "Lady Tarrant? You will forgive me, I pray. But when I couldn't come to your wedding, I hoped you would not mind very much if I made myself known as soon as I could. We were both at Miss Able's Academy. Perhaps you remember me? I am Lady Mary Mountfitchet, Fitzroy's sister."

Joanna pushed back a stray lock of hair and rubbed her hands down over the smock that she wore to work in. She was quite unaware that she had left a smear of paint on one cheek.

"Lady Mary! I remember you very well, and I recall how very kind and patient you always were with us little girls. I'm so glad that you came! Please, come in! Oh, dear! I don't even have a chair in here. Let us retreat to the withdrawing room."

"No, I don't want to disturb your work. In fact, I have come to ask a favor of you that involves it."

Joanna pushed a pile of paper from the top of a crate that had contained canvases. "Then, pray, sit here! Now, what can I possibly do for you?"

"I would like a portrait done. You can do portraits, can't you?"

Joanna nodded, intrigued. "Whose?"

"I would like a painting of Fitzroy."

Surprise turned her back rigid for a moment, and Joanna had to force herself to take a deep breath. "Your brother?"

"And your husband," replied Lady Mary instantly. She coughed into a handkerchief and tried to hide it by laughing.

Joanna felt a surge of agitation as if Lady Mary had brought her bad news. "But he would never agree! He would have to sit for me—pose—for several days, weeks possibly. He doesn't intend to spend any time here at all. I don't see—"

Lady Mary coughed again. Her skin was very white except for a red spot that burned in each cheek. "He has already agreed."

"Then why does he not go to a professional portrait painter?"

"He doesn't have time, whereas you're already in the house,

so he could snatch odd moments. When he came back to town he told me you were a real artist. Fitzroy used to paint, too, so he knows what he's talking about. It would be a very great kindness to us both if you would do it. Please say that you will.''

Joanna had to sit down; for the second time in just over a week she felt faint. Since there wasn't a chair, she just dropped to the floor and folded her legs underneath her skirts. Her mouth seemed dry, her tongue too big for it. ''He used to paint?''

''Yes, he was very good. But then he went away to the war and he gave it up.''

''But why would he want his portrait painted?''

''To please me. Fitzroy spoils me; I suppose older brothers often indulge their little sisters, don't they? I think sometimes he'd do anything I asked, so I'm usually very careful asking. But this time I have an urgent reason.'' Lady Mary stood up and crossed to the window, hiding another cough in her handkerchief. ''My doctors are worried about my lungs. I'm to go to Switzerland—I leave in a few weeks—for a change of air. I'll be there for at least six months. If I take Fitzroy's portrait, I can pretend that I still have him near me, and I shan't feel that I'm so all alone.''

Joanna scrambled to her feet and went up to her new sister-in-law. Impulsively she put her arms around the older girl. ''I shall be happy to do it.''

''And there is another favor, too, that I'm trying to get the courage to ask you.''

''Name it.''

Mary blushed a little. ''Would you also do a portrait of me for Fitzroy? I could come here every day, if you like.''

''I would be honored, Lady Mary. We can start tomorrow, but I shall come to you. You aren't well. You shouldn't have come out. I'll ring for a chair to be brought here, and some tea.'' Joanna crossed to the bell pull. She felt her blood beginning to sing at the prospect of these two portraits. ''Is it very typical of your brother Fitzroy to be this highhanded and let you do the asking?''

Lady Mary laughed, then coughed again. "I'm not sure what's typical of him any longer; he's been so strange ever since he came back from the Peninsula. I only know that I love him. I hope that doesn't sound odd."

Older brothers often indulge their little sisters, don't they? Even the wild, demonic Lord Tarrant, apparently. Joanna wondered briefly what Fitzroy was like when alone with his sister: the man who had smiled so reassuringly at her wedding and enabled her to get through it all; the man who had caught her imagination for a moment at the folly?

"No," said Joanna, with a strange constriction around her heart. "It doesn't sound odd at all."

After Lady Mary left, Joanna could no longer concentrate on her pigments. To do a portrait of Fitzroy! Desire for it burned in her fingertips. She wanted to paint him as he had looked in the moonlight at King's Acton, and she wanted to capture that wild, mysterious humor tinged with the strange desperation that she had seen on his face when he had left her standing at the church door after their wedding. Would her hand reveal more of him in a painting than she had consciously seen with her eyes? With the painful honesty that she brought to her work, Joanna once again faced her feelings about him, the fascination diluting her animosity, the attraction mixed with her doubt. *Fitzroy was also an artist! Why had he not mentioned it?*

She faced the answer with the same candor: *Because you are nothing to him, Joanna Acton, but a nuisance, a problem, a lady he was forced to marry to save his brother. Why the devil should he include you in anything that he is or does?*

After her meal that evening she found herself pacing through the house, looking for signs of him. Though it was only a rented house, this was his home. He had lived here since returning from the Peninsula. Yet it seemed devoid of individual touches. There was nothing that revealed him, neither the arrogant man who had arrived at the Swan, nor a man who used to paint before going for a soldier. Joanna let her candlelight flicker over the books in his study, a selection of authors that any gentleman might own; she studied the paintings, they were all from the previous century, of landscapes or horses, nothing personal; it was a house that he hadn't really lived in, as if for the last two years he had been suspended, belonging nowhere.

"Were you looking for something?" said a subtle voice behind her.

Joanna whirled around. "Yes, you!"

Fitzroy peeled off his gloves and threw them onto a chair. He looked tired, the fine, tanned skin drawn tightly over the strong bones of his face. "You were looking for me? Why?"

"No, not the physical you! I was looking for who you really are—inside all that pride and sarcasm. The man whose portrait I am to paint for his ill sister."

"Dear God," said Fitzroy. "And what did you find?"

"Nothing. It's as if you don't exist in this house. Do you exist in the world?"

He paced restlessly to a writing desk in the corner of the room and began to sort through the small stack of letters there. He looked formal, remote. "I would hope so," he said dryly. "Several people would say I exist only too much, your brother Richard for one. He'd rather see me out of it."

"Yes, but he won't help you leave unless you do something that's outrageously unforgivable. I made him promise."

Fitzroy looked around at her. "Thank you for your kind solicitation, Lady Tarrant. I trust you are finding everything else in the house to your satisfaction?"

Joanna felt a small stab of anger. She had been forced into this match as much as he had, yet surely it was reasonable that she didn't want her brother to dispatch her husband? "Yes, of course. Thank you for the studio. When may I expect you for the first sitting for your portrait?"

He tossed down the letters. "Now, if you like."

"Very well, I can do some preliminary sketches."

She marched from the room and through the corridors to her studio without looking back to see if he was following. Yet she knew that he was there, as she knew without looking that her shadow was there on a bright day, or that her heart beat in her chest without listening for its beat. She could feel his presence in her bones. *He is a man who can never be ignored,* she thought. *How do I capture that in paint?*

As they reached her studio he stepped ahead and opened the door for her. A small courtesy, devoid of meaning, yet she noticed the shape of his hand as he held the knob, a purely masculine hand, as beautiful as a Michelangelo sculpture. Was that the source of her fascination? A craving, an attraction, simply that of an artist for the aesthetic?

Joanna picked up the smock that she had left across a crate and shrugged into it.

"I am surprised that you agreed to this," she said. "It would seem that you are always busy."

"I am. Where do you want me?"

"Over there. Near the window. I had the footman bring in that chair for your sister. But once I begin the painting I shall need you to sit every day. Can you do that?"

He dropped into the chair and sprawled back, looking at her from faintly narrowed eyes. "Name the time."

Joanna pinned a fresh sheet of paper to her board. "Evening is best. Then I can use candlelight to create the same effect each time."

"But I have engagements most evenings, Lady Tarrant. And so will you. In fact we are invited to a ball this Friday. My father and yours will expect that we both attend, and Lady Reed would be devastated not to meet my new wife." It was said with that faint air of sarcasm. It infuriated her.

"Then you must sit for me when we get back." She took a knife and sharpened her charcoal stick, chopping fiercely at the innocent wood. "I find it incredible that you let your sister come to me with her request. A message would have sent me to her; she wouldn't have needed to risk the air. She is obviously very ill. Don't you care?"

"Lady Mary knows that I have things I must do. She also likes to go out when she is feeling up to it. If she is dying, is that a reason to restrict what is left of her life? Rather the opposite, I would have thought.''

Joanna dropped her charcoal. "She is *dying?*"

His voice was level and controlled, but anguish shimmered and darted beneath the surface. "I hope not. But the possibility brings me here to your studio. Nothing else would, I assure you. Now, for God's sake, start working.''

Joanna stared at him blindly. It was as if her own shock and distress stripped what she was seeing of meaning. Then she shook herself. This was the gift that Lady Mary wanted. "I shall start with a profile. Stay just as you are and look at the window frame.''

He remained as still as a marble god while Joanna feverishly let her charcoal sweep over the paper. The line of brow, nose, and chin burned into the white surface. In a set of quick strokes she blocked in the turn of his shoulder and his high, stiff collar and cravat which blocked any view of his neck or throat. His hair lay like a shadow over his forehead. She stepped back for a moment and looked at what she had done. Emotion had distorted her drawing into something far too disturbing. In one violent movement, she stripped the paper from the board and crushed it in both hands.

Fitzroy looked around. "Do I contaminate your art—like the blood of Nessus—poisoning your gift into agony?''

"No, it is not your fault," she said blindly. "Stay like that. I shall start again.''

It would not come right. Every attempt dulled into meaninglessness. Joanna began to hate herself, and her pain threatened to spill over into something embarrassing and public. This was her one gift. She had thrown away every privilege to which she'd been born in order to pursue it: a season in London; evenings filled with frivolity and flirtation; the chance to meet a man she could love, to marry him and bear his children. And now her skill seemed to have seeped away, draining from her fingertips like sand flowing from a broken hourglass, making a mockery of her sacrifice. She tore down the sheet and crumpled it with the others.

"What is it?" he asked. There was genuine concern in his voice.

Joanna threw down her charcoal and walked away from the easel. "Nothing. I am out of practice. Let us try again tomorrow. Anyway, who was Nessus?"

He glanced up at her and flexed his shoulders. "The centaur who carried off Hercules' wife, Deianira. When Hercules shot him down with a poisoned arrow, the dying Nessus convinced her to soak one of Hercules' shirts in his blood, claiming it would act as a love charm. Instead, when she made Hercules a gift of the shirt, the poison caused the hero so much torment that he killed himself."

"And Deianira hanged herself, too, didn't she? I remember now." Joanna paced restlessly. "What do you suppose all those old stories really mean? Centaurs and gods and warriors in bronze armor? Must heroes fight monsters to prove themselves, and must it always end in tragedy?"

"It doesn't matter how it ends," replied Fitzroy. "It is how they conduct themselves in the meantime, and whether the monster is successfully destroyed."

"That is so typical of a man! Of course it matters how it ends!"

His voice was full of mockery. "Nessus and Hercules both died: one for love, and one from its results. But only Hercules is remembered as a hero."

"No one asked Deianira for her opinion."

"She ran away with the wrong man, like you did."

Joanna turned back to face him. "In my case they were both the wrong man, weren't they? And we are not Greek. Our stories are so much tamer: *I, said the sparrow, with my bow and arrow, I killed Cock Robin.* England is not as well suited to high tragedy."

"Yet Cock Robin is just as dead." Fitzroy crossed the room to her easel. Pinning up a fresh sheet, he took up a stick of charcoal. *"Who'll dig his grave? I, said the Owl, with my pick and shovel, I'll dig his grave."* His hand moved rapidly over the paper. "What would Athene think, do you suppose, if she knew that her sacred bird has become a gravedigger in an English children's song?''

"I don't know." Joanna gazed at the strong, graceful line of his arm and the strangely innocent concentration on his face. "Is it merely a children's song? Who *was* Cock Robin?''

"I thought you would be able to tell me that," replied Fitzroy, turning his head to smile at her. "You are the pagan, after all."

Joanna crossed quickly to the easel. Nessus's powerful horse's legs straggled across the turf, his man's torso twisted in the death agony, his hands clutching at the shaft of an arrow fired by a faraway Hercules just cresting a hill top. The creature's head and shoulders lay in the lap of a woman. The entire drawing was fiercely, brilliantly executed with a stunning economy of line and a passionate depth. She could feel the centaur's torment, and his desire for revenge as his lifeblood ebbed away.

And the woman? The wife of Hercules, who unwittingly brought about the death of the two great symbols of male power—centaur and hero? Deianira was gazing away into a remote distance, as if the pain of these inferior creatures meant nothing to her. Black hair lay uncoiled around her face, the face that Joanna looked at every morning in the mirror. Fitzroy had used his own wife as a model for Deianira.

Joanna felt confused heat rising in her cheeks, but before he added features to either hero or centaur, there was a tap at the door. Fitzroy tore down the sheet, as she had done, crumpling it into a ball.

A footman came in with a letter on a tray, and bowed. "For Lady Tarrant, my lord."

"For me?" Joanna opened the plain wax seal. A strand of bright blond hair curled around inside the paper.

"What is it?"

"I don't know." She could not hide her mistrust and distress. "I don't know what it means." She put the paper into his outstretched hand, reading aloud the one line as she did so. *"We have Milly."*

Chapter 8

Joanna sat down on the empty chair, dropping her head forward onto her hands. "What can it mean?" She felt sick and faint, the blood draining away. "Who has Milly?"

Fitzroy savagely crumpled the note. "Your little sister is in no danger, Joanna. It's all right. You must trust me in this."

She looked up. "Trust you? Why should I trust you?"

He watched her steadily for a moment as if regretting what he would have to say. "I have a man watching Miss Able's Academy. He would have sent word. Milly is safe."

Joanna clutched at his sleeve. "You have a man there? Whatever for? Is Milly in peril? For God's sake, why?"

He threw down the crushed sheet of paper, the skin of his hand white across the knuckles. "She is your sister and you are married to me, so I took some simple precautions. There are people who don't like me, that is all."

Joanna leapt to her feet. "And Richard, and Harry, and my sister Eleanor? Are they in danger, too? You married me, saying nothing of this, knowing that it put my family in some kind of jeopardy! You unconscionable—"

He caught her arms. "There is no real risk, merely a little

petty harassment, perhaps. I have made certain of that much, at least, Joanna. Only I am the target, not you or your family.''

"How can you be sure? Oh, dear God! Let us go there now! *Now,* Lord Tarrant!''

Fitzroy studied her face, his eyes dark and soft. ''By all means,'' he said quietly. ''If it were my sister, nothing else would content me. But believe me: Milly is safe and we race off on a wild-goose chase. It will result in nothing more than whimsy and, very likely, a good soaking. Be of good cheer, Joanna.''

Yet he ordered his carriage and fifteen minutes later handed Joanna onto the high seat of the yellow and black phaeton. The exactly correct amount of seriously shiny brass glimmered brightly in the light from the flambeaux. A couple of armed menservants on horseback were waiting to accompany them. In spite of his assurances Fitzroy obviously intended no risk on the journey, but perhaps he always traveled carefully at night. He gathered up the reins and nodded to his tiger. His competence and nonchalance were reassuring, somehow filling Joanna's heart with comfort. The tiger released the horses' heads and swung up behind them.

Fitzroy gave her a sudden smile. ''Are you prepared to rouse Miss Able out of bed?''

"For my sister's sake, I'd rouse the Prince Regent himself!''

He laughed. ''I doubt very seriously if Prinny is in bed this early!''

They drove rapidly along the turnpike toward the school that Joanna had fled less than two weeks before. She clutched the strand of hair. Had Milly been kidnapped to be held to ransom, or hurt in some way? If only, if only she could trust that Fitzroy was right! Yet he seemed so unconcerned and lighthearted, gently teasing her about her schooldays, that Joanna found her fear melting away to be replaced by an uncomfortable doubt—perhaps she shouldn't have demanded this!

Miss Able's Academy lay in complete darkness. It had begun to drizzle, turning the sky an inky black. As they turned in at the gates, one of the servants whom Fitzroy had sent on ahead rode up to meet them, the water beaded on his hat sparkling in the light of the carriage torches.

"I spoke with Vernon, my lord. The little girl's not been approached and is safe in her bed, right enough."

Fitzroy grinned at him, and taking Joanna's hand in his own, brought it to his lips and kissed it. "Nevertheless, we shall rouse the academy, Simon, and create a stir of excitement for the ladies and their noble pupils, shall we?"

Simon touched one finger to the brim of his hat, causing a little cascade of water to run down over his nose. He grinned. "Very good, my lord."

"You were right?" Joanna found herself embracing his strong fingers in return as relief flooded through her. She closed her eyes for a moment. Nothing could come of this wild nocturnal journey now but embarrassment, surely? "I'm sorry. I should not have insisted. We have no need to disturb them!"

"Nonsense," replied Fitzroy. "After coming so far and getting wet, the least we can do is have a little fun, don't you think?"

He helped Joanna from the carriage and into the shelter of the porch, where Simon began a ponderous hammering at the door. There was no reply.

"Keep trying," said Fitzroy.

Several more heavy blows followed. Joanna stood in the porch, while her husband stepped back out into the rain and gazed up at the face of the building. It began to pour in earnest. The horses shifted nervously in the hand of the tiger, and Fitzroy spoke to them, soothing and quiet, water running down over his face and soaking his coat.

"Whatever is the alarm?" cried a shrill female voice suddenly. "I warn you, if you are brigands, we are armed!"

"Brigands in England, Miss Able?" queried Fitzroy, calm and polite. "Lord Tarrant, at your service, ma'am, most certainly not a brigand. You will not, I pray, fire that fearsome blunderbuss? I am here with Lady Joanna, your recent pupil. We have come to visit her sister, Lady Matilda Acton."

A lamp must have been lit in an upstairs window, for yellow light washed over Fitzroy's face, casting his features in gilt.

"At this hour! All decent God-fearing folk are in their beds, sir, and this is a ladies' establishment where decorum and propriety are our watchwords and our guides. You would not gain entrance now, were you good King George himself!"

"I trust I am more in command of my faculties than our sainted monarch, ma'am. I pray you will open this door before my servant takes it into his skull to break it down."

Miss Able shrieked. "I'll have the Watch on you and your men, you rogue!"

"No, no," called Fitzroy. "Not the blunderbuss, I pray you, ma'am."

Joanna stepped out and peered up at her erstwhile headmistress. "I am here, too, Miss Able, and getting uncomfortably wet. Pray let us in. Having come so far, may I not see Milly now?"

"Oh, goodness! This is beyond the bounds of anything! I am surprised you dare show your face on these premises, young lady!"

Fitzroy choked back a grin and tried to look stern. "You are speaking, Miss Able, to my wife, Lady Tarrant, future Countess of Evenham. I'm sure she will forgive your nightcap and gown, and even your fearsome weapon, but she can hardly overlook being made to stand in the rain."

Miss Able clutched at her nightcap and the straggles of hair that snaked below it. Throughout the exchange, Simon had continued to hammer lustily at the door. One by one, other lights appeared in other windows, followed by a succession of young female faces pressed against the glass, until eventually a window at the end of the row on the second floor opened to reveal a bright blond head.

"Joanna? Oh, how splendid!"

Joanna spun about and ran along the front of the house until she was directly beneath the window. "Milly! Are you all right?"

Milly leaned further from the window. "Of course, I'm all right! Why wouldn't I be? What on earth are you doing here?"

"Why do we not discuss that in more comfort?" suggested Fitzroy, taking off his hat and wringing water out of it. "Miss Able?"

Mistress and blunderbuss had both disappeared from the window. A few moments later the front door swung open. Fitzroy and Joanna were allowed to step into the hallowed hallway of Miss Able's Academy for Young Ladies. Milly was fetched from her bedroom, and Miss Able herself soon appeared, hastily dressed in her best bombazine, with her wig on crooked. Joanna was about to be treated to the extraordinary sight of her husband charming this fearsome apparition into smiles and giggles.

Joanna hugged Milly and pulled her little sister onto the hard horsehair sofa.

"Why have you come?" asked Milly. "And in the middle of the night!"

"I had a silly message," replied Joanna. Now, in this ugly, too familiar parlor, her fears seemed absurd. "Has no one been near you?"

"Why should they? I wish they had. It's terribly dull here without you."

Joanna took the strand of golden hair that she had carried from London and laid it against Milly's plaits. The shade was quite different. She hugged her again. "Then I have just made a dreadful fool of myself."

"But I had a message, too!" exclaimed Milly. "I remember it exactly, though I threw it away: *No es oro todo lo quo reluce.* It's just nonsense, isn't it?"

Fitzroy spun away from Miss Able. "So, you see, it was a jest, after all," he said sharply. "Shall we let Miss Able and her pupils return to their beds?"

Joanna looked up at him in alarm. The good humor was gone. His brow had contracted into a dark frown.

"I'm sorry——" she began.

Any malevolence seemed dissolved into pain. "Oh, for God's

sake, don't apologize! Surely your splendid state of wetness is penalty enough?'' He strode to the door. ''Let us go.''

Fitzroy drove back to London through the downpour in an agonized silence. *No es oro todo lo quo reluce.* He did not dare look at Joanna sitting stiffly at his side, in case he should spill out the horror that lay in his heart and burden her with it. *All is not gold that glistens.* Joanna could not have known, but it had been one of Juanita's favorite sayings. Would messages like this keep arriving forever? With most of them jokes, and some of them lethal?

When they arrived back at his house, Joanna fled up the stairs to her room, leaving Fitzroy alone with his servants.

''Begging your pardon, my lord,'' said Simon. ''How did you know for sure, before we spoke with Vernon, that the little girl was safe?''

''I didn't, though it seemed likely.''

''But you were so very jolly with the mistress—''

Fitzroy turned to him, fiercely rubbing a hand over his wet head. ''And why not? Why the devil let her suffer her fears for the whole journey?''

When Joanna came down in the morning he had already left the house. She packed up a portable easel, some sketch paper and charcoal, and ordered a carriage to take her to Lady Mary. Fortunately the Black Earl was out. Joanna did not want to meet Lord Evenham just now. His eldest son seemed too much like him.

Lady Mary was lying on a chaise longue in a sunny drawing room leafing through a book. She looked up with real pleasure when Joanna came in.

''Oh, are you here to begin my portrait? It's so very agreeable of you!''

''Not at all, it's a real pleasure.''

Joanna meant it. She stood at her easel and began her preliminary study of Lady Mary's features with the easy confidence she had always brought to her work in the past, except when the subject was Fitzroy. There was a distinct family likeness between them, clear in the dark hair and excellent bones, in the unmistakable intelligence. Yet, just like her brother, there was a shadow in Lady Mary's expression that Joanna decided she must remove if her painting was to be a success. Lady Mary must be made to relax and forget her troubles.

"Do you like making verses?" she asked, setting down her charcoal.

"Verses?" Lady Mary looked around with clear astonishment. "Oh, I'm sorry! I've moved, haven't I?"

"It doesn't matter. Are you tired? Perhaps we should take a break."

"I've ordered us a little luncheon. Shall we have it now?" Lady Mary stood up and rang the bell, then came over to Joanna to look at what she had done. "Good heavens," she said. "You really are an artist. That's wonderful!" She smiled. "But I think you flatter me. Do I really have such a resemblance to my handsome brother?"

"You are angling for compliments, Lady Mary," replied Joanna instantly. "He is lucky if he has a likeness to you."

A servant came in with a tray and laid out the food on a small table: some fresh crusty rolls and butter, fruit cut into elegant little pieces, a wedge of creamy white cheese. "Caerphilly," said Lady Mary indicating the cheese as she took her seat at the table. "My favorite. Why did you ask about verses?"

Joanna sat opposite Fitzroy's sister and took some bread and cheese. "When we were children, my brothers and sisters and I used to play a game with our grandmother: someone would begin a nonsense rhyme and everyone had to supply a line in turn. It was tremendous fun. I thought we might do the same while I work, to help pass the time."

"But I couldn't possibly!" exclaimed Lady Mary. "How on earth could you invent a rhyme, just like that?"

"Easily! It didn't have to be very good, you know, just funny. The last time we were all together at Acton Mead—that was my grandmother's home, but it's Richard's now—we did one about my little sister Milly. John and Eleanor started like this: *'There once was a creature called Milly who went out whene'er it was chilly.'* Then Richard added: *'But although we had snow, the sled wouldn't go . . . ' ''*

"Oh, good heavens! And someone had to provide a last line? What was it? I'm intimidated already!"

There was a movement behind them. Joanna looked around and felt her heart constrict. Fitzroy stood in the doorway. He was watching her. Joanna couldn't understand the expression in his dark eyes, so she looked away, chin high, as he came into the room, his boots soft on the thick carpet.

"Intimidated, Mary mine?" Fitzroy leant over his sister and kissed her. "What nonsense. Never say an Evenham can't match an Acton when it comes to absurdity. How about: *'Since the white wasn't snow, but Caerphilly?' ''*

Mary looked up at him and laughed. "Sledding in fields of cheese? What wonderful nonsense!"

Fitzroy pulled a spare chair over to the table and sat down. The shadow was completely masked now. He seemed determined to be civil, even generous, but Joanna felt wary. She had allowed herself to be too vulnerable, and received nothing but disdain in exchange—yet he had not hesitated to drive her to Miss Able's, and she owed him something for that.

"Which I understood to be the idea! But neither is it good enough yet for Joanna?" Fitzroy winked at her. "Then how about: . . . *'for the chilly filly, Milly, willy-nilly.' ''*

In spite of herself, Joanna laughed. "Not obscure enough, sir! Mine would have been: *'Since Harry won't push it, now, will 'e?'* But before I could say it, Harry himself came in and tossed off an ending as neat as you please: *'Since she couldn't tell flat land from hilly!'* and no one could top that, now, could they?"

Lady Mary clapped her hands together. *"Because Milly forgot how to, poor silly."* Then she blushed, though she was still grinning. "Now one about you, Joanna!"

"Who can describe Lady Joanna? / As she dines upon white bread and manna," began Fitzroy immediately.

"Oh, there are no rhymes left at all!" cried Lady Mary.

"She'll force down the mess, / in the cruel wilderness," added Joanna.

Fitzroy didn't hesitate. *"Joanna's eaten manna, hosanna!"*

Joanna's voice clashed with his. *"Eat manna, I declare, but I canna!"*

Within five minutes the table was in an uproar of laughter. Caught up in the merriment, Joanna fought to top her husband in flights of word play, punning and rhyming, trying to cap every absurdity with a fresh one. It felt strangely innocent and natural, to play and have fun as if only the moment mattered. This was a side of him she had never imagined, let alone witnessed, a man who could set aside everything else to be merry with his sister.

"Enough," said Fitzroy at last. "Alas, I must go." He stood and kissed Lady Mary once on the forehead before striding to the door. Then he turned and winked at Joanna.

Still shaking with hilarity, Joanna looked across at him as he stood poised in the doorway, one hand on the jamb, the other pressed flat over his heart. *This is how he should be— laughing, free!* The tousled dark hair, the span and vigor and power of every line of him, truly carefree and relaxed for the first time, the longing to capture it in paint caught at her heart. *This, this is how he should be!*

Yet as she watched him the faintest hint of distress seemed to darken his expression, blurring the purity of the moment, flooding her with frustration. She was being closed out again!

"Until tonight, Joanna," he said, the merriment dying out of his voice.

Joanna felt her question stick in her throat. "Tonight?"

"When I shall pose for you."

"Oh, of course."

He dropped his hand as if it hurt him, the fingers clenching unconsciously into a fist. "Then tomorrow is Lady Reed's ball. As newlyweds we must put in an appearance. Our fathers require it, so that we may face down any last shreds of gossip." The rest of his reply was tossed over his shoulder as he walked away, and the innocent children's rhyme seemed to be bruised with anger: " *'Who'll sing a psalm? I, said the Thrush, as she sat on a bush, I'll sing a psalm.'* "

The dressmaker arrived that afternoon, and Joanna began to order the wardrobe she would need if she was to make an unexceptionable Lady Tarrant, and fulfill her new role in society as a married lady. While the woman fussed and measured and held up swatches of fabric, Joanna thought hard about Fitzroy. What on earth had he done that Richard found so unforgivable? What haunted and drove him so mercilessly? Why did he no longer paint when he had such brilliant talent of his own?

"Mrs. Price," she said at last. "Do you know that old nursery song about Cock Robin?"

The woman's pale blue eyes looked up at her client in surprise as she pulled a couple of pins from her mouth. "Why, of course, my lady! The bullfinch has my favorite verse: *'Who'll toll the bell? I, said the Bull, because I can pull. So Cock Robin, farewell.'* Why, I've sung it to my children often enough, bless me!"

Joanna looked down at her. Mrs. Price was a warm, motherly person. It wasn't hard to imagine her singing rhymes to her babies—as Helena no doubt sang to little Elaine. The memory of her niece's sleeping face brought a sharp, unexpected stab of pain. Joanna crushed it and made herself think about the problem at hand. "Yes, we used to sing it when we were little, with my grandmother. My youngest sister, Milly, would cry over it. What do you suppose it means?"

"Why, nothing, my lady. All a lot of nonsense, isn't it? Birds and beasts talking and murdering, and giving each other Christian burial? Just doggerel for children, that's all."

"Is it?" asked Joanna.

She could still hear Fitzroy's mocking voice. *You are the pagan, after all.*

Would she be able to draw him tonight, or was she doomed to be blind where her strange new husband was concerned? Surely she could not fail Lady Mary in this?

"Do you prefer the ivory trimming or the rose, my lady?" asked the dressmaker. "The ivory compliments your complexion very well, but the rose brings out more color, I believe."

Joanna shrugged and tried to concentrate on the dresses. Although she and Fitzroy were not to share their lives, she was to accompany him to Lady Reed's, and for no reason she could fathom she wanted to impress him.

Fitzroy came into her studio very late, with the gloss of fatigue and distress plain on his features. Once again he sat in the chair and Joanna stood at her easel. Very slowly and carefully she began to draw him. There was a slight irregularity to the shape of his nose that she hadn't noticed before, and the hint of a dimple marked the corner of his mouth—or did he have a very small mole there, hiding in the shadow? She let her charcoal float over the paper, as if the stick were actually touching him with a faint, soft caress. The shapes molded and formed: the curve of his cheekbone, the deep curl of his lip, the entrancing outline of his ear with the black hair curling carelessly over it. A deep, warm pleasure began to build in her, a soft, sweet flush creeping over her limbs to settle heavily in her belly. Yet somewhere, on a deeper level, an unease crept in with it. Joanna was barely aware of her feelings. Lost in concentration, she forgot her fears. Yes, tonight it was coming! She had not lost her skill!

At last she stepped back and looked critically at what she had done. It was a good likeness, capturing not only his features but his mood and something of his dark power. Yet it was not the memory of a beloved brother that anyone would want to take to Switzerland. Surely Lady Mary would want him carefree and untroubled, as he had seemed that morning! The portrait must capture Fitzroy Monteith Mountfitchet filled with gaiety and laughter. She closed her eyes for a moment, seeing clearly how it must be: his intensity and intelligence affirmed and clarified by humor, not this grim, tight man harassed almost to despair by his mysterious duties.

Joanna stared at the drawing, trying to place what else made her so uncomfortable. Every line spoke of that bone-deep fatigue and its dark shadow of distress, as if her charcoal had unwittingly trespassed too deeply, seen too much. The result was disconcertingly intimate and revealing—a blatant, dishonorable invasion of his privacy—exposing him, vulnerable, human, as if she had deliberately set out to uncover any personal weakness and shout it to the world. Oh, Lord, in its way this was worse than her disaster of the night before!

Without thinking—the vision of what she wanted burning away any other consideration—Joanna left the easel and rushed up to him. "This is no use! You are too tired and preoccupied." She seized his arm and shook it.

Fitzroy shrugged off her hand. "I did not sit still enough?" He rubbed his fingers over his face. "I'm sorry."

Joanna caught again at his sleeve, confused by her own shame and embarrassment and anger. "No! This is how I want you to sit, but bright, unclouded, as you were this morning, not stiff with weariness. Relax, for once! Can't you take off your cravat?" Impulsively she reached for it and pulled out the knots, wrenching away the strip of linen. "I'll rub your neck."

He sat arrested, his collar open to reveal his strong throat, and gazed up at her, his clear incredulity edged with dark humor. The man she had momentarily exposed in her drawing disappeared.

"*Do* you want me, Lady Joanna?" he asked, and laughed.

She barely heard him, caught up in her vision of how his portrait must be and her distress at what she had done instead.

"I want to paint you perfectly, so that Lady Mary will be made happy and lighthearted to look at it! I used to rub my brother Harry's neck when he'd been practicing his marksmanship too hard and the muscles were tight. Father would goad him until you'd think he'd just break like a brittle piece of glass, yet I could ease it for him. Let me help you, for heaven's sake! What on earth do you do all day that leaves you looking as if you had just swum the Atlantic?'' She tossed aside the cravat. "Exhaust yourself in a bawdy house?''

Fitzroy sprawled in the chair as hilarity began to transform his features. Joanna saw it with triumph.

"And what the *devil* do you know about bawdy houses, Joanna?''

She was still swept away by her idea of the portrait she could do of him. She could hardly think of anything else, and he was already part way there, moving into laughter, burying that terrible desolation. She perched on a low crate and tugged him from the chair. "Not much, I admit. Sit down and lean back on my knee. Yes, like that. Now, think of nothing but warmth and relaxation while I work out all this damned tension.''

It was the most extraordinary thing he had ever done. But Fitzroy obeyed her, slipping from the chair to sink onto the hard floor at her feet. She hadn't thought about the discomfort of that surface, had she? A small gurgle of genuine mirth moved somewhere deep in his chest. Then he leaned his head back onto her smock, his cheek resting against the smell of oil and pigment and some other higher, wilder scent that was Joanna's alone. The scent he had smelled on her when he had kissed her at the Swan Inn, and that drifted about her on their wedding day—as if she walked always amid the wildflowers of a high moor.

"So you can still laugh,'' said Joanna dryly. "Just drop your head forward and relax.''

He crossed his arms on his upraised knees and laid his forehead on them. She folded down his shirt collar. Fitzroy felt the touch of her hands on his neck, then had to bite back his reaction as she pushed closer so that she had one knee on each side of his body. Her strong fingers began to massage the tight muscles at the base of his neck. It felt wonderful. Fitzroy allowed himself to drift on the sensation as she rubbed and probed, forcing the knots to dissolve one after another, the tension sometimes exploding in an exquisite burst of pleasure, sometimes merely diminishing gradually until it faded away.

What an extraordinary creature! *His wife*. Her thighs were

soft against his body. He knew her breasts moved, round and inviting, just above his head as her hands thrust and kneaded. Dear God, what an enormous, appalling innocence lay beneath her offer to do this! She had no idea of the effect her ministrations would have on him. She thought of him as a brother, for pity's sake, rather than Fitzroy Monteith Mountfitchet, reputedly the most dissolute rake in town! Desire surged in him, in an urgent, compelling torrent.

Fitzroy recognized it with pain, for he knew he must suppress it. The next night he was going to find out if Lady Reed was expecting him in her bed in trade for the secrets that might save Wellington's life. He closed his eyes and tried to picture Lady Reed. She was beautiful, worldly, and experienced. He had no doubt that it would be delightful to bed her. Yet all he wanted was Joanna, his innocent wife, and under the circumstances it would be the act of a blackguard to touch her. The irony of it left him breathless. Ruthlessly, Fitzroy forced himself to concentrate on his quest for Lord Grantley, crushing this strange awakening before he should disgrace himself.

His flesh felt extraordinary under her fingers, smooth and fine, yet firm and hard with muscle. Joanna concentrated on finding the bunched knots and easing them. She worked in silence, still in a fury of concentration, but slowly, inexorably, a different, deeper emotion began to replace her concern about the portrait. It was as if a slow flush spread from his neck and shoulders up through her hands and arms to set a fire in her blood. She tried to ignore it.

"Now let your head fall back," she said. "So I can work around the sides."

He dropped his head back into her lap, the weight partly supported by her skirts, his eyes closed, without saying a word. His head was a little turned, one cheek lying against the softness of her inner thigh. Joanna had no idea what he might be thinking, but the taught lines were softening on his face and the hint of a smile played at the corners of his lips—not that bitter, sarcastic grin, but a smile of real pleasure.

Joanna reached to the muscles on each side of his neck and

rubbed her fingers along them in long, sure strokes. Yet this
man wasn't Harry! He was that monster who had ravished her
mouth at the Swan Inn, mocked and insulted her, then sworn
to ignore her for the rest of her life. How could he also be the
man she had seen that morning at his sister's, quick wit soaring,
released by laughter? For her portrait had revealed him to
be suffering, vulnerable, a man she didn't want to have to
acknowledge.

His head in her lap felt strange, almost as if he belonged
there, yet it was creating an echoing weight somewhere deep
inside, a heat and heaviness. The supple strength of his body
against her knees disturbed her—why should she tolerate that?
Joanna didn't understand it, and it wasn't altogether comfort-
able. She stopped rubbing, meaning to push him away, and
discovered why he was lying so still against her legs, his breathing even and deep. Fitzroy had fallen asleep.

Chapter 9

Joanna felt frantic for a moment. What on earth should she do? Leap up and let him fall to the floor? Shake him awake? Or study him, study him for the portrait that she had agreed to do for his dying sister. She looked down as he shifted a little and sighed, then tentatively she touched his hair. He didn't move. She ran her hand lightly over the dark curls, sensing every fiber as it moved beneath her fingers. *He had lovely hair.* What an odd thing to think about a man! She examined his face, the eyelids closed over those dark eyes, the stress and tension flattened away by sleep. It would be appalling to wake him, a clear act of barbarism. Why invite him to don that sarcasm and defensiveness once again, when just for a moment he had found respite from the tragic weariness that seemed to contaminate his every waking moment?

Softly she moved her forefinger to his jaw bone, down the sideburn that outlined his cheek. The skin of his jaw was a little rough, prickly under her questing fingertip, alluring in its very masculinity. The small dark shape at the corner of his mouth, where a dimple might well appear, *was* a mole. More boldly, she traced his eyebrow and the inviting line of his nose.

Fitzroy slept on, in the dead, cold sleep of real exhaustion. His shirt had fallen wide open at the neck, revealing the beginning of the soft, dark hair on his chest. *How I long to touch it!* thought Joanna. *Oh, dear heavens, I am shameless!*

In a strange agony she sat on the crate and let him sleep, while her legs pricked with pins and needles, and the hard edge of the wood bit into her flesh. Her hands lay gently on his shoulders, passively feeling the slight rise and fall of his breathing, while her own heart fluttered unevenly in her breast, making her limbs languid and her blood fiery.

Joanna had no idea what drove the demonic man that she had unwillingly married, but she knew that it rode him hard and without mercy. Surely the least she could do was let him find rest for a moment, without demands from her? She let her mind drift, barely aware of the shadowed room with her easels and supplies, remembering the times he had seemed to be something different for a moment—something deeply compelling and attractive, even potentially kind. The images shifted and stirred against her half-closed eyelids.

One of the candles guttered and went out, and Fitzroy moved a little, then murmured. ''Ah, sweetheart.'' He rubbed his cheek on her skirt, then turned to bury his face against her thigh. His arms slid around her and he ran both hands up her legs and over her hips, pulling her into his embrace. ''Let me love you.'' It was an undertone, said on a breath like a sigh.

Joanna fell against his chest without resistance, her legs long gone to sleep and her back stiff. Fitzroy cradled her in his arms with a tenderness that belied every notion she had ever held about rakes. His head rested on her shoulder as his fingers gently touched the side of her neck. Slowly they moved to her chin, trailing heat, touching the corner of her mouth with his thumb in a delicious firing of her senses. Joanna melted against him, wanting more, longing for this exploration to go further, lost in the strange half dream of the moment.

''Do with me what you will,'' she whispered, barely aware that she had spoken. ''I'm your wife.''

Fitzroy opened his eyes. Joanna saw them widen in shock,

and in the next moment he had pushed her away and leapt to his feet. "Bloody hell!" As if her presence burned him, he turned away, dropped into his chair, and ran his hands back over his hair. He was shaking.

"It's all right," said Joanna, sitting up. She felt awkward and lost, and immeasurably defenseless. "You fell asleep, that's all."

"For God's sake," he said brutally. "It's not all right. I thought you were someone else, obviously. Please accept my apologies."

There was no way to cover her vulnerability and humiliation except with anger. "Someone else? Who? Your first wife, Juanita? Or one of the millions of women who've suffered because of you since she died?"

"Millions?" It was said with a sharp upward inflection, a hint of savage humor that belied his expression.

Joanna struggled to her feet. "Hundreds, then, or tens. What does it matter? Do you take pride in punishing females because Juanita betrayed your love by dying?"

He looked up at her with nothing but distaste, the humor warped into mockery. "What the devil do you think you can know about my marriage to Juanita? *Betrayed your love!* Where did you learn that phrase? From some gothic novel? Pray, spare me your schoolgirl interpretations of things you know nothing about. Good night."

Without giving her a chance to reply, Fitzroy thrust away the chair and stalked from the room. The door slammed behind him. Joanna sat on the edge of the crate and wondered why her eyes burned, yet tears refused to come. Dry eyed she went to her easel and tore down the drawing, ripping the paper to shreds. Why on earth should she care, when Richard believed that because of some appalling transgression of honor, he barely deserved to live?

In the morning Joanna woke early. She had several hours before Lady Mary would expect her, but she could not paint.

The studio she had longed for seemed barren, so Joanna took her sketch paper and went outside. The garden was laid out neatly, with a walled space for vegetables and fruit, and a small sweep of lawn running into a little copse of trees on the opposite side of the house from the stables. The garden had no more personality than the house. Joanna wandered along a path through the trees, noticing the light and shade, listening to the rustle of the leaves. An odd warble of sound rumbled in the background, low and sweet, beckoning her. Joanna recognized it before she reached the neat little shed with the small arched openings and the doweled perches: the cooing of pigeons.

A man with brown curls was leaning against the trunk of a nearby tree, watching the birds ruffle their feathers and peck at grain. As Joanna came up, he turned and grinned at her. A pigeon nestled in his hands.

"The dove of peace?" Quentin gently stroked the bird's feathers. "Fitzroy likes paradox."

"Oh," replied Joanna. It seemed incredible. Fitzroy kept pigeons at the bottom of his garden? "Are these his birds?"

"It's a hobby we shared as boys at Evenham Abbey." Quentin opened his hands and the pigeon flew away. "But Fitzroy takes it very seriously now. That's why he lives out here, instead of taking a townhouse in Mayfair."

Joanna watched the bird soar up into the blue sky. "Oh! Will it leave and be lost?"

"No. It will come back. This is its home loft, where it was born. It would come back here even if it had to begin the journey in Scotland. Would you like to hold one?"

He strode up to the pigeon loft and opened a cage. The pigeon inside waited tamely as Quentin slipped his hands around it and handed it to Joanna.

She felt the rapid beating of the small heart beneath the rust and ivory feathers, the bloom on the plumage silky under her fingers. The pigeon nestled against her hands, closing its round black eyes.

"Why does it have leather thongs on its legs?"

"Because it was brought here from Belgium. Don't let go, or it will fly home across the Channel."

Joanna clutched the bird to her breast. "Did you want to see Fitzroy? He isn't here."

"But he will be." Quentin's voice was quite casual, but he watched her closely. "I wondered if he was still enamored of Lady Carhill."

Joanna looked at him blankly, the pigeon quivering in her hands as it opened its eyes. "Lady Carhill?"

"The lovely countess, Elizabeth. Her husband neglects her, an open invitation to a rake. While you and I were racketing north on your ill-conceived escape from Miss Able's Academy, Fitzroy was being entertained in her private boudoir." He winked. "I have it on the very best authority. News of our flight must have interrupted his little *rendezvous*. No wonder he was so evil-tempered at the Swan!"

"Here." Joanna held out the pigeon. "You had better put it back."

Quentin took the bird and released it into its cage. "So does he still pursue an interest there? It would be a trifle *outré* for brothers to share a mistress, don't you think?"

"I'm sure I don't know," replied Joanna. "You must ask him."

The green eyes smiled at her. "You have no opinion on Fitzroy Mountfitchet, Lady Joanna? Good God! Everyone else seems to feel very passionately about my brother, one way or another."

"Do they? Because he likes to be impossible, I suppose. But all of this quivering emotion seems to be getting in the way of anyone seeing him clearly, doesn't it?"

She turned and marched away through the trees, brushing away a trace of angry tears. So Fitzroy had a mistress. It was what she expected, wasn't it? Lady Joanna Acton had entered a marriage of convenience, as her mother had. Surely she could develop that same worldly, uncaring attitude? Yet why couldn't she understand him any more clearly than all those others? Joanna closed her eyes. The artist had seen something that the lady could not fathom. She was sure that it was not pleasant dalliance with a mistress that occupied his days. He was doing something dangerous and exhausting, something that was a burden to him: a burden he apparently didn't share with anyone. There was no reason at all, of course, why he should share it with her.

"The bays, George, right away! In the phaeton."

Joanna stopped. It was Fitzroy's voice. She had walked blindly through the garden and was almost to the stable. Several loose boxes stood in rows around two sides of a cobbled yard, the horses peering out over their half doors. A small cottage crowded up against the stables and the carriage house, obviously home to Fitzroy's head ostler and his family. A woman peeked from the window at the sudden clatter of hooves and the opening of the carriage house doors. Her husband, George, ran to obey his master's instructions, giving his own to a handful of stable lads.

Sheltered by the trees Joanna watched as Fitzroy swung from the back of a lathered gray. He looked harassed and tired, but he gave the horse a pat. As a lad took it by the reins and led it away, Fitzroy paced up and down the cobbles, swinging his riding whip against his boot. The door of the cottage opened. The woman, large with child, smiled and spoke a soft greeting to him as she held out a tankard. To Joanna's amazement Fitzroy grinned, took the tankard, and drank. As he began to hand it back to her, a small boy, still in short skirts, ran from behind his mother and launched himself at Fitzroy.

"Well, now, Master Tom!" Fitzroy picked up the child and swung him high in the air. "And how do you do today, sir?"

"Horses!" squealed the boy, giggling. "I give 'em an apple?"

"Ah, you like my gray, then, Tom? But see, your papa is bringing out my team." He turned and let the child watch as the two magnificent bays were harnessed to his phaeton. Tom confidently wrapped his plump arms around Fitzroy's neck and giggled again.

"Ready, my lord," said George.

"Here, Tom, go to your mama, for I must be away." Fitzroy swung the boy into his mother's arms as she blushed a little and curtsied. "Thank you, George. Your lad's a credit to you."

George gave him a huge grin. "It's very kind of your lordship to notice the youngster."

"Notice him!" replied Fitzroy. "I could quite easily adopt him, if I thought that his mother would give him up. Don't stint on apples from the store, now, will you?"

Fitzroy exchanged his short crop for the driving whip which George offered, and swung himself onto the phaeton. As he gave the team their heads and bowled out of the yard, he took the time to wave and smile to the little family.

Joanna walked away and dropped onto a marble seat near the lawn. She could almost hear his implacable voice: *I most particularly don't want children.* Why? Why had he said it? What on earth was she to make of him? It seemed the most unlikely attribute for Fitzroy Monteith Mountfitchet, but he was obviously wonderful with children and liked them. So why did he not want his own?

The only answer that came to mind was that he didn't want children with her, and of course he would never sire bastards. Joanna leaned her head onto her palms and forced herself to face it. Her art was the most important gift in her life. But something had changed in her since she had made that absolute statement to her mother. She had shed tears over baby Elaine because a strange longing had seized her heart and would not let go. She did want to paint, but she also wanted babies. It was a strange and desolate revelation.

Fitzroy spun his bays around the corner of his property, only to be forced to pull them up sharply. One of the horses reared a little, and took a steady, firm hand to bring back under control. Quentin, mounted on a black gelding, blocked the road.

"For God's sake," snapped Fitzroy. "I'm in a devilish hurry!"

Quentin swung his horse out of the way so that he could

ride alongside the carriage. "You are always in a damned hurry, brother. I want but one word from you. Lady Carhill? May I pursue her?"

"Chase any lady you like!"

"But I rather thought you had a proprietary interest. You don't wish to court her?"

"Devil take it," said Fitzroy. "I do not. If there is any lady that I would really like to woo, it's my wife. Make what the devil you like out of that!"

Fitzroy whipped up his team, leaving Quentin staring thoughtfully after him as the phaeton disappeared in a cloud of dust.

Joanna wore her wedding dress to Lady Reed's ball. Mrs. Price had made some alterations to it, taking out the lace insert at the neck so that it swept low across her breasts, shortening the sleeves, and trimming the ivory silk at neck and hem with an elegant border of dark brown piping. Her new dresses weren't ready yet, and her life at Miss Able's Academy hadn't prepared her with many ball gowns.

Fitzroy did not take her. She had not seen him since he had driven his team of bays from the stable yard. He had not joined her in Lady Mary's drawing room later that day. Instead his sister received a bouquet of flowers and a charming note of apology. Joanna traveled with her mother, though she and Lady Acton discussed nothing but fashion during the journey. They were on their way to a society evening, that was all, and as the new Lady Tarrant Joanna must put in an appearance. If Joanna's mother had either concern or curiosity about her daughter's hurried marriage, she did not express it.

Fitzroy was already there. Joanna saw him as soon as she entered Lady Reed's ballroom. He was taller than most of the men, with an easy, commanding presence that could never be overlooked. As if drawn to notice her in exchange, Fitzroy glanced in her direction. He gave her a quick, impersonal nod, his eyes bleak and his face rigid, then returned his attention to his companion. Fitzroy was engaged in a very obvious flirtation with a petite redhead, apparently their hostess.

Lady Acton's eyes narrowed a little, but she said nothing as she took her daughter about to introduce her to the company. Joanna had no reason to care, did she? Theirs wasn't a real marriage. Fitzroy could flirt with any female he liked, and he had given her permission to take lovers if she wanted. However, Joanna had no desire to take a lover, though it wasn't long before her dance card was filled. She moved through waltzes and country dances with a succession of young men, some of them old friends of the family, some total strangers. She could not imagine beginning an affair with any of them.

Through all of it, she watched Fitzroy. His flirtation was growing more serious. A shameless intimacy was developing in front of the eyes of everyone there: a touched hand, an inclination of the head, a certain way of smiling. Lady Reed seemed to be melting, as if she were a small planet spinning too close to the sun. Fitzroy dropped his dark head to the flame of her hair and laughed at something she said.

Joanna closed her eyes. Of course he had mistresses. That had been understood from the beginning. But he could not! He could not do this so publicly!

She glanced back at him. Lady Reed had allowed him to slid an arm about her waist. Fitzroy touched one finger to her lips and let it linger there for a moment, then he led her from the room. The eyes of most of the crowd watched it happen, before some of those eyes moved to stare at Joanna with curiosity, or sympathy, or concern.

As soon as she could, without it being obvious, Joanna left her partner and the ballroom. She felt the intense, angry humiliation of it, though she didn't want to care. What an outrageous betrayal! He had promised to keep up appearances in public, hadn't he? Obviously this was his idea of maintaining his reputation—that of a rake—and he had no concern whatsoever for hers.

She entered the small powder room set aside for the ladies and dropped into a chair, afraid she might cry, bawl like a child, and determined not to do so. Someone came in behind her.

"I'm not sure whether to envy or pity you, dear child," said a woman's voice in her ear. Joanna looked up to see a beautiful blond smiling archly down at her. "I am Elizabeth, Lady Carhill, a particular friend of your husband's. All of us adore him, of course, though it's very hard to imagine being married to him, and I'm sure we can't understand why he should wed a child fresh from the schoolroom at a moment's notice. Should it fill our hearts with covetousness or compassion? What is he really like—is it glorious or dreadful?"

Joanna sat in her chair, stiff and frozen. *What on earth was this?* "I'm sure I don't know what you mean."

Lady Carhill opened her fan and toyed with the silk tassel on the handle. "A man like Fitzroy? On your honeymoon? Of course you know what I mean. But when he was so desperately in love with his Spanish wife . . . It must be very difficult for you."

"No, not at all," replied Joanna. "Why should it be?"

Lady Carhill laughed a little unsteadily. "Well, we can all envy a girl who has the right to claim the brilliant Lord Tarrant as her own, but alas, it's rather sad to see her so obviously neglected while he disappears into private quarters with Lady Reed." The slight odor of wine colored her breath. "Lady Reed! Of all females! I was told she would be next. But perhaps she has the headache and he merely comforts her?"

"Perhaps the pain is his," said Joanna sharply. "And she comforts him!"

"No doubt she does." Lady Carhill gave a deep sigh, ruefully tilting her blond head to one side behind her fan. "And if Fitzroy wants a woman with enough experience to do it right, I suppose Lady Reed has plenty of comfort to offer. He was mine the last time, then he will bed Lady Kettering next Friday. It is all arranged."

Joanna stood up. *So this is what they mean when they talk about a man being a rake? A different woman every week, and in public, with no shame at all!* She wanted to go home. Not to Fitzroy's house, but to King's Acton, back to the safety of her childhood and a life lived in innocence now forever shattered. Leaving Lady Carhill nervously folding and unfolding her fan, she marched back into the hallway.

"Do you think he is down to her petticoats by now?" asked someone with a hint of petulance.

Joanna turned to find Quentin grinning down at her. He was clearly three sheets to the wind. He winked at her like a conspirator.

"I imagine the petticoats were shed some ten minutes ago," said Joanna, her color high.

"Don't you want revenge?" Quentin stepped closer. "I should, if it were me—even though I didn't love her—if my wife did that in front of the entire *ton.*"

Joanna felt hideously vulnerable, though she was determined not to show it. "What kind of revenge?"

"What's sauce for the goose is an entire feast for the gander, I should think. How he would hate it if you paid him back in the same false coin!" Quentin touched her cheek with his fingers.

Joanna had very few reserves left. She was afraid she would shatter and make an embarrassing scene. The temptation to allow Quentin, or anyone, to take her in his arms and hold her was almost overwhelming. From some deep well she dredged up another few moments of courage. "Are you offering yourself? You think I should start an affair with my husband's brother? If it is *outré* for brothers to share a mistress, surely it's unseemly for them to share a wife! Fitzroy was forced into this marriage to save your neck, for heaven's sake. He never claimed to love me. Good Lord, does everybody hate him so much?"

"I don't hate him." Quentin moved his folded knuckles to her ear. He was still smiling, very handsome and a little disheveled. "I just hate to see what he's doing."

Joanna firmly pushed his hand away. "Do you? I'm sure I

don't see why." She felt the humiliating tears threatening to spill down her cheeks.

"By God," said Quentin. His green eyes narrowed as he enfolded her fingers in his strong palm and held tightly to her hand. "Don't say that, in spite of his malevolence, you've fallen under his spell, too. For God's sake, my dear girl, he'll break your heart!" Quentin was very foxed, with the clear confidence and muddied judgment of several hours of heavy drinking behind him. He carried her fingers to his lips and kissed them fervently. "Run away with me, Joanna!"

"Run away with you? Are you mad? I thought only this morning you were planning the conquest of Lady Carhill?"

"I was," said Quentin, turning her hand palm up and kissing the inside of her wrist. "But my present mistress must be discharged first, and to run away with you now would infuriate her! Perhaps then she would release me from her clutches."

Joanna choked back a small, bitter laugh. "I had no idea that being a rake was so complicated."

Quentin pulled her into his arms. "Yes, it's delicious. Never take a lover who's not English, Joanna. Damn it if you aren't too good for Fitzroy! Don't let him destroy you as he's destroyed the others! Leave him, why don't you? He's more the devil's disciple than I am!"

A man spoke from the shadows in a voice as cold and biting as a winter wind in a graveyard. "Last time we had true love in a tavern. Is it now to be a cuckolding in the corridor?"

Chapter 10

Joanna spun about to see Fitzroy soberly staring at her as she stood wrapped in his brother's arms. Lady Reed was nowhere to be seen.

"It's only solace," said Quentin, releasing her. "What the devil did you mean by what you said to me this morning? If you insist on such a public neglect of your wife, Fitzroy, the horns will no doubt sprout quickly enough."

"For God's sake, go away, Quentin." Fitzroy seemed infinitely weary. "I don't think Joanna can take much more."

Quentin stared at him for a moment, then with a wobbly bow to Joanna, left them.

Fitzroy stalked up to her. As the light caught his features she felt her heart catch. Her artist's eye pierced his cool control to the turmoil beneath. *Like the vampire,* Joanna thought suddenly, *caught out in the open at dawn—on the edge of dissolution—eyes reflecting an incredulous shock and an infinite regret. While I stand here in my made-over wedding dress, feeling sorry for myself. What, what is happening?*

"Joanna, I have nothing to say but that I am most deeply, sincerely sorry for this whole shabby business. You shouldn't have come, but I knew of no way to avoid it without causing even more comment. May I take you home?''

The quietness in his voice frightened her, for it threatened to disarm her completely. It would be easier to cope with that bitter, sarcastic man who had first surprised her with Quentin.

She turned away from him, lifting her chin. ''It would be the most convenient way to avoid more scandal, wouldn't it? Is my public humiliation to be on a regular basis or just every Friday?''

He caught her arm and turned her to face him. ''Why Friday?''

''It doesn't matter. Perhaps I didn't quite understand our bargain when we made it, but I did promise not to interfere in your life. Bed any woman you please. Why not a new one each week? It's nothing to me.''

His face was set, rigid. ''Who told you?''

''Lady Carhill. Oh, fiddlesticks! I am more than ready to leave.''

In a cold anger Fitzroy snapped his fingers for a servant and ordered the carriage. A few minutes later he helped her into the plush interior in silence. Then to Joanna's astonishment, he slid an arm around her shoulders and pulled her against the warm strength of his body.

''There aren't apologies enough in the language, Joanna. But I'm sorry that Lady Carhill chose to take out her frustrations on you. None of this is your fault.''

Joanna lay enfolded, dry-eyed, his heart beating steadily beneath her cheek. She was angry, and wretched, and filled with miserable indignation. But his mouth against her hair left her mesmerized, drowning her sorrow and her hurt in a sea of longing.

''Well?'' The word conveyed an exquisite archness of tone. ''And how was he, our puissant Fitzroy Mountfitchet?''

Lady Reed looked up, her face pale. The red hair was a little disordered, as if carelessly bundled back into its pins. Her friend was idly wafting her fan, the large sapphire on her finger catching the candlelight in a blaze of blue fire. The two women sat alone in a small private parlor away from the noise and bustle of the ball.

"Glorious," she whispered. "And incorrigible. Why did you suggest that he'd want to become my lover? Why? I did everything just as you said, and I know he desired me quite desperately. He's a man, after all! Yet in spite of everything I made him do, he didn't seem humiliated, and he would not bed me. In the end he was merciless, in that cold, implacable way that he has, mingled still with ineffable charm. I don't know if he's quite human. But it was as if some part of him wasn't even there so that I had no power over him, while if he'd so much as snapped his fingers I'd have licked his damn boots."

The fan stopped moving for a moment, though the candlelight still danced and glittered on the ring. "He *is* humiliated, Lady Reed, and the damage is sinking deeper every day. More deeply and more permanently than even he may think. Did you see the little wife, her eyes like saucers? He will hate himself, loathe himself, for doing this to her. This sudden marriage adds such a delicious piquancy to our game, don't you think? And as an additional delight, we have Richard Acton waiting in the wings, not even aware that he has more than a walk-on part."

"I don't care about the game you're playing. I just wanted him, that's all, and I thought I could punish him a little for not similarly desiring me. That's why I agreed to your demands, as well as it settling my gaming debt. But why do you want to hurt him so much? All this seems a pretty savage revenge for some minor lapse of gallantry!"

The fan closed with a snap. The soft accent became more marked. "A minor lapse? For God's sake, for what he did in Spain, death would be too easy."

But Lady Reed laid her red head on her arm and began to weep.

* * *

Joanna stared down at him, despising herself for wanting him to stay after what he had just done. "You are going out again? Now? It is almost dawn. Why?"

They had not gone to her studio when they came back from the ball. Joanna could not paint. She had far too many strange emotions boiling and seething in her to do anything but go to bed and try to forget it all. Fitzroy had brought her back to their house, escorted her to the door of her room, and turned away. But he was not heading toward his own room. He was going back down the stairs that led onto the street outside. Before she could stop herself, this deadly question slipped out into the silent hallway of the house and hung over Joanna like the Sword of Damocles.

Fitzroy was instantly arrested. He stopped and turned around. "Does it make a difference?"

She didn't want to show so little pride, to open herself for another wound, but the words came out anyway, clipped and angry. "Aren't you going to explain?"

"I can't. But not because it's you doing the asking. Try to believe that. Nothing I do is a reflection on you. Try to sleep, Joanna."

And with an odd, crooked smile he picked up his hat and saluted her briefly, before he opened the front door and disappeared.

Fitzroy rode fast into town. It had been worse than he could have imagined with Lady Reed, ugly, destructive, a travesty of everything he had ever felt or desired about women. He could taste the foulness of that shameless manipulation like ash in his mouth, poisoning the blood. It would not matter if he was the only one being damaged. But there was Joanna, with her brave defiance and unexpected compassion in the face of his outrageous behavior. He had not wanted to marry her, but she moved him more deeply than he could understand. All he wanted was the chance to find out why, to court her and discover more about her. Instead he was pursuing women he did not want, slaughtering his wife's innocence and faith in the world. This was worse, far worse, than Juanita.

Lord Grantley was in bed. His servant hesitated for only a moment before allowing Fitzroy into the house and sending a message up to his master. *Helen of Troy* was the password. Half an hour later, Lord Grantley faced Fitzroy over a pot of coffee in his private study.

"This had better be urgent, Tarrant. I have a set of state functions today, and could have used my sleep."

"Urgent, my lord?" Fitzroy glanced at him, his face ravaged by dark sarcasm. "I have just abandoned my new wife after a most edifying scene at Lady Reed's ball. If I hated Joanna, I could not have done her more hurt. The honor that I owe my name ought, at the very least, to demand discretion when I pursue other women. Instead I have left her shattered by my public betrayal. Sadly, Lady Reed would have it no other way. But is it urgent? No, no more than usual. Yet I cannot go on."

The older man's glance was sharp, with very little compassion. "Pray, stick to the facts, sir."

Fitzroy ran his hands back through his dark hair. "Listen. Almost every day I get another of these mysterious missives. They send me on a wild-goose chase that always ends in some minor humiliation or embarrassment of one kind or another. I've been halfway to the coast, for God's sake, and to Buckinghamshire and back in a day. There is absolutely nothing to show for my efforts but a steady exhaustion that is beginning to eat at my bones." He reached into his pocket and pulled out a folded sheet of paper. "This is today's mission, delivered by hand though no one in my household saw the messenger. It will take me into Hertfordshire on another bloody fool's errand, yet I'm afraid to ignore it in case this is the one that matters, or in case another death awaits at the end, instead. The man who killed Green hanged himself, effectively closing that trail. But I am no nearer to knowing who murdered Herring or

Flanders, and there is no hint of a plot against Wellington that I can discover.''

Lord Grantley dropped his lids over his eyes and leaned back in his chair. ''According to Herring's message there won't be until you bed the right lady. I am to assume from your unfortunate state that it was not Lady Reed?''

Fitzroy looked up and laughed, with a wild, bitter undertone. ''It was not. Trojans and Greeks mean nothing to her. Yet it would seem that she is in on the game.''

''What game, sir?''

''A game of cat and mouse, my lord. By God, what an apt expression! Have you ever watched a cat with its prey, tossing and batting at a living creature? The mouse ends up in a paralysis of terror, longing for the final blow of the claws or bite to the jugular, only to be toyed with again and again.''

''What of it, sir? It's the game we played in the Peninsula to force the French to give way, isn't it?''

''But this time I am the mouse and the cat is invisible, crouching somewhere in the dark. Lady Reed went much further than Lady Carhill; it was not pretty. But because she might have replied that Helen's smile was only for Paris, I had to go along with it, whatever degradation I might feel, however dishonorable or vile my part in the play. And at last she let slip that she had been put up to it.''

Lord Grantley sat up and slammed his hand palm down on the table. ''By whom?''

Fitzroy stood up and began to pace, his hands clasped behind his back. When he stopped and turned to face the older man, he was smiling, an empty, courteous smile. ''She wouldn't say. But I gather that a group of society ladies have a little wager concerning me, as some kind of retaliation for the cruelties perpetuated on their sex by heartless rakes. If nothing else were involved I would say the entire game is simply that, and that we shan't find out anything sinister concerning the Iron Duke's safety. No dastardly plots, no assassins, nothing but a few ladies suffering from *ennui*.''

"For God's sake! Killing your men seems a very absolute way of revenging womankind on a rake.''

Fitzroy dropped into a chair and stared at his hands, pressed palm down on the table in front of him, the fingers spread. "Exactly, my lord. Flanders, Herring, and Green, God rest their gallant souls. *My* men. And my wife's little sister used as a decoy to deliver an empty message. That is why I dragged you from your bed. I must tell Joanna what is going on. Or I can't go through with any more of this.''

Lord Grantley stood up, towering over Fitzroy. With the flat of his hand he gave the younger man a stinging blow across the face. "That is not a challenge, sir, for you to meet me at dawn,'' he hissed. "But a reminder that you have an obligation to do your damned duty! You will not go mewling to your wife. God knows how she might react, what she might give away!''

Fitzroy touched the fingers of his left hand to his jaw, where the skin had gone livid. "Should I thank you, my lord? I cannot retaliate, of course. Our respective positions insure that. But no doubt it was deserved. I have done the same to more than one green soldier who threatened to lose his nerve before a battle.'' He gave a wry grin. "Now I know how it feels.''

"I don't question your nerve or your courage, Tarrant,'' said Lord Grantley, leaning forward with an awkward commiseration, as if embarrassed that he had lost his temper. "But we cannot risk what might happen. The very fate of Europe might be involved. Yet you think that this entire imbroglio may be personal, that it doesn't need to involve Whitehall, that Wellington isn't in danger?''

"I do, my lord.''

Lord Grantley drummed his fingers on the table top. "And I do not. I cannot take the risk that you are wrong. You will continue with the charade, sir, in spite of your imprudent wedding. You will go to Lady Kettering's affair and do whatever is asked of you. For God's sake, it cannot be that hard to bed a pretty woman, and this marriage was arranged—was it not?—one of convenience.''

Fitzroy did not reply for a moment. Then he stood up and bowed. "If I am to ride to Hertfordshire today and be back in time to visit my sister, I must go home and change."

"Your sister, Lady Mary?"

"She is ill, my lord, possibly dying. I visit her every day that I can."

"My dear fellow!"

"It is one of the reasons why I resent all this so damned much." Fitzroy pulled on his gloves. "There are not enough hours left in each day. Incidentally, I have taken over the care of Herring's family. I have hidden them, in case innocent women and children might be the next target. Flanders and Green were both single, thank God. But there were other men who served under me in the Peninsula. I cannot protect them all, were I to ride the length and breadth of this island every day, though I am doing what I can. You know, if she wasn't already with the angels, I would say that this is just the kind of game Juanita would have enjoyed. It has the very mark and stamp of her; in fact it reeks of it."

"Juanita? Oh, your first wife, of course." Lord Grantley looked distinctly uncomfortable, but no stone could be left unturned and Fitzroy had just raised the most unholy suspicion in his devious mind. "There's no question that—?"

"That she died? None at all, my lord. I was there. You might say she died because of me." Fitzroy stopped in the doorway. "Unless we are being beleaguered by a ghost?"

Joanna did not see Fitzroy at all the next day. She visited Lady Mary and worked on her portrait. It was easy to take pleasure in this painting. Their visits were becoming ever merrier and the face that was taking shape on the canvas glowed with laughter. Joanna stood back to look at it, and found an answering glow in her own heart. It would be the best she had ever done. So she was leading the life of a spinster while married to a rake. It didn't matter as long as she could do this!

Nor did Fitzroy come to her studio that night. Joanna waited for him, nervously pacing, until at midnight she doused the candles and went to bed. So he could not even keep that promise and sit for her every day! Yet in the morning she came down the stairs to find him waiting. Joanna stopped and looked at him, surprised, her heart beating a little fast. He seemed drawn, preoccupied, as always. But as she stood on the stairs, lost for words, Fitzroy grinned up at her, the corners of his mouth supple with a laughter that she could not trust.

" 'There was a roaring in the wind all night; / The rain came heavily and fell in floods; / But now the sun is rising calm and bright; / The birds are singing in the distant woods,' " he quoted without preamble. "I thought I would take you and my sister into the country today. If you would like."

"Good heavens!" replied Joanna tartly. "How I am honored, to be sure! What on earth brought about this sudden change of heart?"

He still sounded amused, but there was some strange, deeper undertone. "We can visit Mary's old nurse, a gentle and harmless creature whose day will be gladdened by our arrival. Or at least by Mary's arrival. Mary will love it."

Joanna would not let him escape so easily. "And what about all the other business that usually keeps you so busy?"

"I have taken care of it by working through the night. But I have recently received a lecture about doing my duty. Surely escorting my wife and sister on a rustic outing is dutiful enough?"

"And I am to believe the person exists who dares lecture you?"

He leaned on the newel post as if considering this. "There are many, Joanna. You among them. And now you are about to object that it didn't rain at all last night."

"How did you know?" She laughed. It was impossible to stay hostile when he was looking up at her beneath his lashes like that. "Very well. I was. *The rain came heavily and fell in floods?* It did not. *There was a roaring in the wind all night?* Stuff! It was exceptionally calm and peaceful."

"Oh, no, my dear, it stormed. Graves yawned, spirits roamed, and wolves wailed and howled like banshees. I can still hear the noise of it.''

Joanna gave him a very keen glance. ''On the contrary. The night was perfectly still. How the devil did you spend it that you thought otherwise?''

He glanced away, the amusement gone. ''In unholy enough pursuits, of course.'' She knew he would not say more and was proved right. As he looked back at her, he changed the subject. ''I would be grateful if you would allow me to act the gallant, and take you and Mary away from this Godforsaken town for just one day.''

Joanna gave him a formal curtsey, practiced often enough for Miss Able. ''I should enjoy it above all things, sir. Pray, allow me a few moments to change.''

Fitzroy drove west out of London in a barouche borrowed from his father, the highstrung bays in harness. Joanna watched the confident tact and authority with which he handled the horses. Once again she noticed his hands and the set of his shoulders, limber, graceful, intensely masculine. Why was he so impossible to paint?

Under a tasseled cream silk parasol, Mary leaned back on her seat and exclaimed enthusiastically about the beauties of the spring countryside. ''Oh, look, Fitzroy! Lambs! May we stop for a moment?''

Fitzroy instantly pulled up the horses and held them steady, while the ladies watched newborn lambs cavort in a pasture. Joanna pulled out her pack of paper and began to make rapid sketches—a page filled with gamboling, tumbling lambs, and the stolid ewes mumbling their cries through mouthfuls of cud. They stopped again for a tree full of blossom, for nesting swans, for two young children fishing in a pond.

It was bright and warm, the sun climbing strongly in the sky, when they reached a small thatched-roofed village straggling along its mill stream. Soon Joanna found herself being introduced to an elderly lady who sat in her best parlor like a robin on its nest, Lady Mary's childhood nurse, now retired to the village of her birth. They took tea, which Fitzroy had brought, and chatted of sane, ordinary things, while the old lady patted Lady Mary on the knee and smiled at her.

Joanna let them talk, making a few quick sketches of the nurse and her quiet room. She was unaware that Fitzroy watched her, or that his eyes followed her hands moving over the paper with an odd longing.

"Come, Joanna," said Fitzroy at last. "Let us take a stroll and leave these two friends to their reminiscences."

For Lady Mary's sake, Joanna took his proffered arm and left with him. Dappled sunshine mottled the dry dust and rough cobblestones of the village street. It was quiet, almost hushed, as if the dogs had forgotten how to bark and the thatched houses held their breath, afraid to awaken the baby.

"Who, do you suppose, managed to slip this serene moment unnoticed into the normal bustling country routine?" asked Fitzroy quietly.

Joanna could not afford to be charmed, to be beguiled by this unexpected truce or this calm, bright day. Only two nights before he had publicly seduced Lady Reed in a manner guaranteed to humiliate her. It still hurt. "I don't know. I have been wondering how you fit this entire outing into your outrageously busy schedule."

They turned off the street and began to follow a path that wound down through a birch wood.

The answer was taut. "So have I. Don't make me question it. Life is nothing but moments, anyway. Take each one as it comes, for God's sake."

Joanna took her gloved hand from his sleeve and turned to face him. "What fustian! Life is a great deal more than moments. Everything that happens takes meaning from what has happened before and from the expectations we bring to it. By your philosophy, Lady Mary simply sits with an old woman, and it wouldn't have mattered that you brought her here. I do understand why you did it, you see—in case there is never another chance for either of them. But it is the years of shared memories that make it meaningful—the baked apples on the nursery fire, the stories told to a half-sleeping child—and the trust in mutual love and caring.''

A bird flew away through the trees in a hiss of wing beats. Fitzroy looked back down at her with something close to anger. ''By God, are we allowed nothing pure and fresh, untainted by thinking and recollection?''

''It's impossible! When Lady Mary looks at an apple tonight it won't be the same as one she looked at yesterday. *This* apple will have the aura of childhood about it, bubbling and hissing in the flames, tender and wholesome, or it will be half red and half green and poisoned by a jealous stepmother, the magic apple of a fairy tale. Nothing exists entirely by itself. Everything comes trailing its retinue of associations and memories with it.''

''Can't an apple simply be an apple?'' He was carrying a cane. With the end he sketched rapid shapes in the dirt. A circle, a stalk, two leaves. ''What the devil is it when you draw it? Just a shape, a fruit, without all this trail of remembrance!''

''No,'' said Joanna, passion rising in her voice. ''It becomes what I bring to it. No human being ever saw just a fruit, unless he were a saint or a mystic.'' She grabbed the cane from his hand and sketched a curve like a bite out of the fruit before handing it back. ''Snow White bit into something luscious and innocent, but the wicked stepmother gave her a deadly poison that made her appear dead. Which was the real apple?''

Fitzroy leaned against a tree, sweeping the cane through the shapes in the dirt, scattering the lines. ''They were both the real apple, two halves of one whole. Oh, God! By your argument we are forever doomed by our prior experience. Nothing can be new and innocent. There can be no forgiveness and no salvation.''

She couldn't bear what she heard in his voice. ''Why doomed? We are made by what we have done, but must we be cursed by it? Snow White was rescued, wasn't she? Kissed by a prince?''

He looked up, straight into her eyes. Her heart seemed to stop for a moment, then lurched wildly.

"We know Snow White. We have been shown her life: the time in the castle with the wicked stepmother; her naive, kind-hearted days with the seven dwarves; the more innocent, indeterminate period while all life was suspended in the glass coffin. But the prince has no former existence at all in the story. He has never seen a woman sleeping before; he doesn't even accept the finality of death. Hadn't you noticed? He isn't real. If he was, he would never have believed that he could raise Snow White from the dead."

"Fiddlesticks!" Joanna knew she should turn away, flee this man and this moment, but her attention was caught, straining to understand. "He just believed in the healing power of love, that is all."

They were standing far too close to each other. His dark, heated gaze threatened to singe her.

"Did he?" said Fitzroy softly. "Did he believe that a kiss could cure anything?"

Joanna felt the roaring of awareness in her ears. Every nerve seemed to sing, shout for her attention. His lips were infinitely beautiful to her—as he formed the words "Snow White," as he took a breath—every detail highlighted, magnified, fascinating. She knew what those lips could make her feel, if he wished it.

You have eaten the poisoned, forbidden apple, sang a high, wild voice in her ear, *and only the kiss of a prince can save you.* Then the words spoken eons, ages ago, by a child came rushing in like a storm surge: *a woman can't do anything of her own, nothing real anyway, if she's gone soft in the head for a man and children! So if it has to be marriage, then very well, let it be to a self-centered, arrogant bastard like Fitzroy Mountfitchet. At least he will leave me alone!*

Joanna longed to believe it. She longed for the desire to be left alone. But this man who had swept into her life like a demon could not be exorcised from it. *Could* not? She did not *want* him gone. She did not want him to leave her alone. She

Jean R. Ewing

wanted his children. Joanna stepped closer, lifting her chin, offering herself.

Fitzroy gently touched her face, as if he might unwittingly lean forward and press his burning mouth onto hers.

A sharp crack shattered the air.

Birds flew up from the trees in a thunder of wing beats.

Fitzroy lunged at Joanna and flung her down. She hit hard onto the damp ground, the smell of bruised grass and dead leaves flooding her nostrils. He landed on top of her, pressing her into the earth, while he cursed under his breath.

"Damnation! Damnation!"

The air was crushed from her lungs. Fitzroy was heavy, and hard, and ruthlessly covering her body with his own. Joanna wanted to turn her head, but wet grass was stuck to her cheek.

"What?" she tried to say.

"Lie still," he whispered. "Someone is shooting at us."

Chapter 11

A second ball thudded into a tree above their heads, then there was silence. Fitzroy moved, quietly rolling away. As Joanna took a deep breath she heard the faint sound of something sliding, hard and metallic. Afraid even to turn her head, she lay pinned on the ground, a small stick pressed uncomfortably into her side.

The undergrowth rustled, the leaves shaken by something living. Joanna heard it lunging past, then circling and coming back. She pressed her lids shut as the rustling came closer and stopped, only to be replaced by a loud, damp panting. A large drop of saliva landed on the grass next to her face. Swallowing her fear, Joanna looked up. A bright yellow face with a pair of honest brown eyes grinned back. A golden retriever, tongue lolling, put its face close to hers. She smelt the scent of its breath and wrinkled her nose.

Someone whistled. The dog looked up and barked.

"It's all right," said Fitzroy.

Joanna sat up, rubbing grass and dead leaves from her skin and hair. "Are you quite mad?"

Fitzroy was sitting with his back against a tree trunk, staring up at the canopy of leaves overhead. Sunlight caught the strong line of his chin and throat. He held a naked blade in his right hand and he was looking at it. The light glanced from the bright steel, running along it like fire. So it had been a sword cane that he carried. Richard had one, too. Joanna supposed most of the Peninsular officers did. As she watched, Fitzroy thrust the blade back into its case, gave the handle a twist, and stood up, once again a gentleman with an ordinary walking stick.

Joanna scrambled to her feet unaided. "Mad, lunatic, insane, fit for Bedlam!"

Heavy footsteps crashed through the trees, a bush shivered, and a man in leather gaiters appeared before them like the great goat god, Pan: a Pan with a bluff, shiny, weather-beaten face and black whiskers under a felt hat. He carried a double-barreled shooting piece over one shoulder.

"Good Lord!" he said.

The dog trotted over to him and sat down by the gaiters, gulping the pink tongue back into its mouth.

"Your dog, sir, has not found your bird," said Fitzroy casually. "Perhaps because you didn't hit it."

"Good Lord!" said the rustic again. "I was shooting at pigeons, sir!"

"If you were to aim a little higher next time? Then you might bag your supper instead of causing alarm to innocent ladies and gentlemen." Fitzroy lifted his cane and pointed to a scar in the bark of a nearby tree. "The trace of your ball, sir." He moved the cane higher and indicated the tree tops. "The pigeons were up there."

"Well, I'm blessed!"

"An excellent dog, sir, but a villainous aim."

"I'd like," replied Pan, turning very red and panting now like his dog, "I'd like to see you do better, sir!"

"With pleasure." Fitzroy took the gun from the man and primed and reloaded each barrel in turn, ramming home the balls that Pan gave him from a pouch at his waist. It was done with a rapid, deadly precision.

"Don't," said Joanna. She didn't trust him. He looked wild.

Beneath that careless, sarcastic humor, she could sense a great swell of anger, like the sea.

Fitzroy raised a brow and winked at her, before turning back to the rustic with the dog. "Pigeon pie?" He lifted the gun. "Or shall we take the mistletoe from that oak over there?"

He fired one barrel. The dog raced away, reappearing in moments with a small oak branch in its mouth. The clutch of mistletoe was growing at one end.

Pan rubbed a large hand over the back of his neck. "Bless me, sir. You are a fair shot. Very fair, indeed. You could bring down a bird very clean, I dare say."

"Do you mean that?" asked Fitzroy. He swung the open mouths of the gun toward the fellow. "Can you trust your own judgment? Pray, stand still, sir, lest my hand shake."

The dog dropped the branch and barked.

Joanna screamed as Fitzroy fired point blank at the man. Pan had no time to move. He stood frozen, whiskers stark against his suddenly white face. The smoke cleared away. A neat round hole punctured the felt hat near the crown.

"For heaven's sake!" Joanna rushed up to the man. He had taken off his hat and put one stubby finger through the hole. "I'm so very sorry, sir. Indeed, my husband will pay you compensation for your alarm!"

Pan of the black whiskers shook his head slowly. "Well, I'll be! The very devil of a shot, indeed! No need for blunt, ma'am. No need at all." He looked up at Fitzroy, the color flooding back into his face. "Fair's fair, right enough, sir. I'm sorry if the lady had a fright—for I surely did."

Setting his felt cap firmly on his black hair, the man snapped his fingers at the dog. With a quick salute, he turned and stomped off through the trees. The golden retriever looked back once over its shoulder at Joanna and Fitzroy, before bounding away after its master.

Fitzroy dropped to his heels against the nearest tree and began, quite helplessly, to laugh.

"This is madness!" Joanna stared down at him. "You *do* always carry your own storm with you, don't you?"

"No doubt I do, but our friend with the dog could have killed you."

"By accident! But you very nearly murdered him deliberately!"

Fitzroy looked up at her, shading his eyes against the light. "Do you think so? Then which is worse? A murder resulting from bungling and incompetence, or a lesson deliberately given? He was in no danger from my shot, I assure you. Indeed, had he ducked, I'd have missed the felt hat altogether."

"And who on earth are you to teach him a lesson?"

"An officer he recognized from more difficult days, of course. He was a sergeant, and a damned incompetent one, too, though he never served directly under me."

"You knew him?" She was incredulous.

Fitzroy grinned up at her. His hands hung relaxed, a wrist supported by each knee, the back of his hands strong and square above the curving fingers. "He'd have been mortified to admit it. I saw no need to let him know I knew him, too. But bearing a weapon and shooting at pigeons in a public wood carries a certain responsibility. Anyway I have a particular fondness for pigeons."

"You keep them at the bottom of the garden."

"Yes, Quentin told me you had found him there. But not only do I abhor the idea of a pigeon being shot down from the sky, it is generally considered unsporting to scatter balls into innocent passersby."

"But it is much worse to hurt someone intentionally!" Joanna was shaking now that the danger was over. "That man meant us no harm at all!"

He stood, caught up his sword cane and scraped the tip along the furrow in the bark. It was very close to where she had been standing. "Though you would have been just as dead. But why should we debate it? You have never harmed a living soul, whether by accident or design. Let us go back, shall we? At least wherever my sister spends time, sanity reigns." Joanna turned away, only to be arrested by something new in his voice.

She could almost have described it as tenderness. "Wait. You have leaves in your hair."

She stood, eyes closed, groping for some understanding, some calm, while his gentle fingers picked out leaves and twigs, the knuckles occasionally brushing the sensitive back of her neck. How could he be so impossible, and then turn her legs into willow saplings with a single touch?

Yet there was no sanity to be found with Lady Mary in her nurse's old parlor.

"Look, Fitzroy!" she said as they came in. "Kittens! May I take one back with me?"

Lady Mary's lap was full of kittens. More tiny balls of fluff crawled and clung to her skirts and shoulders. Fitzroy plucked a mewling puff of orange from his sister's collar and gave it to Joanna.

"What is this?" he asked with a wicked grin. "How can such a creature be both so innocent and a young hunter? In that flat and appealing little head, a kitten carries everything it will ever need to know to be a terror to mice."

Joanna caught the kitten. It opened a tiny pink mouth armed with teeth like needles and cried. Fitzroy gave her another one. She sat down. He placed a third on her shoulder.

"Let them be," she said sternly. "Let them be innocent while they may! For unless they are taught by their mother, they never will catch mice. Instead, they'll just become fat old toms sleeping by the fireside. Not everything is determined, Fitzroy!"

He gave her a grin that touched something deep in her heart. "Well, thank God for that."

They drove back to London with Lady Mary's kitten safely ensconced in a basket. Yet after delivering the ladies to their respective homes, Fitzroy called for his gray to be saddled and left again. Joanna did not want to admit to herself how much she longed for her husband to show her the attention he showered on his sister. She only knew that she could never be indifferent to him. She waited until past midnight before she went to bed. Fitzroy did not come home. How was she to finish a portrait of him if he didn't sit for her? And what was she to do with her new, strange feelings for him?

When he reappeared the next morning, it was as if their day in the country had never taken place, or if by taking a day away from town he was now driven twice as hard to make up for it. He apologized stiffly for missing their appointment in her studio and assured her it wouldn't happen again, but he was distracted, almost demonic. She couldn't understand him.

Yet almost every day after that, he joined her and Lady Mary, often still dusty from the road or with the drawn, attenuated look of a man who had gone an entire night without sleep. He seemed to shrug it off, shedding the fatigue like a coat. Joanna slipped aside to make sketches of him, while he laughed and teased with his sister and they played with the kitten. He brought Lady Mary little gifts: meaningless, charming things, like feathers or shells or an unexpected, whimsical surprise—a chocolate confection in the shape of a heart, or a speckled bird's egg. Joanna watched them together with an odd hunger while she let her fingers fly over the paper, catching the tilt of an eyebrow, the cut of his jaw.

Then, back at her studio, she would study the drawings she had made of him and wonder who he was. For the image of the man now flowing from her fingertips onto the paper was of a Fitzroy Monteith Mountfitchet who didn't exist: a man full of love and gaiety and quick wit. The vision of it filled her imagination. From the sketches Joanna blocked out a final version on canvas. It showed him half-turned toward the viewer, his head tilted back a little, with his shirt open at the collar and the hair tumbled over his forehead. A smile lurked at the corner of his lips as if he were about to wink at the world. It was what she had dreamed of and longed for. She had succeeded only too well in her desire to give Lady Mary a portrait she could treasure—this was going to be superb.

So when Fitzroy stalked into her studio at the end of each day, drawn, sharp, dark with fatigue, she could use him as a direct model for his throat, hair, and clothes, refining the colors and shapes of his skin and features, while painting his expression in truth from memory, leaving the grim reality behind. She found herself obsessed with this portrait, for while it was entirely her creation, it felt like a great truth, more true in its way than the first dark drawings she had destroyed.

Joanna worked in silence. She asked him nothing more about his life, or where he went every day. She did not offer to touch him again, to rub his neck or offer any kindness, though he would pull off his cravat himself and toss it aside with obvious relief. Yet sometimes she would look up from the canvas to find him watching her with an intense craving: the look of a man dying of thirst, gazing at a desert mirage. She couldn't understand it, for he would instantly veil his expression with indifference. Their marriage took on the pattern that he had promised.

You won't get my attention or my interest. I shan't be available to you, or supportive of you. I shall always be preoccupied with other concerns that I will not share with you. Is that what you want?

So how on earth could she tell him that it was not what she wanted any longer? That it moved and disturbed her to see him so filled with anguish? That she lay in her bed every night filled with covetousness that only Lady Mary knew glimpses of the magical man she was creating on her canvas? That while she resented and despised the husband who had humbled her at Lady Reed's ball, and was infuriated by the cavalier who had shot a hole in a rustic's felt hat, she was falling in love with a painting?

For Lady Kettering's dance, Joanna wore one of her new dresses. She stood for several minutes and stared at her reflection in her mirror. The dark hair, and the eyes that seemed to her too intense for beauty, were unchanged, but she was not the same girl who had run away from Miss Able's Academy only a few weeks before. There were little shadows of stress at the corners of her mouth, and a new watchfulness veiled her expression. It was as if something of her husband's mood was rubbing off on her. Words from Cock Robin tumbled into her thoughts. *'Who'll bear the pall? We, said the wren, both the cock and the hen, we'll bear the pall?'*

She walked down the stairs alone to wait for the carriage. Once again her mother would escort her. No doubt Fitzroy would arrive there separately, as before. Joanna knew quite clearly what to expect. *He will bed Lady Kettering next Friday. It is all arranged.* She had entered this marriage thinking she wanted his indifference. How could she have guessed that it would hurt so very much?

There was a large grandfather clock in the hallway. It reminded her of the timepiece at Miss Able's. It had stood like a sentinel at the entrance of the school, keeping strict time, the drill major of her hours and days, the martinet clock hands and the great brass weight in the walnut case. Joanna closed her eyes and remembered it, remembered why she had run away—and remembered Fitzroy driving her there through the dark, in case there was a threat to her little sister, Milly. Now her days were her own to order as she pleased. She had a studio, and she was doing good work. She had no excuse at all to be miserable.

There was a knock at the door. Ah, her mother, at last! Joanna stepped forward to see the footman gazing down at a small brown-haired woman in a black dress and cloak.

"Please, is Lord Tarrant in?" asked the woman.

"Now what would the likes of you be doing at the front door?" replied the footman. "The tradesman's entrance is round the back."

"No, I have personal business with Lord Tarrant," insisted the woman with quiet dignity. "My name is Mrs. Morris. I am sister to Ned Flanders—as was his groom in the Peninsula. He would want to see me."

"His lordship is not in."

The footman began to close the door, but Joanna stepped forward. "Wait!"

They both looked at her in clear surprise.

"I am Lady Tarrant, Mrs. Morris," said Joanna. "May I help you, instead? Please come in."

Joanna led the brown-haired woman into a private room and ordered her some tea. They made an odd contrast: Joanna dressed for a ball; Mrs. Morris in her plain black dress and stout country boots.

"My brother died recently." Mrs. Morris was dry-eyed, composed, but Joanna saw clearly how it hurt to say aloud. "I was going through his things and came across this." She held out a small parcel. "He said to me once that if anything happened to him, I was to bring it to Lord Tarrant."

Joanna took the parcel and turned it over in her hands. "Then of course I shall make sure that he gets it. Is there anything else I can do for you, Mrs. Morris?"

The small woman stood up and smiled. "No, thank you, my lady. Lord Tarrant has been more than kind. He settled a very generous sum on Ned's family when he was killed. It's been quite a help at our farm, and to my sister in town—that's where I'll be staying tonight."

"Your brother was killed? I am so very sorry."

Tight lines appeared on Mrs. Morris's forehead. "He got in a brawl and was stabbed. Heaven only knows why! Ned was never much of a drinking man, for all his years as a soldier. But there you are. Wondering won't bring him back. Good evening, your ladyship."

As soon as Mrs. Morris left, Joanna heard her mother's clear tones, then the deeper voice of a man. Oh, dear Lord! Her brother Richard! He had come to town! In a panic Joanna shoved the parcel underneath a cushion on the chaise longue and hurried out into the hallway.

"Well, sister mine?" Richard grinned at her and swept her into a hug. "How is married life treating you?"

Joanna gathered every ounce of courage she possessed.

"Very well. As I predicted to you, I'm loving my freedom. What are you doing in town, sir?"

"Helena sent me to make sure that all is well with you and that Tarrant is keeping his word. Mother is being coy about things, as usual. Is he behaving like a gentleman, Jo?"

"Of course," said Joanna bravely. "Why shouldn't he?"

"Then I shall happily escort you and Mother to Lady Kettering's ball. But if your husband fails to behave impeccably toward you, I can't promise not to run him through on the spot."

It was casually said, but Joanna held no doubts about the depth of Richard's distrust of Fitzroy. This was disaster!

"Now that you're here, don't let's go to this silly ball. I'd much rather we stayed and caught up on all the news. How is baby Elaine?"

"Our darling child is well and crowing. But I'm counting on this evening, Jo. I hear Lord Kettering has a mount for sale that his wife has outgrown. I thought the beast might be interesting. And if I can't arrange that, everyone else in town who has an eye for good horseflesh will be there. It's too good an opportunity to miss."

"But you can visit them all in the morning if you are looking for a horse," insisted Joanna. "Anyway, I have the headache. I don't feel at all like going! Please stay here with me!"

"No, I think I must go. I'll come and see you tomorrow."

Joanna looked up at her brother. His mouth was set in a determined line. He wasn't in London to search for a horse. He was going to Lady Kettering's ball because Fitzroy would be there. Had rumor of the scandalous scene with Lady Reed reached all the way to Acton Mead? Oh, Lord! If Richard witnessed Fitzroy do the same with Lady Kettering, there might be bloodshed right there between the waltz and the Boulanger. Though neither Richard nor Fitzroy would be armed, she wouldn't put it past her brother to seize the bow from the hands of the first violinist and use it to stab her husband to the heart.

"Then I'll come, after all. The headache isn't so bad."

Richard escorted the ladies out to the Acton carriage. As

Joanna was handed in next to Lady Acton, her mother leaned close and whispered in her ear. "I shall do my best, my dear child, to help you to keep them apart. I could not prevent Richard coming, I'm afraid. So could you ask Fitzroy to be more careful of public appearances, perhaps, if he plans any major indiscretion tonight? I do not want to see Richard hurt over the worthless rake you have married."

Fitzroy assessed the situation at a glance: Lady Kettering waiting with ill-disguised impatience, tapping her fan, tossing her glossy brown curls, as she talked with some friends; Lady Acton briefly meeting his eyes, conveying a distinct warning and something very much like a plea; Joanna, his lovely, brave, forbidden wife, dancing with her brother, her eyes anxiously scanning the room; Richard, his jaw set, as alert as he had ever been in Spain on patrol against the French.

What the hell was Lenwood doing in town? And tonight of all nights? How the devil was he going to handle this? To be called out by Richard Acton, a man he admired and liked, over Lady Kettering was the ultimate madness.

Fitzroy stepped out of sight behind a pillar for a moment as the deadly absurdity of it threatened to undo him with derisive laughter. Lady Carhill was beautiful, at least. Delectable Lady Reed had even been a little in love with him. He had been left with the feeling that she had hated what she was doing as much as he had, that she really wanted something very different and had become trapped in the ugly masquerade with him almost by mistake. In another life perhaps he would joyfully have taken her as a mistress, instead of leaving her desolate, her hands empty. Unconsciously his fists clenched.

For tall, graceful Lady Kettering with her perfect profile was entirely predatory. Fitzroy had no desire at all to pursue her. Yet he must. In spite of Lady Acton's silent plea. In spite of Richard's probable retaliation. And in spite, God help him, of Joanna. He wasn't sure when it had begun, this craving for his wife. She was lovely, of course. But it was more than that. It was her courage and her humor and her passion for her art. Every night in her studio while she stood at the easel he would watch her: the graceful lines of her body, the mass of coal black hair, the way her tongue would sometimes slip onto her bottom lip as she worked in a fever of concentration.

If he owed a debt to the gods for Juanita he was prepared to pay it. But why must Joanna suffer also, and Green and Herring and Flanders?

"Dance with me, quickly!"

Fitzroy looked around. Joanna stood at his elbow, her face a little flushed.

For the first time in his life he was dumb with shock.

"Come on!" insisted Joanna. "Unless you want bloodshed and weeping and flocks of dark ravens!"

Fitzroy took her hand and led her onto the floor. It was a country dance, involving a great deal of walking up and down and spinning of partners.

"I'm sorry," hissed Joanna, "that it's not a waltz; it would have been easier to talk."

The steps separated them for a moment, but the next movement required Fitzroy to lead Joanna down the center of the aisle of dancers then spin her about at the end, a moment when a private word could be exchanged.

"I wanted Richard to see you behaving gracefully toward me in public, at least. Then when you disappear, I'm coming too. Don't look so astonished! It wasn't hard to arrange."

Fitzroy swallowed hard. "And what, dear wife, have you arranged?"

"Lady Kettering will be waiting in the summerhouse. You and I will go out into the garden, then you can join her while I hide in the bushes. Richard mustn't know, you see. For though he'd prefer you to have a mistress—indeed he expects it—any public display of lubricity will make him think he has to act heroic on behalf of his sister."

"You spoke with Lady Kettering?" Astonishment left him searching for balance.

Joanna was gazing up at him with wide, dilated eyes. "Why not? She was so surprised she agreed right away."

"Joanna. You can't do this!"

The steps of the dance spun them apart.

When Fitzroy next took her hands Joanna grinned at him. "Why not? However despicable I may find him, I'd rather lead my husband to his lover than his death—or Richard's death, which counts more."

There was no time for him to reply.

The dance was over. Clinging to his arm, Joanna steered Fitzroy out of the ballroom. From the corner of her eye, she saw Richard watch them leave. Her brother turned to his partner with a set jaw, and a frown sending a deep crease between his eyebrows, but he could hardly object if his sister took a little air with her husband.

The garden was cool and moist, dew beading already on the leaves and trailing vines.

"The summerhouse is down there," said Joanna, pointing. "Lady Kettering gave me very precise directions. I pretended to believe that you had business with her; it disarmed her completely. She's wondering whether I am simple-minded or merely immensely naive. I'll be lost in the maze—it's behind the shrubbery to our left."

Joanna knew quite clearly what she wanted. She wanted Fitzroy to forget Lady Kettering. She wanted him to tell her so: *Devil take the shrubbery, Joanna! My only desire is to stay here with you.* And then he would relax and laugh, and offer her something of himself that he otherwise shared only with Lady Mary. Perhaps he would even kiss her again and take her, dizzy and enflamed, into his arms. Instead he inclined his head very slightly and smiled at her in the moonlight—a smile devoid of pleasure or intimacy, echoing nothing but anger and despair.

"There is nothing that I can say, Joanna. I'm so sorry."

He spun about and left her. She watched him for a moment striding away down the path toward the summerhouse. Then

Joanna walked blindly through the shrubbery to lose herself in the maze.

Lady Kettering was leaning gracefully against a marble column. Fitzroy caught her from behind and spun her to face him.

"Now," he said. "No games, my lady. Do you have information for me or not?"

She gave him a coquettish smile. "Ah, Fitzroy. You are so very formidable! Are you threatening me?"

"If you like."

"But if I have information, sir, you must pay the price for it. *Let Helen but smile, and Trojans and Greeks war to the death.* How foolish men are to fight over women. After all, *Helen's smile belonged only to Paris.*"

He thrust her up against the wall of the summerhouse, taking her hand and kissing her knuckles. The gesture mocked her, insulting. "You have just allowed my wife to be used in your nasty little game, my lady. It is the one thing that I cannot forgive. I will pay no further price. If you wish to give me a message, give it. Otherwise I shall walk away."

Lady Kettering ran one hand along his jaw. "And let Wellington die, and leave a poor lady bereft? You could not be so lacking in chivalry, Fitzroy."

He smiled. "You have heard, perhaps, what happened in Spain to my first wife, Juanita? Don't think you can trust me to be gallant or spare you because of your gender. Tell me now, Lady Kettering, what you know."

"So you are a brute, after all," she hissed. "I hardly believed it; now you have proved it to be so. Very well. Let go of me and I shall tell you. But the price will still be owed and I shall make sure it's collected. If not now, then later."

"What do you know?" he said, implacable.

"I have a set of instructions for you. They were given to me just this afternoon. If you wish to save Lord Wellington's life, listen carefully."

* * *

Joanna sat down on a small marble bench and peered up between the high, thick hedges at the thin wedge of night sky. A faint mist silvered the air, so that the stars were veiled. She shivered and closed her eyes. Fitzroy and Lady Kettering! Her throat hurt. Why did he do this? She could understand Quentin, perhaps, tied to a wife he couldn't live with, avoiding commitment, becoming a rake. But Fitzroy? What drove him? What drove any Don Juan? For if he simply found every new woman irresistible, why not her? Was she so unattractive, so very undesirable to him?

Or was it, as Lady Carhill had said, that he was still in love with his first wife? She must insist, as soon as the opportunity presented itself, that Richard tell her what had happened. How had Juanita died?

Chapter 12

"After Theseus slew the Minotaur with the aid of Ariadne, he abandoned her. What do you suppose is the moral of that story? Never trust men in mazes?"

Joanna's voice almost betrayed her. "Fitzroy!"

She could not face him. A hideous embarrassment was turning her face red, as if she might be throttled at any moment.

He dropped onto the marble bench beside her, and idly picked a blade of grass from the path at their feet. "Lady Kettering has returned to the ball room. I don't suppose you care, but apart from kissing her hand, I did not touch her." He spun the grass blade about between his thumb and forefinger. "Even I, as hardened to depravity as I may be, could hardly consummate a rendezvous with a lover that was arranged by my wife, could I?"

"Why not?" replied Joanna immediately. Her heart had already leapt back into its more usual orbit, beating a crazy rhythm of gladness. *I did not touch her!* Oh, it did matter! "Wasn't she pretty enough for your jaded tastes?"

He gave her a shrewd glance, a small smile beginning to play at the corner of his mouth. "No, I find her very pretty,

Joanna, though I don't like her. She has promised to renew our rendezvous at some later date.''

Joanna fought for the courage to keep her voice calm, to feign indifference. "Oh. Well, that's all right, then.''

She could sense the warmth and strength of him, sitting next to her in the darkness. Moonlight touched his profile, making him seem metallic, perfect, and completely unattainable. Joanna stood up.

"Do you want to go back?'' he asked.

"To the ballroom?'' She wasn't sure what he meant.

"No, home. I have about as much desire to dance any longer as Hercules had to face the hydra.''

Home. The formal rented house. It was the only home he had, of course. "By all means,'' said Joanna. "Richard is probably breathing fire in the ballroom by now. Let's escape and go to my studio. I can't get your eyebrows to come right.''

He reached up and very gently ran one thumb across her forehead, smoothing down her eyebrow. Then he abruptly dropped his hand and stood up.

In silence they walked back to the house. Throughout the carriage ride home, Joanna watched him, his mouth and his eyes, as he leaned back against the squabs, locked away in that place she could never reach, offering her nothing in return for her sacrifice.

He is an arrogant, self-centered rogue! They had been the words of a child, understanding nothing. And what had her mother said? *You are not selfish, Joanna. You are just filled with too much passion and too much burning longing for life.*

Fitzroy shifted a little on the seat and closed his eyes. Joanna saw the tension limning his jaw.

Damn him! He has become part of my life. Can't he understand that, and give me something—one drop of notice? Or share anything of his concerns and his torment? I'm his wife!

Fitzroy sat in the chair, casually posed with one arm along the back, his cravat abandoned, shirt open at the neck. Candlelight caressed his smooth skin, casting him in gold. Joanna, once again in her old dress and smock, hated him with a clear passion, and knew her emotion was only an imposture for desire.

"Why don't you paint anymore?" she asked as she mixed some pigment on her palette.

The reply was distant, preoccupied. "I have too much else to do."

"It seems to me a kind of cowardice."

He looked up at her, cocking a brow. "Does it?"

Something was burning in her, something she had kept banked at Lady Kettering's. But now a lonely, hot wind was stirring the embers and fanning them into flame. "Yes, it does. To give up a gift like that shows an appalling failure of spirit, doesn't it? What else can account for wasted genius? Only a craven loss of nerve, when, who knows, if you followed your talent you might prove to be a master?"

The supple voice remained casual, impersonal. "But what if you were to make decisions in your life based on faith in that talent, and discovered that you weren't a genius, after all?"

His very coolness infuriated her. "Does that matter? As long as our effort is genuine, brings pleasure, fulfillment, who cares about society's judgment? All art is a risk, isn't it? We might show the world how mediocre we are. So it's safer not to do it. It's the same with your superiority and sarcasm. It shows nothing but a fear of letting your guard down, in case people see you for what you really are and remain unimpressed. Is that what happened in Spain for which Richard could never forgive you? A base act of cowardice?"

He stood up, the lines of his back stiff. "Perhaps."

Joanna marched up and down, violently stirring the paint. His casual response to this unforgivable affront to his honor only fueled her blind rage. "Just as you gave way to your father over our marriage. I think you have no bravery in you. Rakes don't, do they?"

His voice was quiet, intense. "Courage is what you did tonight at Lady Kettering's. You think I didn't know, didn't recognize that, or appreciate the spirit that it took? What's happening now is the aftermath, like soldiers rioting after a battle. Don't do this, Joanna!''

"Don't do what? I have never made any demands on you. I have honored the terms of our contract. But you have used me at every step. You left me at the church door after our wedding, and foolishly at the time I thought it rather splendid. But it meant that I was left without any support to face your father and mine—hardly the chivalrous act of a gentleman.'' It was a weak argument, but the anger in her threatened to flame out of control. "You take it for granted that I'll be complacent and cooperative about your mistresses—but what about my pride and confidence? All those women! So beautiful and desirable. Lady Carhill was ready to weep over you!''

He came up to her, crossing the room in a few long, rapid strides. "What can I do, Joanna?''

She looked into his eyes, forcing herself to meet that devouring gaze in spite of the mortifying sting under her lids. "I have swallowed my humiliation that I am the only female on this earth that you don't want. But it's too hard—it makes me feel like the ugly stepsister, when every night you go to the ball with a different Cinderella. Should I chop off my heels and toes to fit them into the slipper, so that you'll notice me, too?''

He caught her by the wrist and tossed her palette aside, spilling paint as the wood cracked. Colors ran riotously together, a reflection of her wild, pure anger.

"Notice you! Every night I sit in that damnable hard chair and watch you poring over your painting, giving all your love and generosity and courage to a dumb piece of canvas, while barely looking at my face as if it pains you to see me. And why not, when I have behaved to you as I have? Yet Lady Carhill, Lady Reed, Lady Kettering, they mean nothing—nothing! Not one of them has been my mistress, though I don't expect you to believe it. Why should you? Compared to your passion for art, I am a mere cipher in your life. What the devil does it matter what I do?''

"But it does, because you married me and there is no one else."

"You should take a lover," he said, but the words seemed to choke in his throat. And suddenly he laughed, with that wild, bitter self-derision, yet his dark eyes were locked on her face. "Though if you did, I would want to kill him."

She didn't know if she believed him, but the words fired a fierce joy in her. *Not one of them has been my mistress.* Joanna stared back up at him, her heart in her eyes. How could he mean it? "I shall never take a lover," she said. "You are my husband. Shall I go to my grave a virgin?"

His grip changed on her wrist, softening, fervent. "You don't know what you ask, Joanna, what it would mean. There'd be no turning back. Dear God, I didn't expect it to happen." His fingers moved up her arm, over the fabric of her dress to the bare skin of her neck. "My feelings don't matter, they have never mattered, yet I had no idea that you were being hurt by my inattention."

She knew what she risked. *So let that one kiss be the first and last expression of lust between us. Even if you invite me, madam, it will never happen again.* Yet she couldn't help herself! "And you think that's all it is? A little wounded pride and vanity? Why did you say you would never touch me again? What else can it be, except that I alone am hideous to you?"

The candlelight flickered as he studied her features, his gaze fathomless, the tension in him palpable. His voice seemed dragged from him, as if it pained him to speak, yet it pulsed with intensity. "Ah, no, dear heart, you are infinitely lovely to me." An odd half-smile lit his face as he gently touched her cheek. "I was angry with my father, and distracted by other claims. But love is a far higher, sweeter thing than lust. I saw at the Swan that you are beautiful and brave, but I didn't think I would be so vulnerable to you. Dear wife, I desire you passionately, with a man's hunger for a woman's beauty and with all the ardor of my soul." His hand slipped to her jaw, his bent fingers caressing her throat. "Thoughts of you envelop me day and night. You have fired a longing in my blood that

I can't quench. I find you enchanting—oh, God, what a dearth of words there are in the language! I burn for you! But I cannot act on it.''

"Why not?" It was a whisper.

He hesitated, as if searching for the words. "Richard told you the kind of work that I did in Spain. It's not over just because we're no longer openly at war. I am caught up in something degrading and vicious that I don't understand, and I cannot tell what may be required next. I can see no way out of it, but I fear the planned end is my death. At first it didn't matter that much. But it matters now. I love you, Joanna, and I know what we risk. Which makes it all impossible.''

All her concentration centered on the sensations he was creating on her skin. The rest barely registered: *The planned end is my death. I love you.* They seemed only words to Joanna, the melodramatic claims of a rake. To how many women had he professed love? She didn't care. Tears ran openly down her cheeks. *I burn for you!*

"So you do dangerous work. I have guessed as much. No man would come from a mistress looking as you do. But we all risk dying, every day. It's an overwhelming reason to live in the meantime—you said as much yourself about your sister. Your restraint is empty, Fitzroy. I'm your wife. If you love me, then prove it, damn you!''

"How the devil?" asked Fitzroy quietly, his voice dry and throaty. "When it is my own heart's desire—how the devil do you expect me to refuse you now?''

Slipping his hands to her waist, Fitzroy pulled her into his body. Joanna closed her eyes as his lips met hers. She would be burned! Surely, surely, the incandescent flame would sear her, scald her to the soul? Joanna held back nothing of her confusion and her desire, letting her mouth move under his searching lips and tongue, trembling, hot, beautiful.

They slipped together to the floor, Fitzroy supporting her easily with a hand at her waist, pressed together, devouring each other. He rolled her onto her back as he kissed her eyelids and hairline and throat. With her hands held above her head in one of his, he ran his fingers over her hair with a tenderness that touched deep into her heart. She would be consumed!

"Let me touch you, Fitzroy!" She wanted to explore him, as if her fingers on his jaw and neck would help her find out who he really was.

"Here," he said, opening his fingers and kissing the corner of her mouth. "I release you, wife, to have your wicked way with me."

Joanna touched his face, the slight roughness of his shaved jaw, the smooth column of his throat moving under her fingers. She had so longed to do this! A deep spring of joy washed away her anger. Tentatively she stroked his upper lip. He caught her fingertip in his mouth, soft and warm, and caressed it with his tongue. She moved her other hand to his back, feeling the firmness and the strange strength of him. Boldly she pulled the shirt out of his waistband and ran her fingers up his naked spine.

"Like that?" she asked, breathless, ravished by the flex of his muscles under her hand.

"Or like this?" He smiled down at her, infinitely desirable, his eyes as dark and wide as a night sky as his fingers moved over her skin.

Joanna gasped, her eyes closed, lost to anything else as the sensations he created flooded through her veins. "Yes! Oh, yes, Fitzroy!" They rolled over together, her smock soon discarded, her dress unbuttoned, his hands on her skin a revelation of delight. She longed to do the same wonderful things for him. Blushing furiously, she whispered, "I want you out of this shirt!"

Fitzroy pulled away, the dark hair falling over his forehead, his eyes dilated into blackness.

"Oh, damnation!" he said and laughed—a carefree, wild laugh, filled with gaiety.

"What?" Joanna sat up, her hair tumbling down around her shoulders. "What is it?"

Fitzroy rocked back onto his heels and held up his hands. "Paint! We are getting covered in paint. Look!"

They had crushed her abandoned palette beneath them. Bright pigments were everywhere, wild streaks of color running across the floorboards, and on their hands and faces and clothes.

"Oh, no!" Joanna looked at her palms. "Burnt sienna and cadmium red."

Fitzroy ran a finger across her cheek. "Prussian blue. It looks like woad, my pagan princess."

She ran one finger through a wash of paint and giggled. "We are tattooed, like savages."

He leant forward and kissed her gently, his lips barely touching hers then parting again softly. "Let me take you to bed, dear heart, or tell me to go to hell forever. I am mad, perhaps. No, I know I am mad to do this. Stop me, for God's sake, for I don't believe I can stop myself."

"I want it," whispered Joanna, shaking in his arms. "I want you. Don't abandon me now. Devil take tomorrow and tomorrow and tomorrow. We are married, aren't we?"

Married. There had been one other time when he had taken a virgin to her bridal bed, wanting it to be the most memorable night of her life. He had felt an exquisite tenderness for Juanita, and a fierce, burning passion. Now he felt it again, even more brightly this time, blazing with a purer flame, and had a second chance, perhaps. Fitzroy knew he ought to walk away, that he was breaking the bargain he had made with himself. Joanna had no idea how absolute this was. Yet he was trapped and there was already no going back. However unwise it might be, he was helpless in the face of an all-consuming desire. Joanna was his wife. He wanted to make her a gift. And if he did not do so now, he would instead give her a wound that might never heal.

Fitzroy picked her up off the floor and carried her out into the corridor, kicking the doors open and closed behind him. He carried her into the great master bedroom and set her down on the bed.

"Now," he said. "I am about to make love to you in earnest, Joanna. I give you my soul to dance upon, if you like. Make merry with my heart, wife. It is yours. I want to touch you

until you melt away, but I shall be melting with you." He
smoothed the tangled hair away from her face, his eyes impenetrable. Then he took one of her hands and laid it palm to palm
with his. Their joined pulse throbbed, hot and wild. "This is
the meaning of desire, sweetheart. To be carried together on
the flood tide. Never doubt, whatever happens later, that everything you feel tonight is real; that I love you; that I am feverish
with my passion for you. But tell me to stop if you want. For
I can't promise anything else. I can't promise to be with you,
or to be a good husband, or even that we can ever do this again.
'The world is too much with us.' Yet dear God, I hope you
won't send me away now!"

"I don't care." Joanna reached up her paint-stained hand
and touched the enchanting line of his jaw. *My husband.* Slowly
she trailed a line of yellow ochre along his chin. "Now is all
that counts."

Foolish words. Joanna woke in the morning to a disordered
bed, the pillows streaked here and there with paint. Her smock
and her old dress were neatly folded on a chair, and Fitzroy
had gone.

She touched a place where the colors had smudged together,
blue and ochre and crimson. *Now I am married.* Pushing back
the covers, she looked at herself, naked, her limbs dappled with
paint like a savage. How did she let it sink in? The meaning
of it. *To be carried together on the flood tide.* Pretty words
that had swirled into deeper and deeper layers as the night
unfolded. Until she had cried out and buried her face in his
shoulder, enfolded and pierced to the heart. *I love you, Fitzroy.
I love you. I love you.* And demonstrated it to him again and
again.

What if he did not return it? She had trapped him, hadn't
she? What if he had taken her to his bed out of pity, or duty,
or masculine pride? Oh, dear Lord, that was the risk she had
taken by inviting him—she would never know.

And Fitzroy was gone. As she expected. He had gone back

to that harried, tormented, mysterious life that he led, leaving her still closed out.

She climbed out of the bed. There was a note on the dresser: *Joanna. Remember. Whatever happens later, I love you.*

The words of a rake, whispered to a myriad women, to soften them and make them pliable—as she had become? It hadn't mattered so very much, until now.

The paper lay on a slim volume of Wordsworth's poetry. Joanna idly turned to the page that was marked by a ribbon and scanned the familiar lines about Proteus and Triton, the poem he had begun to quote that evening in the folly at King's Acton. 'The world is too much with us . . . We have given our hearts away, a sordid boon! . . . The sea . . . The winds . . . It moves us not . . . Great God! I'd rather be / A Pagan suckled in a creed outworn . . . '

She set down the book and heard Fitzroy's voice as clearly as if he were still there in the shadowed chamber: *You are a pagan, Joanna, whether you know it or not.*

And last night he had proved it. For the sea had surged in her, the wind had moved. Fitzroy had taken her to that world where Nature's gods dance beneath a wild moon, and nothing remained but the purity of creation. She would never be the same again. *You don't know what you ask, Joanna. There'll be no turning back.*

She had thought herself in love with him because he was beautiful and mysterious and wild, but that had been only a pale shadow of the love she knew for him now. *I give you my soul to dance upon, if you like.* What if he hadn't meant it? When now she did.

Features crazily marked with paint looked back at her from the mirror. Did it show? This transformation, this awakening?

Joanna took a long bath. Though she scrubbed her face till it shone there was still a faint blue shadow under the cheekbone.

She dressed in her smock and made ready to go to her studio, but was instead summoned away by a servant. Her brother Richard was waiting in the drawing room, pacing back and forth. He smiled as she entered the room. But the smile died.

"Joanna, dear child, is that a bruise? By God, if he has struck you—"

She came up to him and kissed his cheek. "Don't be silly, it's paint! Prussian blue, a slightly too permanent pigment. Do I look as if I've been beaten?"

"No, you look luminous, as if you've—Are you happy, Jo?"

"Of course, why shouldn't I be? I have everything. Now, sit down, brother, and tell me about things."

They talked for a few minutes about generalities, avoiding the one topic which lay like a monster between them. At last Richard stood and took up his cane. He was making ready to leave.

Gathering her courage, Joanna forced herself to say it. Out loud. Now there was no turning back. "Richard. How did Juanita die? You do see that you must tell me, don't you?"

He spun about, the cane gripped hard in his right hand. "I'd rather not, Jo. It's all in the past, irrelevant now."

Joanna felt the tension straining in her. "He is my husband, for better, for worse. I think I have the right to know."

She could see the struggle in him, the desire to leave it unsaid, but Richard sat down again, carefully laying aside the cane, and faced her. "Do you insist on this? Whatever it says about him?"

"I do. I must, Richard!"

"Very well. Life in the Peninsula wasn't easy, Jo. Many officers' wives stayed safely behind in the towns. Yet Juanita came with us on every campaign. She was always charming, exquisite. She carried an aura of culture and brilliance with her, even in camp. Any of the officers would have done anything for her. There was a general envy of Tarrant, I'm afraid."

"Did he love her very much?" Joanna couldn't keep the emotion out of her voice.

Richard steepled his fingers together and dropped his head onto them. "I believe anyone in the regiment would have said he was besotted. He shared everything with her. Yet she confided to me that he was unfaithful at every opportunity."

Joanna closed her eyes against the pain. "Go on, Richard. You can't stop now."

"We had made camp near Orthez. They had an argument over something—I was coming back from the horse lines when I heard the noise of it, though not the words. I assumed he'd been unfaithful again and Juanita found out. She tore out of their tent and took a horse, riding away as if the hounds of hell were at her heels. I mounted and followed her. Tarrant caught up with me within a few miles and begged me to go back, but we rode on together. He seemed frantic. I assumed he was afraid that harm would come to her. The French were camped pretty close by, after all."

It is only a story, Joanna told herself, *about long ago and far away.* "Then it was foolish to ride out alone like that. Was she often impulsive?"

"Impulsive? No, I don't think so. She had hinted before that he was cruel to her, but I always had the impression that she felt a fierce loyalty. She was Spanish and he was her husband. Something very exceptional must have made her run away like that."

"But you found her?"

"Her horse was tied outside a ruined farm. There were other horses in the barn. We heard them whinny. Tarrant reacted with that feral, derisive humor that he'd developed. It made me want to knock him down. We crept up to the farmhouse and managed to look inside without being seen. A group of partisans were arguing in the local patois. Juanita was sitting on a chair near the door, very pale."

"Partisans? On our side, then. Why didn't you identify yourselves and rescue her?"

"A French patrol appeared at the end of the lane and opened fire. After that it was nothing but confusion. The partisans were firing from the farmhouse; the French dismounted behind a stone wall. Tarrant and I took what slim shelter we could in the ruins of the porch. Meanwhile more French arrived and the partisans rushed out of the house to scatter behind whatever cover was available. It would have been madness to let the enemy pin us inside. As Juanita ran out, Tarrant caught her and thrust her behind him. She cursed at him.''

Richard stopped and looked down at his hands.

"Go on," said Joanna. "I have to hear this, Richard."

He looked ill, drawn and tired, the crease deep between his blond brows.

"Juanita panicked, I think. She tried to break away to her horse, shouting something. It was drowned by the noise of our weapons. One of the partisans on the other side of the yard took aim at her as she ran—he couldn't have known she was a British officer's wife, after all. The man was too far away to hear if we had shouted, yet Tarrant saw it all clearly and he had just reloaded. He's a superb shot. He could have winged the fellow and spoiled his aim, even though it would have exposed his own body to French fire for a moment. But he laughed as the man fired at his own wife. I was the only one close enough to hear him. *'We can die by it, if not live by love,'* he said, then he dropped like a stone, getting himself to safety behind a wall. Juanita never made it to her horse. He willingly sacrificed her, rather than risk himself. She was killed instantly.''

"Oh, dear God. And no one else could stop it?"

"I tried. My shot missed. Then somehow I was knocked over the head. It was moving into hand-to-hand combat. A skirmish like that is nothing but chaos anyway, and it was getting dark. I learned afterward that the French finally scattered and Tarrant got me away. He carried me back to camp unconscious, slung over my horse's back.''

"Did you never confront him? Ask him why he let it happen?"

"Of course. We had been close friends. He looked at me with that bitter sarcasm and said: 'Don't preach to me about chivalry, please, Richard. It is better like this. I was mad to marry her.' '' Richard stood up and crossed to the fireplace, poking fiercely at the coals. "He seemed to be playing host to the devil.''

"Yes," said Joanna faintly. "I have seen him like that.''

"Oh, God! When I tried to express sympathy over her death, he laughed aloud. 'Do you really believe that a black-hearted rake could bring a Spanish wife back to England when he is heir to an earldom? What the devil do you think the Black Earl would say?' I had hoped that he could offer me some reason, some excuse for what he'd done. Instead, I wanted very badly to kill him and I told him so."

She had no idea where the strength came from to continue, but now she had to hear it till the end. "Did you call him out?"

"He had been wounded in the leg in the skirmish and was in the hospital tent." Richard gave a wry smile. "And he had saved my life, of course. So I had to content myself with avoiding him, instead. I wish I hadn't had to tell you this, Jo. And I wish to heaven you hadn't married him. I did tell Father, but he didn't care."

"Oh, dear Lord!" Joanna looked at the curtains. A tiny pattern of flowers was worked into the fabric. "Why?" she asked blindly. "Why did he save himself and let Juanita be killed?"

Chapter 13

After Richard left, Joanna sat on the chaise longue and thought about it. She had taken Fitzroy into her arms and her heart. Yet he had not hesitated to abandon his first wife to save his own hide. Then he had joked with Richard, her own brother, the man who had witnessed it, with that violent, wild levity. She had seen that he was driven and haunted. She had not thought him capable of this!

She lay back, putting her hands over her eyes. There was a crunch and rustle. Joanna jumped up before she remembered: Mrs. Morris, and a package for Fitzroy. She felt behind the cushion and pulled it out, a small, flat parcel wrapped in brown paper. Something that Mrs. Morris's brother Ned Flanders, who had been Fitzroy's groom and had died in a brawl, wanted his old Peninsular officer to have. Yesterday it had seemed none of her business, but now, after what Richard had told her!

And after what had happened with Fitzroy last night. He had warned her. There was no turning back.

Joanna crossed the room to Fitzroy's desk and found his paper knife. She cut open the brown wrapping and tore it away. Inside lay a book with shabby leather covers, marked with a moldy water stain. It would seem to have seen serious wear and bad weather. As she opened the cover to look inside, the footman stepped into the room to announce a visitor.

Joanna thrust the book into her pocket as the lady swept in.

It was Lady Carhill, impeccably dressed, her blond hair arranged in an enchanting confection of curls beneath a smart little driving hat. There was a faint dusting of powder across her face, but it was not enough to hide the redness around her eyes. Lady Carhill had been crying.

"Lady Tarrant," she said, holding out one hand in a pleading gesture. "Something dreadful is going to happen! Can you come with me? Now? My carriage is outside."

Fitzroy sat quietly on his exhausted horse and surveyed the house. Lady Kettering had given him explicit instructions. He had followed them to the letter. A trail of meetings and journeys, exhausting and absurd, had finally resulted at six that morning in directions to this forgotten relic of a more dangerous age. Yet by riding like the devil he was here an hour early. The Peninsula had taught him that it usually paid to reconnoiter the ground before facing enemy fire.

Yet he had the unholy suspicion that his mysterious enemy would know that and would be counting on it, reading his mind, guessing his every feint and counterattack. It had been happening ever since this vile business began. Forcibly he was reminded of similar times in the Peninsula, and the deaths to his comrades that had resulted.

He had ridden not more than ten miles from London, but this place was as secluded as it had been in the fifteenth century when it was built. It was a fortified manor house, the crenellated battlements reminiscent of a castle, yet the windows defended only by heavy wooden shutters. Pond weed grew thickly in the sluggish remains of a moat enclosing the garden. He smiled. The bridge across the moat was the only entrance. It was no doubt being watched. If he moved out of the trees which shielded him, his unknown enemy would know he was coming.

Yet he didn't relish the idea of facing whatever lay inside with his powder wet and his pistols useless, his reactions slowed by wet clothes, assuming he survived the attempted crossing. The bottom of the moat would be feet deep in soft mud and the water was thick with coiling plant stems and roots—too deep to wade, and a very nice death trap for a swimmer.

Leaving his horse tied in the trees, Fitzroy crept through the woods on foot, studying the land and the house, learning what he could. The shutters were closed, hiding anyone who might be watching behind them. The front door under its narrow porch had been designed for defense, not welcome. At the back of the house lay a small stable block. A dun horse looked out over its half door and shook its head against flies. The rump of a companion gleamed dully in the next stall. The stable created the only blind spot on the moat for watchers in the house. Fitzroy felt no surprise that a couple of burly servants sat together in an empty stall near the dun horse, playing cards, stopping every once in a while to listen. If he plunged into the moat behind the stable, and emerged, dripping, they would catch him.

No trees grew conveniently over the moat; no forgotten boat lay tied in the weeds. Fitzroy scoured the woods for some old shed, perhaps, from which he could break away a board. He found nothing but an abandoned woodsman's camp and the ashes of his fire. A clearing had been made there for coppicing. Saplings and shoots from the stumps of large trees grew densely together, thin and tall as they reached for the sun. The strong, supple young growth was used for everything from broom handles to sheep hurdles. He almost turned away before the answer came to him: *sheep hurdles!*

With the sword from his cane Fitzroy rapidly cut a swath in the coppice, choosing the longest, most flexible poles. He worked in a fever to weave them together into a strong mat. Then he made another. They were awkward to carry to the moat, for the woodsman's road led off in the opposite direction and Fitzroy had to twist his way through the undergrowth with his burdens. It was the work of half an hour, perhaps, and the crude hurdles would never have held sheep, but Fitzroy had to trust that they would hold him for long enough.

Silently he ran back to his horse. He led the animal to the opposite side of the grounds from the stable and with a quick word and a pat, let it loose. As he had hoped, sensing the other horses his mount whinnied and crashed into the willows at the edge of the moat, searching for a way across. The watchers at the stable leapt up and ran toward the sound as Fitzroy raced back to his hurdles.

Moments later he was leaning against the stable wall. Only his boots were a little wet. Round one to him, perhaps?

Joanna sat next to Lady Carhill as the chaise rattled away from town. She was still wearing her old dress and her artist's smock, her hair in a hasty bundle. Her companion made a stunning contrast, blond, elegant, beautiful. Joanna did not notice. She was fighting the fear and confusion she had felt ever since Lady Carhill burst into the house.

"Is my husband in danger?"

My husband. Until death do us part. Fitzroy!

"I don't know." Lady Carhill pressed a handkerchief to her eyes. "I don't know!"

"Where are we going?"

Lady Carhill turned to look at her. Her lovely face was puffy. "I can't tell you. I won't tell you! There! Why did you marry him when his heart still belonged to Juanita, why?"

Joanna glanced down at her paint-stained lap. "Do you think he still loves her?"

"I know he does," snapped Lady Carhill. "That's why he wouldn't—"

"What? Wouldn't what?"

"Become my lover, if you must know! He wouldn't!"

Joanna felt her heart skip, like a colt allowed out of the barn. So what Fitzroy had told her was true. "But I thought you said—" Her voice cracked a little. "At Lady Reed's—"

"Oh, you silly girl! I was jealous of you! But how foolish

that was. All that lovely gallantry and flirtation, and all the while he was hiding a broken heart. Has he bedded you yet? It makes no difference. You will never have any more of him than I did. None of us will. He belongs to a dead woman.''

She was sixteen. I married her. So why had he let her die?

Fitzroy reached the wall of the house by dodging from bush to bush in the garden. The men were beating about in the undergrowth opposite his horse, who was now peacefully grazing. The original medieval inhabitants would never have allowed their grounds to become so overgrown. No doubt four hundred years earlier the stone walls had been smooth, as well. Now the stone was pocked with weathering; here and there iron ties had been driven through the masonry to support the structure. It was just enough to give him hand and footholds to the roof. Once there he quickly found what he expected: a doorway in a corner turret that would lead him unseen into the house. He had just opened the door when he heard the carriage.

He flattened himself against the wall and watched it turn to cross the bridge. Fitzroy recognized the horses: Lord Carhill's nags. And then he saw the face behind the glass. Hair black as ebony, skin white as snow, lips red as blood, her mouth set and her chin held high, it was Joanna. Memory flooded him; weakening him for a moment: dark hair spread riotously over a rainbow pillow; white skin—like cream touching coffee—against his; carmine lips swollen and sweet with her generous passion. Only last night he had made her his wife. Yet, while she still slept, he had abandoned her for this dark mistress, intrigue. *Joanna, dear heart, what the devil are you doing here?*

Lady Carhill and Joanna stepped from the chaise. Somewhere below him the front door opened.

''*Muy buenas dias,*'' said a soft female voice in the pure Spanish of Madrid. It seemed as familiar as his own mind. ''*Hagan ustedes el favor de entrar.*''

Please come in.

In an agony of grief, Fitzroy heard Joanna. ''Why, good

heavens! What an extraordinary surprise! How charming to
meet you again.''

And the soft reply: *"El gusto es mío."*

The impact hit like gunfire: a numbness, followed by unimag-
inable pain. Fitzroy allowed himself to feel it without question
for a moment, letting the shock sink in, concentrating on
allowing it to dissolve, relaxing, breathing, fighting for equilib-
rium.

It was what she had said to him, bravely gulping back tears,
from the ruins of a stable in Badajoz. Fitzroy closed his eyes.
Screaming, shots, the roar of flames in the background. Soldiers
drunk on battle shock and wine reeling through the streets.
''You are safe now, señorita,'' he had said in Spanish. ''Pray,
come with me. I promise to protect you from this rabble. It
would be my pleasure.''

And holding out her elegant little hand, Juanita had replied,
"El gusto es mío." The pleasure is mine.

For one brief moment Fitzroy almost feared for his sanity.
But I saw her die! Then he stepped into the dark well of the
turret and ran headlong down the stairs.

Fitzroy followed instinct and the faint trace of voices as he
made his way through the dim house. From the cracks between
the shutters, light fell in brilliant, narrow bars across each room,
casting the rest into deep shadow. He stumbled into a side table
and an upright chair. He even pulled his pistol and threatened
a tall candelabrum in the shape of a goddess. The voices were
clearer now. He dragged aside a heavy tapestry and found
himself in a musicians' gallery above the great hall. Darkness
spread below him. Only two sets of candles had been lit, and
bars of sunlight striped the room like the marks from a flogging,
but the rest was gloom, impenetrable as the grave.

Joanna sat near one stand of candles. She looked grim and
determined and worried. Lady Carhill had taken a chair behind
her and was nervously twisting a handkerchief in her lap. A
gentleman stood near them, leaning with false nonchalance
against a wooden post, black with age. Fitzroy knew him

instantly, a man who lived in his dreams, whom he would know in the dark by the sound of his footfall: his brother, Quentin.

Their hostess sat in a high-backed chair at the head of the room. Her dark hair was hidden by a black lace mantilla, the midnight eyes lost in shadow. One bar of sunlight slashed strongly across her lap, highlighting the richness of her dark red dress and striking brilliance from the ring she wore on her finger: a sapphire surrounded by diamonds. Fitzroy acknowledged it and the memories it brought back: the engagement ring that a young British officer had given a girl he found crying in the ruins of a sacked Spanish town, a family heirloom, a symbol of love.

Unless we are being beleaguered by a ghost? Thank God, thank God that he had crept into the house this way, had these few minutes of forewarning in private. Had he come to the front door as instructed, he would have been thrust suddenly into this shadowed room, eyes still blinded by the daylight from outside. What might he have done in that moment of shock?

"He will be here soon," said the soft voice, the Spanish accent faint and elegant. "Shall we have wine while we wait?"

She rang a small bell in the charmingly imperious gesture that Fitzroy remembered, and with a graceful nod signaled the servant who entered. The man reappeared moments later with a tray and wine glasses. He set them on a large oak table, bowed, and retreated. Quentin stepped forward and poured the wine. Each of the ladies took a glass, while he swallowed three in rapid succession.

"About time, Señorita Gorrión," said Quentin, at last setting down his empty glass. "Devilish thirsty work, destroying a man." Fitzroy heard the desperation in it, and the bravado. Quentin would always try to cover his emotions with sarcasm. It was a family trait, of course.

"Will you greet your brother foxed, sir?" asked the Spanish voice with a hint of amusement.

"Good God." Quentin poured yet more wine. His hand was shaking. "I had better or he won't recognize me."

"I'm not sure you will recognize him," she replied with a small laugh. "I doubt he will be boasting his usual elegance. My moat is remarkably slimy."

Fitzroy watched Joanna, her face stark and white at this threatened humiliation to him. Why the devil had she been brought here to witness this? Anger burned in him, clear and bright, yet he knew he could not allow his concern for her to deflect him from what he must do now.

"So you don't think my brother will come to the front door like a gentleman?" Quentin studied his wine. "What do you plan when he arrives, señorita?"

Fitzroy struck a spark from his tinder box and lit the brace of candles standing in the gallery. The tiny flames flared for a moment in the draft, causing them all to look up at him.

"Can the words of a crooked hunchback speak for her, Quentin?" he asked softly. "Richard of Gloster, the most twisted villain in history: 'Plots I have laid, inductions dangerous, / By drunken prophecies, libels, and dreams, / To set my brother Clarence and the king / In deadly hate the one against the other.' I am not the king and you're not Clarence, but as brothers we can make do, I suppose, when drama is about to unfold." He perched casually on the railing and stared into the darkness at the lady Quentin had greeted by her maiden name: Señorita Gorrión. *"Must* you foment discontent, *mi corazón?"*

Joanna looked up, heat flooding her face at the sound of his voice: Fitzroy! He sat above them, his face oddly lit by the dancing candlelight, apparently casual, calm, in command. Then he was not hurt. Not yet. Only she, only she was wounded to the heart!

Doña Juanita Maria Gorrión Navarro, Fitzroy had said, *a nice Spanish lady.* Juanita, Fitzroy's first wife, his first and only real love, was here in this room, when he thought he had seen her die.

But Quentin had known who she was, had greeted her by

her maiden name—Navarro would have been the name of her mother, Gorrión her paternal surname. How long had Quentin known? At Fenton Stacey? At the Swan? During the wedding at King's Acton? When he had offered to run away with her after Lady Kettering's ball? Quentin had allowed his brother to commit bigamy so that he wouldn't have to, leaving Lady Joanna Acton nothing more than a mistress, like all the others, except poor Lady Carhill, who'd had nothing.

The Spanish face was a pale blur under the lace mantilla. *"Ah, mi esposo. Como le va, mi querido novio?"*

"Contrary to your prediction, I am dry," said Fitzroy. "Your moat had a regrettably jaundiced look, so I preferred not to swim. And the henchmen who were supposed to be my welcoming party were sincerely offensive to my sensibility. But here I am. Allow me to join you."

How could he? After two years, how could he greet Juanita like this!

"Of course. I invited you here," she said in her softly accented English. "You were welcome to arrive at the front door, but melodrama was always your style, wasn't it?"

Joanna caught her breath as Fitzroy swung over the edge of the musicians' gallery. Light played oddly across his lithe back, casting monstrous shadows, a vampire arriving by moonlight, ruffling the curtains, bringing the scent of power and ruthlessness into the maiden's bedchamber. He let himself drop easily to the floor and gave them all a small, correct court bow.

"As it is yours." Fitzroy laid down his cane and took a glass from the tray. "Is the wine poisoned?"

The shoulders beneath the mantilla shrugged, the movement clearly discernible in the shadows. "Everyone is drinking it. Did you think I would poison them all, just for you?"

He turned to her and saluted her with his filled glass. "Why not? Tragedies often end with the stage littered indiscriminately with corpses. Enough innocent men have died already to make a very promising start."

"But they all loved you, Fitzroy *querido*, while everyone here hates you: your brother, your mistress, and your poor little wife who isn't a wife at all. What a disgrace! A scandal! How could you do it? Betray noble Richard Acton's sister into harlotry? You *have* taken her to your bed, haven't you? I was told that you had sworn not to, but knowing the carnality of your nature—'' She stopped with deliberate provocation.

Joanna forced herself to breathe. She glanced at Quentin and Lady Carhill. They seemed suspended, like spectators at a play. *This cannot be real,* she thought. *Richard also saw her die!*

Inevitably her eyes were drawn back to Fitzroy. He sat carelessly on the edge of the table, swinging one booted foot. He took a frugal sip of his wine. ''Did Quentin tell you that? How very fraternal of him! As Richard of Gloster said, ''Inductions dangerous!'' Shall we start at the beginning? You greeted my wife at your door as if you were old friends. Where the devil did you meet her, Joanna?''

Joanna gulped at her wine. ''At the house party at Fenton Stacey.'' She was amazed that her voice came out of her throat. Yet it seemed ordinary enough, even calm. ''This lady came there one day. Her name was given only as Mrs. Barton-Smith. We talked about art. Indeed, it was she who told me about Harefell Hall.''

''Ah, now I see.'' Fitzroy smiled at her. It was the smile he had given her on their wedding day. *Take courage!* it seemed to say. Joanna couldn't understand it. ''And was that when you became her lover, Quentin?''

Quentin blushed. The color rushed up from his high collar and cravat to flood into his brown curls. ''Does it matter?'' he replied.

Joanna watched Fitzroy. The pitch of his voice appeared exactly calculated to make any other man want to knock him down. ''My dear brother, I really don't care whom you bed, but this does seem just a trifle indiscreet, doesn't it?''

Quentin seemed to melt. He slid down the post and dropped into a chair. A tremor passed over him. ''If you must know, I didn't know until today who she was. She told me she was a widow, Mrs. Barton-Smith, as Joanna said. And then she told

me about you. I have not wanted to believe that my own brother
is such a bastard, but every day you have proved it.''

"Cleverly done, *mi corazón*,'' said Fitzroy, turning to the
shadowed figure in the lace mantilla. ''I imagine it was easy
to persuade Quentin to run away with Richard Acton's sister.
I wondered what the devil had persuaded him to such an odd
act of gallantry. It must have seemed perfect to you.''

Joanna closed her eyes. Oh, dear Lord! Juanita had used her,
pulling the strings like a puppet master, encouraging her to run
away from Miss Able's with Quentin, all to enmesh Fitzroy in
disaster? What else had she orchestrated? It made simple Joanna
Acton totally irrelevant, didn't it?

"It was exquisite. *Más vale tarde que nunca.* What better
revenge?''

"And why did Lady Carhill and Lady Reed cooperate? Gaming debts?''

"How did you know?'' cried Lady Carhill, leaping suddenly
to her feet. ''Oh, Fitzroy! I had no idea, none, that it would
come to this! How was I to know that Mrs. Barton-Smith was
your wife? She said she had been married to an officer in Spain,
but that he had died there, and that you had tried to seduce her,
and all the other wives—that you were rapacious, a destroyer of
the weaker sex! It seemed a fair enough exchange to help her
punish you a little. The night of my ball Lady Mary was supposed to find us together—you'd have hated that, wouldn't
you?—but you took the key and left me too soon.''

His voice was gentle. ''You had lost a great deal of money,
Lady Carhill? I know your reputation as well as you know
mine.''

"Remuda de pasturaje haze bizerros gorgos,'' said the soft
Spanish voice.

Joanna looked at her blankly.

"Change of pasture makes fat calves,'' translated Fitzroy.

How could he smile? Joanna watched his hands as he set
down his wine glass, the square palms and supple fingers that
had touched her so sweetly only last night. A fierce pain started

somewhere below her rib cage and ran choking up to her throat. Yet she could not interfere! What rights did she have in this?

"So we have established a charming trail of connections," he went on. "Lord Tarrant, the infamous rake, finds himself on the other end of the chase, forced into an unwanted marriage, seduced into publicly taking mistresses, only to be used and tossed aside in his turn. Meanwhile he is to be harassed, kept guessing, driven mad by red herrings. Exquisite in its simple symmetry. But what about the real Herring and Flanders and Green? Didn't they deserve the retirement they'd earned? Or was it because they were witness to the realities of that first impetuous marriage?"

"Those men? They were scum, *campesinos*. It is beneath me to consider them."

Was she rattled a little? The soft voice was less steady. Joanna suddenly realized that Fitzroy was not playing the part that Juanita had planned for him. She had expected to have the upper hand, to be in command. Joanna imagined for a moment what Juanita must have intended: that Fitzroy would try to swim the moat. Exhausted and drenched he would have been brought into this room without warning to face a ghost. Might his defenses have collapsed under the shock?

Instead, he sounded ruthless, his anger clear. "Because their loyalty was mine? In spite of all the beauty and charm of their officer's wife, they were not corruptible, were they? Was that enough to justify their deaths?"

"It was necessary," she said coldly, "to make you take me seriously."

"Ah, no, there you are wrong, *novia*. I take you very seriously. And I resent it. I resent what you have done to those who could not defend themselves. How the devil do you justify what you are doing to Joanna?"

She laughed and snapped her fingers. "Lady Joanna Acton! So ripe and so innocent at Fenton Stacey! She wanted to become an artist. *You* have made her a harlot, Fitzroy, not I. It was not my fault that you married her! Why did Richard Acton let you live to do it? Does he apprehend how you have been treating his sister? I thought it reasonable to let him know. So what will you do when he calls you out?''

"I don't know," replied Fitzroy. "Perhaps I will ask for rapiers. Richard's good with a blade, but he has a very sorry aim with a pistol. I'm afraid if I were to let him shoot at me he would make a mess of it.''

There was a noise behind them, the murmured words of a servant, the opening of a door. Joanna spun about. A tall man stepped into the room. A thin shaft of sunlight fell across his bright blond hair, so that he flamed like the sun for a moment.

"No doubt I would." Richard tossed down his hat and stripped off his coat. The gold cap on his cane blazed into fire as it also caught the sunbeam. "Lady Kettering has been kind enough to visit and elucidate your behavior the night of her ball. She went into considerable detail.''

"How unfortunate," said Fitzroy. Joanna watched him, the controlled movements, the patient voice. She could not understand what he was doing, or how he must feel, but through her own pain she saw his and ached for him.

The heat of Richard's anger was palpable, burning unchecked below the surface. "Do you deny that you let my sister arrange the rendezvous in the summerhouse?''

"No." Fitzroy seemed merely weary of it all. "Though I am sorry that you were present that evening.''

"And that this was not the first such time?''

"As I'm sure you have been informed by now, no doubt with some inventive embellishments, there was also Lady Reed, but Joanna did not arrange that, she just witnessed it." Fitzroy moved toward the table, also shrugging out of his jacket. "Is it to be a duel, after all, Lord Lenwood?''

Chapter 14

Richard pulled his sword from its cane. "I don't believe you can claim the privileges of a duel, Tarrant. The niceties of seconds and attending doctors are reserved for gentlemen, not for vermin that needs to be destroyed. So by all means let it be blades, sir, and why not now?"

"Richard, no!" Joanna leapt out of her chair. Fear and shock had left her numb for a moment, but the sight of the naked steel sent the blood rushing back into her limbs. "No! Something else is happening here, something more than you've been told!"

His face was implacable, the line deep between his brows. "Stand aside, Joanna! For you to defend him only makes it worse." He stepped forward. "Quentin, for God's sake, keep her out of the way!"

"Richard, you promised! Fitzroy, don't fight him!"

"I think, dear heart," replied Fitzroy gently, "that Richard is not in the mood to listen to reason. Shall I let him impale me? Or shall we fight, like two game little cocks in the ring? Quentin, you have been bloody useless up to now, will you please do as her brother asks and keep Joanna safe!"

As Quentin caught her from behind and pinioned her arms

firmly to her sides, Fitzroy's blade also hissed from its case. He held it up for a moment in a salute, as he had done in the wood where the old soldier had been shooting pigeons, then he vaulted back over the table to meet the full impetus of Richard's attack.

The blades clashed together, ringing steel on steel, then scraped, squealing, as the men broke apart.

"Quentin, let me go!" hissed Joanna. "I shan't get between them!"

"Oh, no, my lady. Orders are orders!"

She struggled, trying to elbow him, but Quentin held her firmly.

Boots scraped on the bare boards of the floor. The two figures swayed back and forth in the gloom, the blades dazzling, firing a brilliant shaft of light whenever they sliced through a sunbeam. Fitzroy backed away from a ferocious series of lunges, working hard, blocking, parrying the lightning thrusts. He was tired, with that bone-deep exhaustion that had been his companion since the day Joanna had first seen him, scowling at her after she'd kissed Quentin at the Swan. It showed in the slight hesitation in his reactions, the blade lifted only barely in time, the split second too long between parry and riposte, as if he moved in treacle and had to drag through the weight of it to move his arm.

But Richard was carried on the pure, high wave of his disgust and his rage, and he was an excellent swordsman, graceful, fast, and relentless. It was just a matter of time before Fitzroy made a fatal mistake.

Joanna decided to faint. She went limp in Quentin's hands, allowing her full weight to sag against him.

"By God," he said releasing her. "She's swooning. Lady Carhill!"

Joanna rolled away and sprang to her feet. "Help me, Lady Carhill," she cried. "It's insane to let them fight in the dark. Let us open the shutters, at least!"

"No!" cried the Spanish voice. "Stay where you are!"

"Oh, fiddlesticks, do what you want!" Joanna raced to the

nearest window. "So I am just a harlot and you are his real wife. Whatever he did, however badly he treated you, if you'd ever loved him you would never have wanted to cause what has been happening to him these last weeks! Does love believe in revenge, and understand such viciousness?"

Joanna grasped the iron bar. It fell back easily. In moments she had flung wide the shutters and flooded the room with light. Juanita dropped the lace in a veil over her face. Fitzroy was trapped up against one of the wooden posts that supported the hammer beam roof. Both men were breathing hard. As the shutters banged open, Richard caught the full force of the sunshine in his eyes and was blinded.

In that moment Joanna knew that her husband could have easily killed her brother, but Fitzroy spun away, only to be forced to fall back yet again before a renewed assault. The blades clattered. Boots rasped. Both men were gasping for breath. Yet in spite of their deadly purpose Richard and Fitzroy, in their white shirts and tight breeches, were partners in a duet of startling beauty. Every movement was strong, lithe, graceful, the steel as elegant as the men as it sliced through the air, meeting and parting in a ballet of death.

The red which blossomed on Fitzroy's shirt seemed only a natural part of it, until he swore, dropped his blade, and started to laugh.

"'Who spoke of brotherhood? Who spoke of love?'" he quoted. *"Más vale ser necio que porfiado.* Better to be a fool than obstinate, they say."

He sank, still laughing, to the floor.

Richard stood over him, pale with shock, his bloodstained sword still raised.

"For God's sake!" shouted Quentin, rushing forward.

"It's all right, brother," replied Fitzroy, giving him a wink. "Richard would no more sink his blade into a wounded man than you would." He winced once. "Sometimes it seems like a damned shame, because sadly the wound doesn't seem to be fatal."

Joanna was there first. She reached into the pocket of her smock, searching for a handkerchief. Her fingers touched the shabby leather of a book.

"Here, hold this!" she said, thrusting the volume at Richard. He threw aside his sword and took it.

Fitzroy lay against the base of a post, half supported by the black wood. Joanna tore open his shirt and pressed her handkerchief to the wound.

Lady Carhill marched along the far wall, frantically throwing open shutter after shutter, while Quentin knelt by Joanna and tried to help her.

"It's all right, Richard," said Joanna. "If Fitzroy doesn't bleed to death in the next few minutes, your restraint may have given him a chance yet."

For a moment, it seemed that everyone had forgotten their hostess. She stood up, the sunlight blazing on her red skirts, and said flatly: *"Quién sabe?* It is a useful thing this English chivalry! So you will live a little longer, Fitzroy Mountfitchet, to know what your foolishness will cost you and your country yet!"

Fitzroy had closed his eyes and dropped his head back. Joanna used Quentin's knife to cut strips from his shirt. She had never seen a sword fight before, nor such quantities of blood. Biting down her fear she did her best to bandage the wound. She heard the rustle of the approaching skirts and saw the dramatic contrast of red silk and black lace from the corner of her eye. Then Fitzroy looked up and Joanna followed his gaze.

"Quién sabe?" he said, mocking. "Who knows?" Their hostess was gazing down at him, her red skirts brushing his boots, the black lace still hiding her face. His voice was edged with an amusement that he couldn't quite hide. "There is only one thing I'd really like to know, madam."

"Which is, Fitzroy *querido?"*

"Who the devil are you?"

* * *

It took Joanna a moment to comprehend. Fitzroy didn't think
that their hostess was Juanita. He had never thought so. It was
the only explanation that made sense. Whether Richard had
thought so, or even noticed her, she didn't know, but Richard
had glanced quite calmly at the lady in the red dress. He did
not seem to believe himself in the presence of a ghost. Their
hostess had been relying on the darkness and the effect of
surprise to fool Fitzroy, a surprise which Fitzroy had circum-
vented by somehow getting unseen into the house. What if he
had not? What if he had believed her masquerade? Joanna
shuddered and closed her eyes. Her hands were sticky. She
heard the soft Spanish voice speaking, as if it were a very long
way off.

"Verdad es verde. My name is Carmen Dolores Gorrión.
Juanita was my sister. She still died because of your cowardice
and treachery. It changes nothing. And my revenge has only
just begun."

For the first time in her life, Joanna fainted.

She heard the low hum of voices, like insects lazily buzzing
outside an open window in summer.

Richard's voice: "It is a diary. Your groom kept a diary, for
God's sake. Listen: 'Whenever Lord Tarrant is away, my lady
is entertaining. Several of the other officers are her lovers. It's
a shameful thing, when he is nothing but kindness to her.' I'm
sorry to have to read this. Did you know, Fitzroy?"

Fitzroy spoke softly, as if with a great regret. "Eventually,
when she told me. *Tomava la por rosa mas devenia cardo.* I
took her for a rose but she proved to be a thistle. She took
lovers from the day of our wedding. Does it change anything?"

"But she wrote to me that *you* were unfaithful!" Carmen's
voice, harsh now, the softness gone.

"We were at war, señorita. I was rather lacking in opportuni-
ties," Fitzroy replied dryly. "There were many more unattached men in the camp than women, and I spent a great deal
of time with Richard and the other intelligence officers on one

mission or another, a hideously masculine pursuit. Of course, you couldn't have known that in South America.''

''So! Yet my sister had cause enough to hate you, and took solace where she could. Was that why you let her die?''

''No.'' Fitzroy sighed, as if his breathing pained him. ''I forgave the lovers.''

''Then it was this,'' said Richard. ''Listen: 'It will only be a day, or sometimes it's later the same night that she lies with one of our officers. She takes a horse secretly and rides out of camp. Last night I followed her. How am I to tell Lord Tarrant? She goes to meet—''

''Enough!''

Joanna opened her eyes and tried to sit up. She almost bumped her head on her husband's arm. She was lying on a high-backed bench with her head pillowed in his lap. Fitzroy's chest was swathed in the makeshift bandage, his torn shirt lying open above it, his eyes burning pools of black under his dark brows.

''Fitzroy! You are all right?'' Joanna asked immediately.

''I'll live. And you?'' She felt the touch of his hand on her hair, fleeting, tender, before he moved his arm aside.

''The book that Mrs. Morris gave me—Mr. Flanders kept a diary?''

''Here,'' said Lady Carhill, holding out a glass of wine. ''Drink this.''

Joanna sat up and took the glass. They were all seated at the big oak table: Carmen in the chair at the head; Richard holding the book that Mrs. Morris had brought her wrapped in brown paper; Quentin at the other end with his head in his hands; Lady Carhill next to him.

Richard began to read once more. ''Lord Tarrant—''

''Enough!'' Fitzroy said again.

Richard set down the diary. ''You knew all this?''

''I knew that she took lovers. She told me.'' His voice was quiet, controlled. ''I discovered why much later. How the devil do you think it makes me feel to publicly admit it now? Yet what Flanders found out, and Green and Herring knew eventually, was what she cajoled her lovers into telling her: our army's secret plans, our strengths and weaknesses. Isn't it obvious? Juanita rode out of camp to meet the enemy and sold the information to the French.''

"And you did not report it to Wellington?'' asked Richard.

Fitzroy gave him a glance of pure incredulity. "She was my wife. Should I have seen her shot for a spy?''

Richard tossed the book aside. "I don't know. So that is why you kept her with you, those last months. You were trying to never give her another opportunity. But she died. I think you are going to have to tell us what happened that night. For Señorita Gorrión's sake, at the very least.''

Joanna felt his hand move against hers. She opened her fingers and let his slide around them. She glanced at his face. Fitzroy seemed calm, resigned, yet the tension was there. He was very pale.

"What the hell makes you think you have the right to demand it? Yet it's for your sake, Richard, not hers, that I will tell you. I came into our tent to find her studying our plans for the show at Orthez—maps, memos; God knows how she obtained them. She screamed at me and threw things before she ran out and almost knocked you down. We followed her together. The partisans intercepted her. Call it native intelligence or dumb luck, but they were suspicious of her. You know the rest.''

Carmen stood up, her black eyes filled with tears. "Yes! We know the rest. I came from South America when her letters stopped and found it out. You let her be shot and saved yourself! Because she carried secrets? What if she did? It wouldn't have changed the outcome of the war. Why shouldn't she hate you, hate all the English? Your men had killed our father and our mother and burned our house. Why shouldn't she have used you to fight back and take revenge? She married you in hatred! She even sent me the ring you gave her!'' She held up her hand. The sapphire and diamonds blazed in the sunshine. "But you, Fitzroy Monteith Mountfitchet, son of an earl, such a perfect example of the English gentleman, let her be shot in the back rather than risk your own hide! So I have tracked you down and found you, and I have done my best to make your existence a living hell. What do you think Juanita's life was like, married to an English lord she despised, taking those loathsome English officers to her bed?''

''Yes,'' said Fitzroy, his control slipping, his face as white as his torn shirt. ''I know.''

Joanna clung to his hand, trying to let him draw strength from her if he could.

Carmen's voice had dropped to a hiss. ''And that's what remains, after all the accusations against my sister and your claim of loving her! She was shot because you were too cowardly to save her life.''

The blood had entirely drained from his face. Joanna could feel him shudder. ''I could not save her. I tried for two years, but it was never enough. Juanita was damaged too deeply. She could not recover. I discovered on our wedding night what had been done to her before I found her in the stable. It was too much for her to forgive. I didn't blame her, but I could not save her.''

''So you let her die?'' Richard dropped his head into his hands. ''Dear God.''

''Yes,'' said Fitzroy. ''It's unforgivable, isn't it?''

Joanna watched his face. His expression was closed, remote. In the person of one English officer, himself, he had tried to make up for the actions of a drunken, looting gang of men, a task impossible. It was war, he was often gone on missions. So for two years, he and Juanita had been trapped together in a hell of their own making. Yet how could he claim he had loved her, when he had taken the easy way out? Perhaps once peace had come, with time and love she could have been healed. Surely it had not been necessary to sacrifice her life? Was that all the value that Fitzroy put on love?

Never doubt, whatever happens later, that everything you feel tonight is real; that I love you. He had claimed her body and soul that night. Joanna couldn't bear it if the love he had expressed to her were only a cipher, shallow, easily forgotten. The pain seemed unbearable. But then it came to her, as if a voice spoke in her ear: *And you tell yourself you love him, Joanna. Then shame on you for your lack of faith!*

"You have not told us everything, have you?" she asked gently. "Why could you not fire your pistol and save her?"

"It's quite simple." Fitzroy had closed his eyes against the humiliation of their gathering moisture. "I could not lift my arm. She had just sunk a knife in my back."

There was silence.

"But you saved my life," said Richard quietly at last.

Fitzroy's eyes flew open. "The partisans saved us both, my dear Lord Lenwood. If you will think about it, I never claimed anything different. As soon as Juanita was killed, the French galloped away. They had come to meet her, after all. The partisans bound me up and propped me on my horse; you were slung unconscious across yours. And so we limped back to camp. I'm sorry about everything I said to you later. I hadn't wanted it to turn out as it did, and once she was dead I saw no reason for anyone else to know what Juanita had been doing."

Carmen stood up, her black eyes blazing. "Juanita was seven years younger than I, the baby of our family. When I went to South America she was still a child. She told me only parts of this. I see now how it was. As for those men, Herring and the others, she told me how they spied on her, scorned her— English scum. It was men like that who ruined her in Badajoz. They deserved to die. Yet my family must still be revenged on England! You, Fitzroy Mountfitchet, are a romantic fool. I have lost interest in you." She crossed to the doorway and tugged at the bell pull. The door opened to reveal a servant. "My carriage," said Carmen. "We return to Spain. Quentin, you will come?"

Quentin gave her a crooked smile. "I don't believe so, *mi corazón*. It was sweet while it lasted, but you have mistaken my feelings for Fitzroy. I don't hate him."

Carmen shrugged. "It doesn't matter. He is nothing, a mere pawn. It was amusing to play with him for awhile."

"You have ordered the murder of innocent men." The ironic

edge was gone. Fitzroy's voice blazed with a pure anger. "Do you think we should let you walk away?"

Carmen smiled. "Of course. For now I will tell you that the game has only just begun. And you Englishmen are helpless to stop it."

"What now?" asked Fitzroy. "Is there further retribution?"

"Of course. You are such a master spy and you have not guessed? Your batman, Herring, told you the truth, Lord Tarrant. Did you think it was just a feint? No, Wellington is the real prize. Only remember when you get the news of his death, that the sparrow has finally won."

Joanna turned to Fitzroy. "The sparrow?"

He lifted her fingers to his lips and kissed them. "Obvious enough, given her surname: *Gorrión,* the sparrow."

Who killed Cock Robin? I, said the sparrow, with my bow and arrow . . .

Carmen opened her reticule and tossed a package of papers onto the table.

"Your precious Iron Duke will die tomorrow in Cambrai. The plans are all there. May it bring you pleasure to read them."

The door closed behind her.

"For God's sake!" It was Richard, leaping to his feet.

"You will let her escape?" Lady Carhill tugged Quentin by the sleeve.

Fitzroy leaned back as Richard tore open the papers. "Sit down, Quentin. She wins this round. Wellington's life is far more important than hers. We must read what she leaves us."

"But the plot is for tomorrow!" cried Joanna. "You cannot get warning to France in time, even if the entire British navy attempted it."

"My dear wife, have a little faith. Well, sir?" asked Fitzroy, opening one eye and looking at Richard.

"It's all here," replied Richard grimly. "Wellington will be ambushed as he returns to his headquarters in Cambrai. They plan to use a crossbow. It may sound medieval, but it's just as deadly as a rifle and completely silent, of course. The assassins will have every chance of getting away with it."

"Oh, no! You will ride immediately for the coast, Lord Lenwood?" It was Lady Carhill, still clutching at Quentin's sleeve. "Wellington must be warned!"

"It's impossible." Richard flung down the papers and ran his hands back through his blond hair. He looked gaunt. "Joanna is right. By the time any man from England arrives in France, he will be days too late."

Chapter 15

Fitzroy smiled at Joanna before forcing himself to stand. "But what you don't realize, dear Richard, is that we Mountfitchets regularly deal in signs and wonders. We have all the birds of the air on our side." With a gasp, he sat down again. "Sadly, I don't believe I can ride."

Quentin gently disengaged Lady Carhill's fingers. He looked grim and shaken. "Then I suppose it's up to me to save the peace of Europe, brother."

Fitzroy nodded to him. "Do it, sir. There's still no time to be lost."

"Quentin?" cried Joanna. "But he has been in league with that woman from the beginning! How can you trust him now?"

"Sweetheart, there are times we must trust what we believe we know about another person's heart. Though we have been apart for most of these last years, we were boys together once."

Quentin tried to grin at her and failed. He was chalk white. "Don't listen to Fitzroy's attempts to reclaim me, Joanna. I'm past redemption, a damned drunkard."

"But you didn't know what she really was!" It was Lady Carhill. Her eyes were enormous. "None of us knew. We were all pawns, weren't we?'' She turned to Fitzroy. ''Those men you mentioned: Green, Herring, Flanders. Carmen had them killed?''

Fitzroy nodded, still watching his brother.

''It's a little disconcerting,'' said Quentin with a desperate attempt at bravado, ''to know that one has taken a murderess to one's bed. You are right to have no faith in me, Joanna. We may have been the unwitting dupes of a vicious woman, but we were not innocent. How the hell can I trust myself?''

''By staying sober, sir.'' Fitzroy smiled with the old deviltry. ''And besides, Richard will go with you. What do you know about pigeons, Lord Lenwood?''

Quentin and Richard left at the gallop to attempt to get a message to Wellington in time. Quentin would dispatch the Belgian carrier pigeons while Richard rode on to Whitehall to inform Lord Grantley. Joanna and Fitzroy traveled back to London in Lady Carhill's carriage. It was a silent journey. Fitzroy slept with his head against Joanna's shoulder. Lady Carhill stared from the windows at the passing countryside and said nothing. They arrived back at Fitzroy's house as the day drew in.

Menservants carried their master up the stairs to the great bedroom. The paint-stained sheets were gone, silently changed by the efficient household staff. Joanna glanced at the slim volume of Wordsworth and the note Fitzroy had written which she had tucked inside: *Joanna. Remember. Whatever happens later, I love you.*

Fitzroy was placed in the great bed, as white as the sheets, his disordered hair raven black in contrast. The doctor came. Fitzroy was bled, bandaged anew, and given a sleeping draught made from poppies. He slept heavily. Nothing more could be done.

Joanna turned when the door opened, and Richard and Quentin came in.

''We sent four pigeons,'' said Quentin with an attempt at

gaiety. "The message is attached to their legs. If they survive hawks and weather they will arrive at their home loft in Belgium in about four or five hours. If Fitzroy's man finds them there as he should, it will be a matter of a couple more hours hard riding to get warning to Wellington in Cambrai. So it is now in the hands of Fate and our feathered friends."

"I shall tell Fitzroy," replied Joanna, "in the morning."

"So how is the fallen hero?" asked Quentin lightly.

Her control snapped. "He is very ill! Don't you care?"

A blankness came over Quentin's handsome features. "I care damnably, as it happens. But what the devil can I do about it now? Do you think that what I have done can be forgotten overnight, like the name of someone you hope not to meet again? Fitzroy is the only brother I have. Believe it or not, I'd rather he lives to rain curses at me if he wants to."

"It was my sword did the damage," said Richard.

"But I was the man he should have been able to rely on, wasn't I? Yet I believed all those lies about him. Now, pray, where is Lady Carhill?"

Joanna blushed, still angry. "She's waiting downstairs. She thought perhaps you would like a ride back to town in her carriage."

"An excellent scheme." Quentin went to the door. He turned as he opened it and tried to wink at her. His eyes were glazed. "We shall know in a day, perhaps, if the pigeons were successful, and by morning if I am. Thank God I am free of Carmen, or should I say Mrs. Barton-Smith, at last. I was afraid to leave her—and rightly as it turned out. Who knows? The knife might have been for my back next."

Richard watched Quentin leave.

"Dear God, what a family!" He was drawn, tired. "Must I apologize? I did not mean . . . You have a damnable husband, Joanna."

"Don't say it, Richard. Fitzroy is everything you feared and more—he's the most infuriating man I ever met. I don't blame you at all for perforating him so liberally. Perhaps a little blood-letting will relieve his evil humors." Joanna went up to her brother and put her arms around him. "But it's too late to nullify our marriage. And I want to have his babies."

Richard kissed the top of her head. "Then there's no more to be said, sister mine. If he's to father nephews and nieces, I don't want his death on my conscience, after all."

"He won't die. I shan't let him. Go home to Helena and Elaine and get some rest. Helena will be worried, since you no doubt rode away like a banshee bent on murder and mayhem. I'll send word to Acton Mead as soon as there's news."

"But first I shall see that you bathe, and we shall both dine. Fitzroy won't wake for hours yet. Go, Joanna. Call your maid and take a hot bath."

She did as Richard bid her because she was too tired to do otherwise. They ate a simple meal and talked quietly about Fitzroy, about long-ago adventures in the Peninsula, and about Juanita.

"I never understood him," Richard said quietly at last. "He must have guessed what had happened to Juanita in Badajoz, yet he married her anyway."

"Don't you see? He married her because of it." Joanna broke the remains of her bread into crumbs. "I don't know whether he really convinced himself that it wasn't true, or if he believed he could make amends. Either way it was the action of a fool. Carmen was right."

Richard silently handed her his handkerchief, before he kissed her again and left.

Joanna went immediately into the shadowed chamber to be with Fitzroy. He slept on, oblivious to her presence, his face white, his breathing a little too fast and shallow. She paced the quiet room, thinking through everything that had happened. There were still great gaps in the story that she knew, but she didn't care any longer.

Fitzroy moaned and moved. Joanna raced back to the bedside. He still slept, one hand flung out on the pillow. *Please, Fitzroy, don't die now!*

She took his hand in her own and held it.

Who'll be chief mourner? I, said the Dove, I mourn for my love, I'll be chief mourner.

What was the nature of love?

Joanna had discussed it once with Helena at Acton Mead.

"Love is not something that happens to you," Richard's wife had said thoughtfully. "Love is something two people create. That initial fall helps, of course, when you believe you have met a prince from a fairy tale. Your heart lifts at the sound of his footfall, you are entranced by the shape of him and the way he moves, you look at each other and feel a melting somewhere deep inside. But real passion is liberated only by trust and honesty tempered by kindness, with eyes wide open to all of his faults, as his are open to yours. Then I believe you can grow old together, and still be in love."

"I don't know," Joanna had replied. "Love must be more than kindness! You make it sound so tame."

"I assure you it's not tame to be kind! Not striking back when you have been wounded takes every ounce of courage and conviction you have! But you must both do it. Otherwise you will burn each other until there is nothing left but ashes. It is when the person you love behaves badly that the first test comes, and you must return generosity for pettiness." She had grinned at Joanna's expression. "I don't mean you should be Patient Griselda! Far from it! I'm talking about compassion and generosity based on mutual respect, and that's something that's earned. It's what real love is, and what makes the deepest passion possible."

It seemed impossibly pious to Joanna. She closed her eyes. Helena was a naturally sweet-natured person. Richard was normally the soul of courtesy and consideration. Of course they could have a civilized marriage!

The quiet spaces of the night closed around her. Still holding Fitzroy by the hand, and sliding her head onto the pile of pillows next to him, Joanna slept.

* * *

She felt strong fingers tighten around her own and opened her eyes. Fitzroy was staring up at her. Sunshine was streaming in at the window. It was morning. And very possibly late morning, the dawn chorus was obviously long over. How long had she slept while Fitzroy watched over her?

"Well, Joanna," Fitzroy said with an infuriating grin. "Now your brother has suitably chastised me, am I forgiven?"

His pulse beat against hers, quick and fast.

"I don't know. I don't know what our marriage means. What about children?"

"Ah." He closed his eyes. "I know what I said, petty, malicious words, aimed only to hurt. I felt such rage at my father for forcing my hand and making me face my destiny. Can you forgive me for that, too?"

She felt an infinite distress. Too much yet lay unresolved, didn't it? "You said I look like Juanita. I can see how hard that must have made things."

"No, Joanna. You are nothing like her." He opened his eyes. "I know you want to be an artist and don't want children. Your mother told me. If you do not abandon me as I deserve and will still allow me into your bed, I can be careful, sweetheart. There won't be babies. But, dear God, I should be honored if you would bear me a child. Crazy as it may sound, I like children."

"I know. I saw you with little Tom. I do want to paint, but I don't see why I can't have babies, too. I should like a son. He would be as black-browed as we are, and just as difficult!"

He gazed at her, with a clear, open astonishment. "And if we have daughters?"

"They will run away from school with ineligible rakes. But children alone don't make a marriage, do they? And what kind of father would they have? How dare you take it for granted that we have a future together!"

There was a slight noise behind her. Joanna turned to see Lady Mary at the door. "Is Fitzroy—?"

"Come in, Mary." Fitzroy released Joanna and held out his hand. "I am."

* * *

Joanna left Fitzroy alone with his sister. Lady Mary came down half an hour later to say that Fitzroy was asleep again, and to share her own news.

"I am still to go to Switzerland," she said, smiling shyly. "But the doctors are confident now of my complete recovery. Indeed, they say that although I have suffered some inflammation and weakness, there seems to be no permanent condition of the lungs at all. A stay away from all the smoke and damp is sure to send me home perfectly well."

Joanna felt the joy of it like a bright quaff of champagne. "Oh, Mary! I'm so very glad! But still, I have something for you." Joanna led Lady Mary to her studio and unveiled the portrait. Fitzroy laughed back at her, lighthearted, filled with joy. "I hoped it would cheer you if I painted him like this."

"But it's wonderful! Perfect! Joanna, you are a genius, truly!"

Joanna gazed at the painting she had labored over. She had thought she was in love with it. Now it seemed shallow, like a watercolor wash that was unfinished. Yet it wasn't a lie; it was just a partial truth. With a certain sense of revelation Joanna realized that the whole truth was what she wanted: a portrait with depth, shadows, and layers of complex glazes. If only she could find her way there.

There was a steady stream of visitors all morning. Knowing that Fitzroy still slept, drugged with opium, Joanna dealt with them all in the formal drawing room, refusing them permission to wake him: Lord and Lady Evenham, stiff, awkward in their mixed commiseration and pride; Lady Acton, shrewdly watching her daughter, but saying very little; a Lord Grantley, who apparently had been Fitzroy's contact in the government. The only exception was Quentin. He stood immobile, facing her, and refused to go away, when all she wanted was to be left alone to go back to the bedside.

"I don't care if he's asleep, Joanna. At least let me sit by him for an hour. I know how you must feel about me and I don't blame you, but in my ramshackle way I've only wanted to help you, because Fitzroy . . ."

He choked and stopped.

"What?" she asked.

His eyes were bleak. "There is no one else, except Mary, that I love in this world."

So Joanna allowed Quentin to go up to sick room and keep vigil alone. It took all of her forbearance to do it. A few hours later he came down and stood in the doorway. "He's asleep again," he said.

She leapt up. The last of the visitors had just left. "He woke?"

"For a moment."

"Quentin, what is wrong?" Joanna rushed up to him. His expression terrified her. "Is he worse?"

Quentin pushed one hand over his face as if to knead away his distress. "No, no. It's not that."

"Then what is it?"

"I asked Fitzroy if there was anything I could do to make amends. I told him I would do anything." He paused for a moment, then with obvious reluctance met her eyes.

Joanna felt ice touch her heart. "What did he want?"

"He asked me to stop drinking. It's the one thing I cannot do."

Pushing away from her, he strode from the house while Joanna raced up the stairs to Fitzroy's room. He still slept.

Later that afternoon a note arrived. It was sealed with scented wax and the handwriting was florid. Joanna put it away in Fitzroy's desk, knowing perfectly well that it was from Lady Reed. But the next letter that arrived truly surprised her, for it was addressed to her and not to Fitzroy.

Joanna tore open the seal and spread out the sheet.

"Madam: When I take on a pupil it is forever, knowing that

I have gloried in the enlargement of her mind and the perfection of every faculty, inculcating the highest standards of moral and virtuous behavior in my young ladies. I beg, therefore, to offer your ladyship my most sincere felicitations on your most happy and blessed union. Your ladyship's most humble servant, Eliza Able.''

Joanna gazed at this in astonishment for a moment, and then she began to laugh. Sitting alone at Fitzroy's bedside, she laughed until she cried.

Fitzroy still slept. Joanna sat beside him, watching and waiting. He seemed feverish and uncomfortable, tossing and turning, filling her with fear. She didn't want to eat, and she couldn't bear to leave him. The doctor came again and insisted that Joanna take the air before she too became ill.

"This won't do, your ladyship. A turn around the gardens before you spend another moment at the bedside!"

The garden was quiet, still and calm. Joanna walked through the trees. Somewhere in the distance a church bell sounded, marking the call to the evening service. *All the birds of the air fell a-sighing and a-sobbing when they heard the bell toll for poor Cock Robin.* As she came up to the pigeon loft, she saw George scattering grain into little troughs and closing the birds up for the night. He smiled at her and asked after the master before touching a hand to his forehead and walking away.

Joanna sat on the top rail of the yard fence and watched the light die away in the west. Cock Robin. A young man, filled no doubt with immense conceit and confidence who had believed he could solve any problem just by wishing it so— yet his motives had surely been driven by compassion? What had happened when that young man had died at the hand of his first wife to become the Fitzroy Mountfitchet she had met at the Swan? She closed her eyes. Had it been inevitable that such simple faith would be broken against reality? If she had a lifetime of study, could she ever understand the rogue he had become? What was she to do now? For she too had begun her journey with such simple beliefs, and discovered a cruel world she hadn't dreamed existed.

There was a rustle and the whirring of wings. Joanna stood up, shading her eyes against the dying sunshine. As if it dropped out of the sky, a pigeon landed on her upraised hand. Attached to its leg was a little leather pouch. With trembling hands she tore it open. A small slip of paper lay inside.

"Success. Plot foiled. All safe."

She carefully set the pigeon in an empty cage and gave it grain and water, then she raced into the house and up the stairs.

His valet met her at Fitzroy's door. "His lordship just woke, ma'am."

Joanna ran inside. "Look!" she cried. "It worked. Wellington is safe."

The dark eyes bored into her. "Then I have achieved that, at least." He sounded infinitely empty. "Though it would seem that everything else I have done has left only desolation in its wake."

"Has it? I don't see why!"

"If I have learned nothing else, Joanna, it's that damage once done cannot be undone. Cruelty masked as cleverness is still cruelty. Oh, dear God!" He sighed and pressed his hands to his face. "I could have confided in Quentin, asked for his help. Instead I disdained him, my own brother. Yet in spite of everything, I've never really been a rake. I was completely faithful to Juanita. I did not take Lady Carhill, nor Lady Reed, nor Lady Kettering to my bed. But I let them be used in this foulness, Joanna. I guessed they were just pawns in some deeper game, but I did not spare them."

Her joy died away. So it was not over. "Lady Reed has written to you. I will fetch it."

A few minutes later she handed him the scented missive. Fitzroy read it through once. "The candle," he said.

Joanna handed him the flame and watched him burn Lady Reed's letter. "The doctor left this for you." She took up a draught laced with opium. "You must drink it."

He looked at her with that old sarcastic ferocity. "Am I safer unconscious?"

It is when the person you love behaves badly that the first test comes, and you must return generosity for pettiness.

"Absolutely," said Joanna. She grinned. "More polite, at least."

She watched him drink the laudanum and saw his eyes close again, before she laid her head onto the pillow next to his and stared dry-eyed at the ceiling.

When she awoke this time, he was still asleep. A shaft of sunlight fell across the pillow, casting highlights of deep sienna in his hair and throwing bold shadows over the planes of his face.

Joanna slipped from the bed and rang for Fitzroy's valet. While the man took over the vigil, she went to her own room to bathe and change and order breakfast. She came back to find her husband sitting up, gazing across to the open window.

"My valet has done his professional best to make me into a gentleman," he said. "I am shaved, washed, and bandaged once again in pure linen. But the important attributes remain unchanged. I have made light of what is serious, and the only question I care about remains unanswered. Do you forgive me, Joanna?"

"I don't know." She stood helpless, staring at him. "I don't know!"

His lids dropped again, shielding the black well of pain in his eyes. "I don't blame you. Do you want to be free of me?"

Joanna thought of all the paintings she had tried and destroyed. He was so lovely to her! Why did she still feel so much confusion?

"I don't know that either! Fitzroy, why didn't you tell me what was going on? Why did you let me go on believing that everything that happened was just your whim? It was cruel!"

"Perhaps I am cruel, Joanna." The words were barely audible. "Merely through carelessness and my own bloody conceit."

"And your own talent—why has it gone wasted?"

"Did I require things to be as they have been? Don't you think that I'd rather have painted than do what I have had to do? Dear God, I could not do both! If that is cowardice, I freely confess it!"

And Joanna's confusion crystallized into the one vital question, the question she hadn't been able to face, let alone formulate. Knowing that she risked everything, that the answer would finally reveal what she had to understand, she forced herself to ask it.

"What would you have done if Juanita had not stabbed you? Would you have risked yourself to save her from the partisan's bullet, or would you still have let her die?"

He looked up at her with his midnight gaze as still and deep as an ocean. "I have spent two years asking myself that question. What would you have done?"

Blindly Joanna walked up to the bed. Fitzroy caught her hand and held it, pulling her down beside him. She felt his pulse under her fingers, fast and strong.

"If I discovered that you were a traitor? That unless you were stopped, you would escape to the enemy with vital information? Oh, Lord!"

"It might have meant so many of our soldiers lives, you see, and yet I loved her. I don't know the answer. I shall never know. I can only be grateful that the choice was taken away. It was her only real gift to me, and I believe that's why she did it."

Joanna sat in silence for a moment, studying his face. She knew every line and shape of it. She loved him. Quite suddenly she saw why. Not just because he was brilliant and handsome and passionate, but because of this. He could not save Juanita from her demons, but he had wanted to. He was convinced she had stabbed him so that he would not be faced with choosing life or death for her. This was not cowardice or lack of honor. It was the opposite. It was an overwhelmingly generous belief.

And in return for her compulsive infidelity, Fitzroy had offered Juanita only loyalty and compassion.

So there had been something of love between Fitzroy and Juanita, after all. It had been doomed from the start because of the war, because of Napoleon's ambition and Britain's reaction to it, because the Spanish were divided in their loyalties, because at Badajoz the British officers had lost control of their men. *She was sixteen.* But Fitzroy understood love.

"Do you still love her?" asked Joanna quietly.

Fitzroy looked surprised. "She is dead. I loved her then, but she is only one part of my life, Joanna, and in the past. If Carmen had not thought up such a devious plot to take her family's revenge on me and on England, I could have let Juanita sleep on, at peace in that part of my memory. I wish I could have helped her, but I failed. I don't blame myself any longer for that. It wasn't because of Juanita that I moved in such a rage when I first met you. It was because of my men, being slaughtered when I was powerless to stop it."

"You should have told me," said Joanna.

"Ours was supposed to be a marriage of convenience. It wasn't meant to matter."

She glanced down. "No, I suppose not." Now only one question remained. Joanna looked up, straight into his eyes, and asked it. "So what do you want now?"

His voice was soft. "Shall I be honest? Honesty is an infinitely worse risk than art, isn't it? But here is the truth, upon my honor: what I want now is for you to take off that dress and get into this bed with me."

She blushed scarlet. "But you are hurt!"

"Yes, I am aware of that," he said dryly. "But I still have one good side. I just want to hold you."

"Just hold me?"

"And maybe kiss you a little."

"Fitzroy! Please, the doctor feared for your life!"

"So you do care, Joanna?"

Joanna knew she would be justified in refusing him. Yet she remembered Helena's words with a new understanding: *not striking back when you have been wounded takes every ounce of courage and conviction you have.* This was not the end of a story. It was the beginning, if she was prepared to find compassion and generosity in herself as well as desire. Now it was her turn to be honest, to risk it. "I care with all my heart, Fitzroy. But I thought perhaps that you had made love to me from charity."

"Charity!" He laughed aloud. It scattered her doubts more surely than any protestations. "Then how very little you know about men, sweetheart! I shall be so very happy to teach you more about a man's desire. But, alas, you'll have to undo those buttons by yourself. I don't believe I can use both hands yet."

"Very well," she said, releasing his hand and standing. "But you must promise not to move too fast and tear your stitches."

"I promise," said Fitzroy.

Joanna slowly undid the buttons on her dress. She let it slip to the floor, leaving her in nothing but her shift and stockings.

"Take down your hair." Fitzroy gazed at her steadily, his eyes as wide and black as the night sky. "I love your hair. I wanted to touch it ever since I first saw you at the Swan."

She reached up and pulled out the pins, running her fingers through her hair and shaking the black strands down over her shoulders. His dark, heated longing as he watched her began a fire in her heart.

"I wish I could take off your stockings. I'd like to peel them down, very slowly, and kiss the back of your knee and your ankle and your instep."

Joanna put one foot on the bed and rolled off her stocking, feeling heat spread from her heart and set flames running through her body.

"You may say what you like," she said. "When you can't act on it."

His voice was gentle, teasing. "Are you so sure that I can't act on it? Now the shift."

It was something that took all of her trust and courage. He hadn't earned it, but she would take a risk and find out whether there really was a future for them, after all. Joanna pulled her shift over her head. She was blushing furiously. She felt helpless and hot and filled with desire.

Fitzroy's gaze ran over her body. Her hair drifted across her breasts, skeins of black silk against snow white skin. He caught his breath. There was no sarcasm or mockery in him now. He was as open and vulnerable as Joanna.

As she saw it, the last shreds of her hesitation melted away to be replaced by a clear, blazing certainty. This man was her destiny and the love of her life. *I give you my soul to dance upon, if you like.* He had meant it. And freely, freely, she was prepared to give hers to him in return. As proud and unfettered as a pagan princess, she smiled at him.

Fitzroy smiled back. ''Joanna, I love you with all my heart. You are my now and my future; the past no longer matters. You are my wife, sweetheart. Unless you demand your freedom. In which case, though it break my heart, I should see that you have it.''

Lifting the sheet she slid into the bed next to him, careful to avoid the bandage, letting him slide one arm about her and pull her into his strong embrace.

''How can you possibly talk such fustian, Fitzroy?'' Joanna moved against his skin, feeling the delectable touch of his fingers, and his lips in her hair. Her blood blazed in a clear, unequivocal response. ''I love you. I don't ever want to be free of you. I want to paint your portrait.''

He smiled again as he touched her mouth with his.

''And I yours,'' he said.

AUTHOR'S NOTE

The nursery rhyme about Cock Robin dates from at least the fourteenth century and is probably much older. It was well known during the Regency, and had been used in 1742 as a satire during the downfall of Robert Walpole's ministry. Some scholars believe it may have been a folk retelling of the myth of the treacherous killing of Balder, Norse god of sunlight, beautiful, wise, and favored by all the gods. "Cock Robin" in Regency slang meant a kind, easy-going fellow.

I am told by a generous member of Britain's Royal Racing Pigeon Association that the sport of training carrier pigeons was far more developed in Belgium than in Britain at the beginning of the nineteenth century. However, a few Englishmen kept and flew pigeons as a private hobby, and it was close to this time that pigeons were first used by professional news agencies. So perhaps Fitzroy saw the potential for these courageous birds to exchange messages with Belgium. (We may assume he visited there either before or after Waterloo.)

Modern pigeons fly at approximately forty-five miles per hour with no wind resistance, and can fly distances of five hundred miles in twelve hours without stopping, so it would have been no problem for Fitzroy's birds to cross the channel in four or five hours to deliver the message which saved Wellington from my imaginary plot. In the spring of 1816 the Iron Duke's headquarters were at Cambrai, which is close to the Belgian border, as Europe continued to adjust to Napoleon's final defeat.

Readers of my previous Regencies will recognize Joanna and Richard. The Acton family first appeared in VIRTUE'S REWARD, released in February 1995. Each of the older siblings earned their story, as you may discover in ROGUE'S REWARD (November 1995) and FOLLY'S REWARD (April 1997). I sincerely hope you enjoy their adventures!

I love to hear from readers and may be reached at P.O. Box 197, Ridgway, CO 81432. A long self-addressed stamped envelope is much appreciated if you would like a reply and more information about my books. My sincerest thanks and best wishes to every one of you!

WATCH FOR THESE ZEBRA REGENCIES

LADY STEPHANIE   (0-8217-5341-X, $4.50)
by Jeanne Savery
Lady Stephanie Morris has only one true love: the family estate she
has managed ever since her mother died. But then Lord Anthony Rider
arrives on her estate, claiming he has plans for both the land and the
woman. Stephanie soon realizes she's fallen in love with a man whose
sensual caresses will plunge her into a world of peril and intrigue . . . a
man as dangerous as he is irresistible.

BRIGHTON BEAUTY   (0-8217-5340-1, $4.50)
by Marilyn Clay
Chelsea Grant, pretty and poor, naively takes school friend Alayna
Marchmont's place and spends a month in the country. The devastating
man had sailed from Honduras to claim his promised bride, Miss
Marchmont. An affair of the heart may lead to disaster . . . unless a
resourceful Brighton beauty finds a way to stop a masquerade and
keep a lord's love.

LORD DIABLO'S DEMISE   (0-8217-5338-X, $4.50)
by Meg-Lynn Roberts
The sinfully handsome Lord Harry Glendower was a gambler and the
black sheep of his family. About to be forced into a marriage of convenience, the devilish fellow engineered his own demise, never having
dreamed that faking his death would lead him to the heavenly refuge
of spirited heiress Gwyn Morgan, the daughter of a physician.

A PERILOUS ATTRACTION   (0-8217-5339-8, $4.50)
by Dawn Aldridge Poore
Alissa Morgan is stunned when a frantic passenger thrusts her baby
into Alissa's arms and flees, having heard rumors that a notorious
highwayman posed a threat to their coach. Handsome stranger Hugh
Sebastian secretly possesses the treasured necklace the highwayman
seeks and volunteers to pose as Alissa's husband to save her reputation.
With a lost baby and missing necklace in their care, the couple embarks
on a journey into peril—and passion.

*Available wherever paperbacks are sold, or order direct from the
Publisher. Send cover price plus 50¢ per copy for mailing and
handling to Penguin USA, P.O. Box 999, c/o Dept. 17109,
Bergenfield, NJ 07621. Residents of New York and Tennessee must
include sales tax. DO NOT SEND CASH.*

LOOK FOR THESE REGENCY ROMANCES

ROMANCE FROM FERN MICHAELS

DEAR EMILY   (0-8217-4952-8, $5.99)

WISH LIST   (0-8217-5228-6, $6.99)

AND IN HARDCOVER:

VEGAS RICH   (1-57566-057-1, $25.00)